Nine for the Devil

Books by Mary Reed and Eric Mayer

One for Sorrow
Two for Joy
Three for a Letter
Four for a Boy
Five for Silver
Six for Gold
Seven for a Secret
Eight for Eternity
Nine for the Devil

Nine for the Devil

A John the Lord Chamberlain Mystery

Mary Reed and Eric Mayer

Poisoned Pen Press

First Edition 2012

10 9 8 7 6 5 4 3 2 1

Library of Congress Catalog Card Number: 2011933447

ISBN: 9781590589946   Hardcover
      9781590589960   Trade Paperback

Poisoned Pen Press
6962 E. First Ave., Ste. 103
Scottsdale, AZ 85251
www.poisonedpenpress.com
info@poisonedpenpress.com

Printed in the United States of America

To Kim Malo
who loved historical mysteries

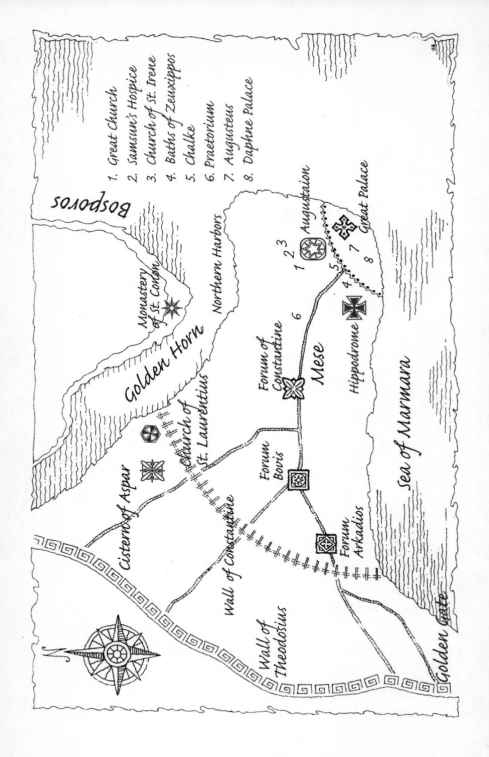

Bosporos

1. Great Church
2. Samsun's Hospice
3. Church of St. Irene
4. Baths of Zeuxippos
5. Chalke
6. Praetorium
7. Augusteus
8. Daphne Palace

Golden Horn

Northern Harbors

Monastery of St. Conon

Augustaion

Great Palace

Cistern of Aspar

Church of St. Laurentius

Forum of Constantine

Mese

Hippodrome

Sea of Marmara

Forum Bovis

Wall of Constantine

Forum Arkadios

Wall of Theodosius

Golden Gate

Cast of Characters

Anatolius *
Lawyer, formerly secretary to Emperor Justinian

Anastasius
Grandson of Empress Theodora

Anthimus
Patriarch of Constantinople from 535 to 536

Antonina
Wife of General Belisarius

Artabanes
Armenian-born general who put down a rebellion in Libya

Belisarius
Justinian's most celebrated general and husband of Antonina

Cornelia *
Met John during his days as a mercenary

Felix *
Captain of the palace guards known as excubitors

Gaius *
Court physician

Germanus
General and Justinian's cousin

Hypatia *
Egyptian who has worked for John and in the palace gardens

Isis *
Former brothel keeper, now head of a refuge
for former prostitutes

Joannina
Daughter of Belisarius and Antonina

John *
Lord Chamberlain to Emperor Justinian

John the Cappadocian
Powerful imperial official, notorious for his tax collection practices

Justinian
Roman emperor from 527 to 565 and husband of Theodora

Kuria *
Lady-in-waiting to Theodora

Manuel *
Personal cook to Theodora

Menas
Patriarch of Constantinople from 536 to 552

Narses
Eunuch who served as imperial treasurer and, later, general

Pulcheria *
A street beggar

Theodora
Roman empress from 527 to 548 and wife of Justinian

Vesta *
Lady-in-waiting to Joannina

Vigilius
Pope from 537 to 555

Prologue

June 548

During the heat wave smothering Constantinople, blades were drawn and blood spilt debating the portent of a series of strange events.

The latest event to exercise the imagination of the sweltering populace was a lightning bolt to the statue of Emperor Arkadios during the same fierce storm that killed three people in their sleep. Loungers at the inn nestled near to the Great Palace between the Hippodrome and the Baths of Zeuxippos, displayed a lively range of opinion, though no inclination to resort to sharp steel to reinforce their arguments.

So far.

"I told my wife lightning strikes inevitably mean disaster," observed a stout patron.

"Disaster for anyone struck," interjected a young fellow seated near the door.

The patron studied the blurry reflection in his wine cup as if it might contain a revelation beyond the fact he had a double chin. "What about the beggar in the Copper Quarter who saw two eagles fighting above the Great Church? And a friend of a friend of mine who works on the docks swears he saw a two-headed snake boarding a ship bound for Italy. These are not things to be spoken of lightly."

"I hear the wife of a high court official gave birth to a monster," said the man seated beside the speaker.

The bald proprietor, cleaning cups with a wine-stained cloth, observed that speaking of monsters, the state of Theodora's health was of great concern. "They say she has bishops praying night and day for her. We all should pray. Imperial deaths mean change, and change means trouble."

"Quite a few will be happy to pray for her to depart and to do it soon," said the man sitting near the door. "What worries me is how will Justinian react if she dies?"

The proprietor set down a cup with a loud bang, picked up another, and ran the dirty cloth around the inside. "There will be changes all right. I wouldn't be surprised if the emperor brought back that exiled tax collector. I hope not. His methods were as persuasive as those employed by palace torturers. I can hardly pay my taxes as it is."

"The Cappadocian? He's safely in Egypt. And if I was him I'd stay there." The stout imbiber took a sip of wine and tugged absently at the folded flesh under his chin. "But there are those at court who will benefit and others who will suffer. You know how Theodora meddles, how she favors her own family."

"Look on the bright side," said his companion. "If she departs, her heretical views might leave the empire along with her. Maybe Justinian will start to bring the heretics into line instead of trying to appease them."

"Let's not discuss religion," said the proprietor. "No matter how many natures we might think Christ possesses, we all worship Bacchus here."

The cup he was wiping slipped from his hand and shattered on the tiled floor.

"Another omen," remarked the stout patron. He started to say more but was interrupted by shouting in the street. Every head swiveled toward the door as a dust-covered man rushed in, scarlet-faced with excitement.

"She's dead! The whore is dead! The Lord be praised!"

Chapter One

Theodora may have been dead to those at the Great Palace and to the patrons of the inn within sight of the palace's bronze gates, but in the empire beyond she still lived. Soldiers camped on the Persian border traded coarse jokes about the former actress, thinking they insulted a living woman. General Belisarius, beaten back by the Goths in Italy, could continue to hope for a few days longer that the empress might sway Justinian to send reinforcements. In Alexandria a monophysite clergyman penned a homily on Theodora's piety, unaware that she had already joined his heretical saints.

Now released into the city, word of her death flowed like a swiftly lengthening shadow along Constantinople's thorough-fares. It reached into taverns and baths, tenements and churches, bringing jubilation, satisfaction, and even sorrow. Borne by worshipers, the shadow fell across the encomium to her charitable works chiseled into the white marble entablature of the church of Saints Sergius and Bacchus, and on the lips of a garrulous ferryman it passed over the whitened bones of her enemies scattered against the sea walls beneath the waters of the Marmara.

By nightfall Theodora would be dead to all who dwelt within the area bound by the capital's land walls. Weeks would pass before she died at the furthest outposts of the empire, from the Danube in the north and Egypt in the south, from Lazica east of the Black Sea to the westernmost part of the African Prefecture. She would go on living for several extra days in Syria, thanks to John the Cappadocian, the former official she so hated. News traveled slowly there because the Cappadocian had substituted plodding mules for horses as a money-saving measure.

Another John the late empress had hated, the Lord Chamberlain to Emperor Justinian, turned away from the newly widowed ruler as the brief meeting of the imperial council ended.

John the Eunuch, as many called him but never to his face, was in his early fifties, a tall, lean Greek, clean-shaven, with high, sharp cheekbones and sun-darkened skin. Age had not grayed his closely cropped black hair. He wore deep blue robes made of the finest cloth, adorned only by a narrow gold stripe along the hem. Dressed less elegantly, he could have passed for the mercenary he had been as a young man or as a desert-dwelling hermit.

"John, please remain." The emperor spoke softly. His bland round and slightly puffy face looked too calm to belong to a man standing beside the body of his newly deceased wife.

The members of the imperial council who had been available at short notice filed out of the cramped sickroom as quickly as dignity allowed—the Praetorian Prefect of the East, the Master of Offices who headed the palace administration, the emperor's legal advisor the Quaestor, and the imperial treasurer. Their hasty departure whorled the haze of lamp smoke, incense, and perfume.

John watched their escape, then fixed his gaze on Justinian. As a count of the consistory John had no specific duties. His work depended on the emperor's whim.

"Excellency," John said. "My condolences."

"Offer a prayer for her soul, John."

This was an order John could not carry out because he worshiped Mithra in secret rather than the god of the Christians. He inclined his head in a vague gesture he hoped would be taken for assent, then looked on uncomfortably as Justinian paced to the foot of the bed and tugged its sheets straighter.

The emperor refused to leave Theodora's side. Did he truly grasp that she was dead?

John realized that now he would never be entirely certain why Theodora had hated him. Perhaps she had not wanted to share the emperor with other advisors. There was no sense of victory. If John felt anything, it was regret that she had departed before he had managed to defeat her. He felt nothing toward the husk she had left behind.

His enemy's death gave John so sense of relief either. He struggled to accept that finally, after more than twenty years, Theodora no longer threatened him.

Justinian paced back to the head of the bed. His pacing was the only sign he gave of agitation. "The evil-doer will eventually be brought to justice before the throne of God. As God's representative on earth it is up to me to administer justice in this world."

"Evil-doer, excellency?"

"The monster who murdered the empress."

The statement took John off-guard. For months the court had observed in horror as the empress wasted away. "Surely the monster was the illness she suffered?"

"No. I won't believe it. She was poisoned."

Despite the hot, smoke-filled air, John felt a chill at Justinian's matter-of-fact tone. If the emperor had displayed any emotion his irrational statement could have been dismissed as a momentary delusion brought on by grief.

"But how could she have been poisoned?" John asked. "We are in the center of Theodora's private residence. Few were admitted to see her." He glanced around the room. Painted angels adorned the walls. A gilded icon depicting the healing saints Cosmas and Damian faced the bed. A chest of inlaid wood sat at its foot. There was a three-legged table with a round marble top crowded by small glass bottles and ceramic pots. As usual an armed excubitor stood outside the only door. "Ask the guard, excellency," John suggested. "He will tell you no poisoner could have gained entrance."

Justinian waved his hand dismissively. "He doesn't know anything. He's new. The other guards—the ones who failed—I ordered executed before you arrived this morning."

The emperor smoothed his dead wife's hair. His features were as motionless as those of the corpse. He might have been wearing a mask to conceal an anguished visage. At times it was not hard to believe Justinian was a demon in human form, as popular rumor had it. Perhaps today he had no anguish or other human emotion to hide but was simply too preoccupied to animate his false face enough into a more human aspect.

"I am also to blame' Justinian went on. "I allowed the murderer to reach her. I remained at her side, and yet, at times I dozed. And food and drink and potions were given to her, under my gaze. I prayed to the Lord that he take me also. My prayer was not answered, or rather it was answered in the negative. To go on living is the penance I must pay."

"You should not torture yourself with such thoughts, excellency," John offered. "The illness simply ran its course."

"You believe that?"

"I do. Everyone does. It is a fact."

Justinian's face remained expressionless. "Nevertheless, I am ordering you to find her murderer. You are an eminently reasonable man, John. When you uncover evidence that she was murdered you will change your view."

John tried not to show his dismay. During Theodora's illness no one had so much as hinted there might be anything except natural causes involved. "I will change my view if I find such evidence. But—"

"You will find her murderer. You must. You won't fail me as her guards did. I am depending on you. The empire is depending on you. Your family is depending on you."

John thought his heart missed a beat as Justinian turned away.

Was the emperor threatening his family with reprisals if John failed?

Justinian bent toward his dead wife's face, ran his fingers lightly across her eyelids and lips, ensuring her eyes and mouth remained shut, John supposed, so that no demons might gain admittance. Would the emperor harbor such a peasant superstition if he were indeed a demon?

"Her pain has ended," Justinian said in a whisper. "Now go and find who did this to her."

Dismissed, John took a last look at his old adversary. The emaciated hands clasped over her chest resembled claws. The face was yellowish and waxy, inhuman. The disease had eaten at her until the flesh that remained stretched tautly over her plainly visible skull. Although her tightly drawn lips were colorless, John could not help seeing, as he had in the past, the red scimitar of her smile.

As he went out to begin his hopeless investigation, John allowed himself a grim smile. It had been premature to think Theodora no longer threatened him.

Chapter Two

"Goddess!" Cornelia cursed. Theodora was gone at last, but she and John were still not free of the empress' interference.

She made certain all but one of the atrium lamps had been extinguished, checked the bolt on the front door, then went up the steep wooden stairs to the second floor. Peter was supposed to have performed the same tasks before retiring to his room, but the old servant had become forgetful.

Cornelia was nervous. There was no telling what disturbances might break out in the wake of Theodora's death.

She strode down the dark hallway toward the bedroom. She could see a streak of light from the bedside lamp streaming across octopi and fish in the blue and green floor tiles. Entering the room she took off her sandals and threw them into a corner.

"And don't tell me I'm bad-tempered, John, " she said. "I know that. But haven't we got enough to worry about with Europa refusing a court physician and wanting me to attend her out on Zeno's estate?"

John was sitting in bed. He picked up the clay lamp to extinguish it as Cornelia turned to take a last look through the open window. The nearby dome of the Great Church, light pouring through hundreds of apertures, radiated an orange dawn into the night sky above cross-bedecked rooftops. Cornelia pulled her linen tunica over her head, and laid it on the chest at the foot of the bed. Only then did the lamplight go out.

She plumped down on the bed so hard it creaked. A muscle in her back joined the bed's protest. The twinge of pain made her curse again. "I'm not as young as I used to be."

"Strange. Watching you, I was thinking you're still the same beautiful young girl I first met. And you still have the same temper. Surely you've attended women before?"

"When I traveled with the bull-leaping troupe. But it's different when it's your own flesh and blood."

"I'm glad you'll be there. After all, it is our first grandchild."

Despite the open window the summer night was stifling. She could hear voices drifting from the city. Patrons leaving an inn, tenement residents sitting outdoors late to escape the heat. From further off came the faint barking of a dog. The sounds emphasized the immensity of the world outside and the comfort of their own room. She pulled John down onto the cotton stuffed mattress and pressed herself against his back. Even though he was as damp as she from the humid air, his skin felt cool, as it always did. He never wore fragrances as did most of the aristocrats at court.

Cornelia would miss the feel of him when she tried to sleep at the estate south of the city. "And then there's Peter," she said, shifting with practiced precision to match her contours to his. "I suggested he might like an assistant to help run the household while I was gone. He was outraged. Said he was still capable of serving his master. Most emphatic that he didn't want help."

"He's proud, Cornelia. I've hinted at a pension more than once but he was quite firm in refusing it. He's a free man and can leave at any time. Even if he is in his seventies, we must allow him his dignity."

Cornelia sighed. "'And you won't dismiss him."

John agreed. "I would like him to retire but I won't force him. It's not as if we give elaborate banquets. He can still manage his tasks and he's been a good servant always. All the same, I can't help but worry. He limps badly when he thinks nobody can see it."

"You might worry a little more about yourself," Cornelia replied. "What about this assignment? How can you find a killer who doesn't exist?"

"Justinian might know more than he is telling me."

"Even if there was a murderer how would you find him? Most of the population of the city would have killed Theodora if they had the chance. And how many at court didn't have reason to want her dead?"

"You could be right."

Cornelia pressed herself more tightly against John's back. Outside two cats fought raucously and briefly. A slight breeze struggled into the room, barely managing to stir the heavy air. "I'd look into her meddling in family affairs, her unwanted matchmaking. Let the imperial torturers go about their work. Let taxes be increased. Let religious arguments thunder back and forth. That's expected. But once you interfere in love affairs, even an empress is treading on dangerous ground."

"You say that because you are thinking of Europa and Thomas and their child. Our own family."

"Perhaps."

"That and listening to too much palace gossip."

"No one at court can help listening to gossip, unless they're deaf." She tugged John's sinewy arm until he rolled over to face her. She could see the faint light from the window glinting in his eyes. "Theodora has always put her own family first, and especially before Justinian's. Look at the marriages she arranged for those sisters of hers, Comita and Anastasia. Their reputations are as bad as hers. Marrying former whores into reputable families is bound to cause resentment. Yet who dare say no to the empress?"

"Not many."

"And not only that. What about those two youngsters she's forced to live with one another? Belisarius and Antonina's daughter Joannina and that wretched boy Anastasius. Joannina will have to marry him now to protect what honor she has left. Everyone knows the match was designed to shift Belisarius' fortune to Theodora's family."

"Anastasius is Theodora's grandson, it's true."

"Son of Theodora's illegitimate daughter. The daughter's well named. Theodora. Like mother, like daughter."

"I don't believe Justinian's foremost general and his wife would murder the empress."

"And there's General Germanus too." Cornelia plunged ahead, ignoring his remark. "Theodora tried to thwart his daughter's marriage, even though it might be the last chance she'd ever have, considering her age. And why? Could it be because Germanus is Justinian's cousin?"

John put his finger lightly to Cornelia's lips. "I do know a little about what goes on at the palace."

Cornelia pushed his finger away. "Not to mention yet another general Theodora wronged. Poor Artabanes! Forced to live with his estranged wife and watch Theodora marry off his lover to one of the empress' wicked—"

She was forced to break off as John inclined his head and kissed her. "I will need to start my investigation after the funeral tomorrow. We can talk about this then, Britomartis."

Cornelia smiled. "Do you think you can silence me like that?" Britomartis, the Cretan Lady of the Nets, was his pet name for her from long ago. Cornelia was a native of Crete and the first time John had seen her performing with a traveling troupe that recreated the ancient sport of bull-leaping the sight of her snared him as securely as fishermen catch Neptune's creatures in their meshes. Or so he had said. Cornelia supposed there were a lot more women called little sparrow in private than Britomartis.

She returned his kiss. "Despite everything, you've never changed, John. You're no different now that you're a great man in the capital than you were as a poor young mercenary at the furthest reaches of the empire."

She felt the muscles of his arm tighten under her fingertips and realized she had inadvertently reminded him of the wound he endured. He had not reached twenty-five when he blundered into Persian territory, was captured, castrated, and sold into slavery like a beast. Tears came to her eyes. For his sake, not hers. Men made too much of their masculinity.

"Oh, John, please don't think of that."

"I wish I could be more for you than…than an old man."

"Old couples are the happiest, they say." She took his face between her hands, hoping he couldn't see the wet streaks on her cheeks. "Besides, we have been together. We have a daughter. Right now, on some battlefield, a young man who has never had those things is dying."

"As always, you are right. Still—"

"Please don't talk, John. Let's forget the past and Justinian. You know how wakeful Britomartis has always been. Help her sleep now, as you always do."

Chapter Three

Theodora's funeral procession made its slow way down Constantinople's main thoroughfare. The colonnades along both sides of the Mese were packed with watchers five and six deep. Most had glimpsed Emperor Justinian, if at all, only from a distance, when he attended events at the Hippodrome or appeared in public for church celebrations.

This afternoon they could almost touch him, if they had dared.

Clad in plain garments without decorative borders or gems, the mourning emperor walked immediately in front of the bier bearing Theodora's coffin. Scarlet boots were his only touch of color. He scuffled through dust and windblown debris as if he hardly had sufficient strength to lift his feet. His head, bereft of crown and bare, was held high but his expression remained blank.

As he passed the crowds a whispering followed him, a snake-like hiss John heard as he marched a few rows in front of the emperor in a line of court officials. He found himself between Justinian's treasurer, the bald, dwarfish eunuch Narses whom John despised, and the obese Master of Offices, who puffed and wheezed ever more alarmingly as the procession climbed the hill atop which sat the Church of the Holy Apostles.

John felt hot and uncomfortable, burdened by the heavily embroidered robes he wore only when ceremony demanded.

It was just as well a sullen sky pressed dark clouds down on the city as if to smother the five domes of the church. A rising wind flapped tunics and cloaks, with gusts carrying away the sound of the hymns sung by the choir trailing the coffin. The wind and lack of sunlight ameliorated the heat and humidity to a small extent.

He would have preferred to be back in bed with Cornelia. He had been forced to abandon that refuge long before dawn. Court officials and ecclesiastics had paid homage to Theodora during the early morning hours. The empress' perfumed and anointed body had lain in the Triclinium, popularly known as the Hall of the Nineteen Couches, on the palace grounds. Any possible echoes of the imperial banquets usually held in the long, many-windowed building were muffled by deep purple drapery covering its walls and the bier on which her coffin rested, covered by a linen cloth of the same color, embroidered with scenes of the Resurrection. Despite Justinian's suspicions of foul play, her death was not unexpected. Preparations for the funeral had been completed for weeks.

Justinian had also prepared for trouble. In case anyone might seek to use the disruption of life to his own advantage, the palace grounds were thick with armed men. When John arrived, his friend Felix, captain of the excubitors, a burly, bearded man, had been patrolling inside the Triclinium, moving from one guard post to another, conferring with those on duty.

Felix growled a greeting.

"I am sorry to hear about the deaths of your excubitors," John said.

"Justinian had no reason to have those boys killed. It was all I could do to keep the rest from revolting." Felix's angry glare moved around the long room filled with elegantly dressed mourners and settled on the dead empress. "They'd rather throw her corpse on the street for the dogs than stand guard over it. The imperial whore reached up out of hell and murdered their colleagues, as far as they're concerned. I can't blame them. You can't stop a disease with swords and spears. Or stop fate either."

John wondered whether Felix blamed the emperor or the empress or both. Usually it amounted to the same thing, or had until now. "Nor can you bring fate to justice, which is what Justinian expects of me," John replied.

"Yes, I've heard. May Mithra stand at your shoulder."

"Have there been any disturbances?"

"None. Not here. I've spent half the night watching over an endless parade of Theodora's pet monophysites. Those heretics are a wild eyed foreign crew and not all of them properly washed." Felix sniffed disdainfully. "They seemed to be genuinely grieving. When Justinian comes to his senses he'll turn them out of that den of theirs in the Hormisdas Palace. Then they'll have something to grieve over."

John noticed an attractive, fair-haired woman surrounded by attendants moving toward the bier. "I see Antonina is here."

"She'll be angry she didn't get what she wanted," Felix said. "Coming all the way from Italy in hopes that Theodora could convince Justinian to give Belisarius the reinforcements he needs to fight the Goths. She arrived too late."

John saw that Felix's gaze lingered on the woman. In the dim light, at a distance and dressed in robes glittering with jewels, she looked the same as she had over fifteen years ago. Back then, Felix was a lowly young excubitor and had confessed to John he had been lured to an unwise tryst with Antonina in this very hall. Did he recall that now? How could he not? Did he ever wonder if fate had smiled, whether it might be him instead of Belisarius leading Justinian's troops in Italy?

John said, "Cornelia tells me that Antonina will be pleased since she can call off that marriage Theodora arranged between her daughter and Theodora's grandson."

"That's a harsh judgment." Felix spoke with surprising brusqueness. "Antonina was Theodora's friend."

There was a stir behind them as the choir took its place and the final detachment of excubitors stepped into line.

Felix glanced back. "A choir of former whores from her refuge singing hymns!"

"Some believe that the dead pay demons at the toll stations on the way to heaven with good works done here," John observed in an undertone. "That refuge of hers will get her through at least one gate."

"Perhaps," Felix admitted in a begrudging tone. "But how will she get through the rest of the gates unless she knows the demons manning them personally?"

John took his leave. He had to be seen going through the motions of paying his respects to the woman who had hated him. Then the funeral procession to the Church of the Holy Apostles would not be long in leaving. Internment needed to be carried out quickly, particularly in summer heat. Although the rich and powerful could afford more perfumes and scented unguents than the poor, once their souls had departed their flesh decayed just as quickly.

Now the long line of mourners was approaching the church. Justinian, pale, stumbled along as if he were an automaton fast running down. The murmur of the crowd along the street mingled with the tramp of excubitors' boots and the monotonous rise and fall of hymns. Clergy brandished censers whose fragrant incense evaporated ineffectively into the pervasive stench of the city. Servants of the imperial household, including several of Theodora's female attendants, all weeping, followed the bier, as did more clergy carrying bright icons whose gold looked dull in the heavy light struggling from the dark heavens. Then came gaudily uniformed silentiaries and mounted scholarae in plumed helmets, minor officials, representatives from palace offices and the charitable endeavors in which Theodora had interested herself. It was a microcosm of both the dead woman's life and imperial power and majesty.

Overhead glowering clouds sank lower and a greenish light began to spill down from breaks in the gray sky. Patriarch Menas waited at the church entrance. His long beard pulling his narrow face down into a sorrowful expression.

"Lord Chamberlain," the patriarch murmured, nodding a greeting.

Was there a hint of irony in the look Menas gave to him?

Probably it was only John's imagination. Menas, like John, had been no friend of Theodora's. A dozen years earlier the new pope, Agapetus, had removed Theodora's heretical ally Anthimus from the patriarchate and replaced him with the orthodox Menas.

Like John, Menas had survived despite Theodora's enmity.

Even if Menas had not intended to convey to John the irony of them both paying their respects to an enemy, it was ironic that a woman who had ordered floggings and torture with less concern than she took over choosing jewelry would rest under the same roof sheltering relics of the apostles, martyrs, and saints, not to mention a portion of what was believed to be the column to which the Christian's gentle god had been tied for a flogging before his slow, tortured death.

John would not have relished tracking down her murderer even if he believed she had truly been murdered. However, a follower of Mithra did his duty. For more than twenty years he had served Justinian. The emperor wanted him to find a murderer and John would do his best.

Was it possible that his duty to Justinian conflicted with his duty to Mithra? John did not think so. Yet there were those who claimed that both the emperor and empress were demons in human disguise. There was no doubt there was evil abroad in the world. A Mithran's life was dedicated to battling evil. Had John been serving the wrong side?

Yes, said the scarred and twisted visage of the demon peering at him from the fringe of the crowd.

No. Not a demon. Not a sign, he realized. It was his friend and informant, the beggar Pulcheria, she of the half-ruined face. Even the poorest of the poor had come to pay their respects to a woman who had lived in splendor.

Or had the beggars come to gloat that though they lived on the streets, they yet lived?

Chapter Four

"Just because Pulcheria is not a demon does not necessarily mean that your seeing her was not a sign," said Anatolius.

"Spoken like a lawyer," John replied.

John had spotted his long-time friend as he left the Church of the Holy Apostles. Anatolius was only in his midthirties but his curly hair, once black, had turned prematurely gray. It distressed him, John knew, but made his visage resemble even more strongly the classical Greek sculptures, bleached of color by time.

Now they sat in Anatolius' study. The cupids Anatolius' late mother had commissioned still cavorted on the walls. He had also retained his deceased father's desk with a skull depicted in its tile top. He did not meet his legal clients here, but in his office.

The room was uncomfortably hot despite the screens to the garden being open. As always in the heat, John drank more wine than usual. Who didn't? He kept adding more water until it was barely palatable, but between the heat and the wine and lack of sleep the past few days he felt as if there were a fog behind his eyes. It was an effort to speak.

Anatolius had listened to John's account of recent events in thoughtful silence.

"I would take you spotting Pulcheria—thinking her a demon—as a sign, John. I know you don't think that way, so consider this. A lawyer naturally gets to know what's on people's minds. Courtiers and senators and senators' wives tell me things they'd never confess to a priest. Lately everyone is frightened. They're all certain Justinian has gone mad. Theodora was his life. He has had to watch her slip away, helpless to save her despite all his power. He is not necessarily the man you knew and I would not trust him. Particularly in regards to this impossible commission he's given you."

"What would be your advice?"

"If you were my client? I would advise you to do what you've talked about for years, pack up and take Cornelia to that bucolic estate in Greece, and do it today. You won't, of course."

John smiled faintly. His friend knew him well. There were very few to whom he had admitted his desire to leave the city and the imperial court some day.

"If you won't think about yourself, think about Cornelia and Europa, and that grandchild who might be squalling even as we speak," Anatolius continued. "You may choose to live like a spartan or some holy man, but nevertheless you are a wealthy man. One day your family will inherit your lands and they may have more use for them than you do. If you fail Justinian, though, he is liable to confiscate everything."

"I could see that if he were still being advised by the Cappadocian, but—"

"The threat is real, John."

"The emperor takes what he wants anyway."

"He can be thwarted. Last year I was approached by a widow, a patrician. She had heard the emperor had taken a fancy to the family estate. It was not a tremendously wealthy family. The widow and her only child, a daughter, were going to be thrown out into the street or rather, since the estate was in the country, into the nearest pasture. I transferred the estate to her daughter, giving the girl a life interest, with the property then reverting to the local bishop. Once the bishop had an interest to fight for, Justinian turned his attention elsewhere." Anatolius frowned. "Forget your estates, John. I hate to mention it, but your family might well be at risk if you fail. Justinian seems to have lost his senses. He's lashing out in all directions. "

"I have survived at court for a long time, Anatolius. I see no reason this time should be any different."

"In the past your main antagonist was the empress. To deal with enemies she and the emperor did not share she had to either work her way around Justinian in secret, or come to an accommodation with her opponents. Consider Patriarch Menas, presiding over things so lugubriously at the church today. A perfectly orthodox cleric who took the place of her handpicked monophysite patriarch Anthimus. Do you think Theodora wouldn't have breathed the fires of the Christian hell on Menas if she could have? But Justinian is orthodox and, in the end, it is Justinian's opinion that counts. So it was Anthimus who vanished, right off the face of the earth. And now, with this investigation, it is you who are likely to find yourself up against Justinian rather than Theodora."

John nodded. He had not told Anatolius about the emperor's implied threat but it was easy enough to guess. "There was a time when we met you'd read me the poem you had composed for your latest love."

"We can both be glad those days are gone." Anatolius brushed a strand of gray hair off his forehead. "Gone, along with my glossy black locks, as someone once called them."

"I'm sure that someone was most attractive. But you penned good verse unlike that acquaintance of yours, Crinagoras. I suppose he is still at it?"

"No. He managed to marry an aristocrat. Her father convinced Justinian to appoint Crinagoras to a position with the Master of Offices. He also lectures on lexicography at the imperial school."

"The young lady must have had execrable taste in poetry."

"Not so young. Her father couldn't believe his good fortune, finally having her taken off his hands." Anatolius ran a finger around the outline of the skull gazing eyelessly up at him from his desktop. "Funerals always make me reflect on the past and the future. On passing time."

"The gods themselves were born of infinite time," John replied. He wiped away a bead of sweat that trickled down the brown concavity of his cheek. A yellow butterfly found its way into the study, fluttered around the painted flowers brandished by several cupids, and recognizing nothing of interest drifted outside again.

"We don't usually think very deeply, do we?" Anatolius mused. "I believe we're designed not to do so. After watching Theodora consigned to eternity I'll brood about death all afternoon and then feel foolish. Just as I'd feel foolish about how deeply I'd loved some woman after the affair ended, but perhaps that's just me."

"I'm surprised you never married."

"I was always too busy falling in love to marry. And then I started late on a career so I've been busy catching up. Some day." He gave John a quizzical look. "That isn't the sort of thing you usually say."

John laughed. "I've been thinking about marriages. Cornelia was explaining all of Theodora's machinations to me. Arranging this marriage, thwarting that one. She believes such actions would give someone a motive for murder."

"She's right." Anatolius raised his gaze to the ceiling thick with chubby, winged cupids. "Eros halts the dance and throws away the bridal torch, if he sees a joyless wedding."

"Nonnus."

"You have read his Dionysius?"

"No, but you recited a bit of it to me a while ago. His verse is much too long and turgid for me, even if he is popular."

A portly, red-faced servant appeared in the doorway leading to the atrium. He was sweating profusely. "Sir, a young woman is here seeking your services."

John caught a glimpse of a slim girl peering around the servant's shoulder. Her light hair was coiled on either side of her head in a style currently fashionable at court. He got up from his seat. "I must go. I have work to carry out."

Anatolius stood also. "Think about my advice, John." He looked toward the doorway. "I will be with you shortly, Vesta.

Why don't you wait on the bench by the fountain? It's cooler there."

When the girl and the servant had vanished, Anatolius gave John a rueful grin. "The fair young ladies now only come to my house on business. Alas."

Chapter Five

Antonina did not look up as Vesta entered the kitchen of the city house Antonina shared with her husband Belisarius on the few occasions they were both in Constantinople together and not on campaign.

"The ingredients you requested, my lady," the girl said, laying a fragrant basket on the table.

"You took long enough." Antonina was stirring a pot of boiling liquid set on the brazier. "I thought you were going straight to the market. Have you obtained only the freshest? It makes a difference and if you wish to learn how to make love potions, you must take care to use only the finest herbs and flowers."

She finally looked up, frowning, and continued. "And how is my daughter? Still thinks she's in love with that young oaf Anastasius?"

"I'm sorry," Vesta faltered. "But—"

"You won't say," Antonina replied, waving her spoon. Drops of scalding liquid fell on the other's clothing. "You may be stupid, but you're loyal. No wonder, if you get to wear your mistress' jewelry!"

Vesta's hand went to one of the dangling silver earrings hung with blue pendants.

"Her father and I gave her those earrings when she was only a baby," Antonia said. "Valueless, in case she lost them. Just be certain you're loyal to the right person, that's my advice. Here, keep stirring this and don't let it boil over. It's a ginger preparation for ailments of the stomach."

She examined the contents of the basket. "You didn't get as many rose petals as I need so you'll have to get more. If my potion wasn't so popular with the ladies of the court I wouldn't need your assistance."

My assistance is an excellent opportunity to spy on your own daughter, Vesta thought, but on the other hand it also means I can tell my mistress what you say and do here. "I tried everywhere."

Antonina laughed. "You can steal roses from the palace grounds easily enough. Go out tonight, pick as many as you can, and bring them to me."

She paused for a heartbeat, staring out the window at the looming wall of the Hippodrome. "Now as to how to make rose water. The rose is a very prettily scented flower, sacred to Aphrodite so the pagans say. Which is probably how it came by its reputation as a kindler of love when used to anoint the skin."

"Yes, my lady."

"It's effective with many men. I remember when Belisarius was—but never mind about that. Set that pot aside. I'll give you instructions and when we have enough rose petals you can try your hand at making a batch."

As Antonia spoke it occurred to Vesta that Belisarius would be advised to be careful what he ate and drink when home on leave. With Theodora now gone and considering Antonina's ambitious nature, she might well be planning to conquer Justinian.

"Pay attention, Vesta!" Antonina was saying. "All you do is take several handfuls of petals and cover them with boiling water in a lidded bowl. When the mixture is cool, squeeze and remove the petals. As simple as that, but the women at court are too idle to make it themselves and too proud to admit their need of it. And that being so, they can hardly order their servants to make it for them. On the other hand, a visit to their old friend Antonina, a hint dropped, a gift given…."

A sly look came into her eyes as she continued. "Does your mistress ever use it, I wonder? After all, it inflames ebbing passions. Perhaps that betrothed of hers has a wandering eye? Has he ever made any obscene suggestions to you, Vesta?"

Vesta clenched her fists and began to wish she could poison Antonina to protect her mistress, or at the very least still the cold voice asking questions she had been ordered not to answer.

Chapter Six

During the night a thunderstorm broke the oppressive heat.

John and Cornelia were startled awake by the crack of a lightning bolt. The strike was near enough to rattle the lamp on the bedside table and the water clock in the corner. John leapt up in time to force the shutters closed against a gust of wind. Then the skies opened. He and Cornelia lay awake, watching flashes of light flicker through gaps between shutters and window frame and listening to rain lash at the brick facade of the house.

John could imagine sheets of water racing along the streets, wisps of straw, rotting vegetables, animal droppings, and other debris swirling and eddying into corners and soaking baked mud to a soft, clinging consistency. As the air cooled, he and Cornelia drew closer together.

Around dawn John rolled reluctantly away from her warmth. Pulling on a light tunic, he went to the window and opened the shutters. Crows strutted around the square dragging long shadows behind them, pausing to peck at morsels washed there by the night's downpour. Their eyes glistened like the wet cobbles.

"I count nine," John told Cornelia, as he turned away from the window. "Nine for the Deofil's own self."

"Deofil?" Cornelia sat up in bed.

"It's the way they say 'devil' in parts of Bretania."

Cornelia ran a hand through her tousled hair and gave John a quizzical look. "Those crows are predicting the devil?"

"It's not much of a trick. Constantinople has always been full of them."

"That's why we should move to that estate in Greece, the one you plan to retire to. I wish you were leaving the city with me today for good. Maybe the crows are telling you it's time go." She had let the sheet fall away and sat worrying at a knot in her hair. She smiled at him to show that her remarks had been meant teasingly.

A shaft of morning light draped itself from her shoulder, across her breasts, and settled against the rumpled sheets under her thighs. John felt a momentary tightness in his chest, no different than he had felt seeing her in the light of dawn decades earlier when he was a young mercenary.

He tried not to dwell on that other life.

Cornelia said, "You remember after we had news that Europa was pregnant we walked in the garden and you saw four crows and told me that our grandchild would be a boy, because the rhyme said four was for a boy?"

"We shall soon know if the crows are accurate."

"The day Theodora died I saw a single crow sitting on the fountain in our garden. One for sorrow, you said. But how many people were sorry Theodora was gone? I wasn't."

"Perhaps the prediction was not for you. Perhaps the crow was meant to be seen by someone else. By Peter."

"What? Would Peter feel sorrow over Theodora?"

"Maybe he is destined to overcook tomorrow's diner. That would make him unhappy."

Cornelia had finished with her hair but she made no effort to get off the bed. "What a funny rhyme for you to carry around in your head, here in the capital so far from its home. It seems out of place."

"Like the head it is carried in," John said. A secret Mithran serving a Christian emperor, the son of a Greek farmer, former mercenary, former slave, a man who had traversed the empire from Bretania to Egypt and Persia. He had spent almost three decades in Constantinople. He carried a map of the city in his mind. He knew the most intimate details of the imperial court and its intrigues. Even so, he did not feel he belonged.

"I don't remember you mentioning nine for a devil before. Is it the last verse?"

"In some versions of the rhyme."

"Are there many versions?"

"Probably as many as you care to make up. Julius was fascinated by fortune telling. He was the friend who introduced me to Mithra. We served together in Bretania. He used to talk to the natives whenever he had a chance. At night, in camp, he'd explain to me, for instance, how I should check the colors of the caterpillars to see if we'd have a cold winter. I'm not so sure some of the peasants weren't just amusing themselves at his expense."

Cornelia leaned forward attentively. "You remembered all the rhymes about crows?"

"Some of them. The rain reminded me." John turned back to the window. Crows still stalked across the cobbles but he didn't count them. "We had had downpours for a week. If you have never been to Bretania you can't imagine what it is like. The bitter chill, the icy fogs. Despite the cold, Julius returned from his patrol full of enthusiasm. He had struck up a conversation with an old farmer who recited this new rhyme. Others Julius knew went to seven, or to ten or eleven. This one, he said, had nine for the deofil's own self and wasn't that strange since there was another rhyme that had nine for a kiss. Not that women don't sometimes turn out to be devils."

"And did he see ever nine crows after that?"

"No. The next morning we forded a swollen stream. We must have done that a hundred times. This time he lost his balance or maybe a devil grabbed his leg and dragged him down. Before I could do anything he was carried away in the current and drowned."

He heard a soft footstep and then Cornelia's bare arms encircled him. He felt her warmth press against his back.

"Come back to bed, John. The carriage won't be here for a while."

Cornelia left for Zeno's estate before the sun had warmed the air. John had requisitioned one of the imperial carriages used to transport foreign dignitaries. Mist rose from cobblestones in pearly columns. John turned away before the carriage clattered out of sight beyond the corner of the barracks across the square. He did not like farewells. Under the circumstances he was glad to have Cornelia out of the city and not within easy reach of the emperor should things go wrong with the investigation.

Peter served John bread and boiled eggs, his lips drawn tight in unspoken disapproval.

"I know what you're thinking," John put his cup of Egyptian wine down on the scarred table. "If the mistress were here we would be having a proper breakfast. But when I was a young mercenary without a nummus to my name I would have been happy for such excellent fare."

"It would have been a proper breakfast indeed for a young mercenary," Peter replied. "When I was a camp cook we usually made gruel." He refilled John's cup. "I intend to visit the market, master. I'm going to see if I can get a really fresh swordfish to grill." The look he gave John was almost challenging.

"Swordfish would be excellent, Peter." John suspected his servant had recalled his fondness for the dish and thought it would cheer him with Cornelia away.

As soon as Peter limped downstairs and shut the door with an echoing bang that emphasized the emptiness of the house, John went his study to contemplate the Gordian knot he had been ordered to unravel. He wished he could solve his problem by waving a sword at it.

He glanced up at the little girl in the wall mosaic and sighed. Years ago he had named the solemn, dark-eyed child Zoe but now knew her real name had been Agnes and she was no more alive than the cut glass from which her double and the scene around her were constructed. Despite that, he continued to think of her as Zoe and she remained his confidante.

In daylight, Zoe stood in a serene country landscape beneath billowing clouds. Later, illuminated by fitful lamplight, the cleverly angled tesserae would reflect satyrs cavorting in the fields and pagan gods rioting in the sky.

"It's fortunate you cannot see what's going on behind you, Zoe," John muttered. "And equally unfortunate I'm just as blind to whatever has been happening behind my back."

He stood at the window. The mists had evaporated, Below, excubitors went in and out of their barracks, whose rain-washed surface gleamed in strengthening sunlight. Beyond the barracks a line of cypresses marked out the perimeters of a garden, more trees embraced a small church, and in the distance lay the Sea of Marmara, above which gulls visiting from the docks and foreshore swooped to and fro.

By now the carriage bearing Cornelia away would have passed through the Golden Gate at the southern end of the city on its way to Zeno's seaside estate. He wondered how his daughter Europa was faring, if Peter would find an acceptable swordfish, then chastised himself for permitting his thoughts to wander. Cornelia would send news in due course, Peter would doubtless find what he sought, and meanwhile he must at least organize a plan of attack for his investigation.

He couldn't very well investigate everyone at court who had nursed a grievance against the empress, let alone everyone in Constantinople.

Who had access to Theodora's sickroom? Not many, so that might be the place to start. But what about those who had some connection with those who had been granted access? A servant, for example, might be working for anyone at court or in the city.

Time slid away as he sank into thought. He was sitting at his desk, still pondering, when a thunderous knocking brought him to his feet. He hurried downstairs. It was Peter, laden down with a swordfish and a basket of produce.

"Thank you, master. It is hardly proper for you to let me in. I was on the wrong side of the door to open it." Peter said as he followed John upstairs.

John was about to reply when Peter gasped. Before John could turn to catch him, Peter fell backwards. He went crashing down the stairs, coming to rest surrounded by pears and several surprisingly intact pots of honey. A large cabbage had rolled into a corner of the atrium and the swordfish reclined next to Peter's out flung arm.

Although he lay flat on his back with his legs stretched straight toward the door, the toe of his left boot pointed at the wall. The sickening angle made it obvious that, unlike the pots of honey, Peter's left leg was broken.

Chapter Seven

"Get hold of his leg above the knee, John. When I tell you, pull as hard as you can."

The speaker, Gaius, the palace physician, had helped John get Peter up to his third floor room. Peter was positioned with his left leg extending past the edge of the bed. John clasped his servant's upper leg while Gaius grasped the ankle.

"Pull!"

The physician was a stout, bald man. His big forearms corded with effort. John leaned backwards as he pulled in the opposite direction.

Gaius' rubicund face grew redder. With a grunt he twisted Peter's leg until the grotesquely misplaced foot returned to its normal position. "I think we've got it. Let go."

John thought he could hear bones snap back into place, but surely that was his imagination. He looked with concern at Peter, whose face was calm but as waxen as that of a corpse.

The servant smiled weakly. ""Don't worry, master. For all I can feel, my leg might have been amputated."

"You still have your leg," Gaius said gruffly, positioning the splint under it. "The tibia and fibula were both broken right through, but cleanly and that's fortunate for you. Help me with these bindings, John."

"I am sorry for the trouble, master," Peter said.

"You'll be back on duty in a few months," Gaius told him. "Your leg will be good as new."

The servant sighed. "Can you make the rest of me new as well?"

Seated at John's kitchen table, Gaius looked up from his cup. "I'm grateful for your assistance in helping me set Peter's leg, but not for this terrible wine of yours. Not that I would ever refuse to drink it," he added truthfully. The physician had spent so much of his life with his bulbous nose buried in cups it had taken on a wine-dark color. "You'll have to tie Peter to his bed for several weeks."

"That will be difficult," John replied. "He'll try to get up before you're out of sight."

"For now, the draught of poppy potion I gave him will make him sleep. He may not be as difficult as you anticipate. After you left us alone I frightened him into agreeing not to get out of bed until I give him permission."

John asked how this remarkable feat had been accomplished.

"Oh, quite easily. I told him he would probably faint if he did and if we found him apparently dead on the floor I would have to establish if he was still living by extreme methods, such as thrashing his chest with nettles or pouring vinegar into his mouth. According to Peter, vinegar tastes no worse than your awful wine. So I went on to the possibility of onion juice squirted into the nose and horse-radish rubbed on the tongue. That got his attention. I didn't have to mention any of the more stringent invasive tests. If the healing goes well, his leg should remain much the same length as it always has been. If not, it'll be shorter than the other and he'll limp."

"He's already does, but thinks nobody's noticed."

"It's age gnawing at his joints. I'll bring something for that tomorrow."

John nodded. His own joints ached on damp mornings like this. "You've heard Justinian has ordered me to find out who poisoned Theodora?"

"Yes. Word gets around fast. I'm under suspicion, needless to say." The physician drained his cup and reached for the jug. "I attended Theodora until the day before she died, and it was not an easy illness. That last week she was asking for more and more poppy potion and yet it hardly seem to lessen the agony."

"Could anyone have poisoned it?"

Gaius considered the question. "No. I make it myself from tears of poppy and it never left my hands between completion and delivery to the sickroom. I've served as palace physician long enough to know it's the only way to avoid problems."

"Do you think she was poisoned?"

"No. She was gravely ill. I saw no signs of poisoning. It would have been impossible. Who could have poisoned her? It's not like anyone could walk in and invite her to have a drink or eat a honey cake. No, I'm certain it wasn't that, despite what Justinian says. Though if the emperor says a thing is so, as far as we're all concerned it is so."

"He expects me to prove it."

Gaius shook his head. "It was a wasting disease, John. There were all the characteristic signs as illness ran its course. Marked loss of weight, yellowing of the skin, increasing pain."

He shook his head and took a gulp of wine. "The pain was unimaginable. Several times Justinian summoned me, begging me to give her something stronger. You could hear her screaming all the way to the end of the corridor. I tried to explain to him that there was a limit to the amount of painkiller I could administer and that it could only deaden the agony so far. He was frantic."

"The emperor is used to having his own way."

Gaius nodded. "By a week ago it was obvious she was not long for this world. At the very end the pain subsided, mercifully. The last time I attended her she was drowsy. Until I got close enough it was hard to tell if she was still alive, her breathing was so shallow. Her pulse was strong but slower than it should have been, her pupils contracted. She seemed rational, but kept falling asleep. Most likely she slipped into a coma during the night and never woke up. I've seen it before. I knew what the outcome would be from the beginning."

"I take it no one would have considered the possibility of murder if she were a shopkeeper or a minor functionary?"

"Or even if her husband were rational."

After Gaius departed John visited Peter, finding him half asleep in his whitewashed room. Sunlight poured through the window across floorboards polished by wear and touched the large wooden cross mounted on the wall above the bed.

"I have instructions from Gaius that you must remain in bed for some time." John told him. "It would please me to know you will follow them. That being so, you are going to need help for a few weeks."

"Yes, master," Peter replied in a faint voice. "It was my own fault for not scraping the mud off the soles of my boots at the door. Slipped on the stairs, you see. Careless." He rubbed his forehead where a large bruise was beginning to swell. "What happened to the swordfish?"

"I rescued it and I shall grill it," John replied. "I don't know if you'll feel like eating? Soup perhaps?"

The elderly servant looked horrified. "But master, it is not fitting for you to cook or wait on me!"

John pointed out he had cooked his own meals many times in his days as a mercenary and there was nobody else to care for Peter with Cornelia away.

"If I may suggest it, master, would it not be possible for Hypatia to return until I get back on my feet? If someone else must work at my brazier, well, admittedly she over-spices the food but after all, she is from Egypt. She is familiar with the household. We've known each other a long time, and she takes directions well."

John concealed a smile. Peter had chosen the person he already had in mind, a young woman who had worked in the household in years past. Actually, not quite so young now, he reminded himself. In her mid-thirties. Since leaving John's employ, she had been working in the imperial gardens. "An excellent choice, Peter. I'm certain it can be arranged."

"Thank you, master," Peter closed his eyes. "I hope she will not be too irritated with me for not cultivating her herb beds as well as I should. I am afraid our garden is not as beautiful as it was when she looked after it."

"It will soon revive. Now you should worry about your own health. Try to rest."

John went back to his study.

It did not occur to him that anyone might think it odd for a high official to be caring for a servant. Over the years Peter had become part of his family. He was certain Hypatia would agree to help.

If only his investigation could be resolved so easily.

Chapter Eight

John did his best to ponder the task Justinian had set before him but he was preoccupied with other matters. He ended up wandering the house, hoping he would not be summoned by the emperor, and looking in on the sleeping Peter.

Late in the afternoon he opened his eyes, realized he had fallen asleep at his desk, and went to the kitchen to prepare the swordfish Peter had purchased.

Though not as tasty as it would have been had Peter been able to cook, the meal was passable. Unlike many men in his position John knew how to clean and braise a fish. Peter could barely keep his eyes open. He dozed off after a few bites and several slurred compliments on John's culinary skills.

When he was certain Peter was sleeping soundly John left the house to look for Hypatia in the palace gardens. Hours later, as sunset approached and golden-red light gilded the western sides of trees and bushes, he wondered if he had begun his search too late in the day. The gardens were extensive. They sloped down to the sea on terraces, a vast, bewildering array of vegetation—lawns, shrubbery, copses, meadows, beds of flowers and herbs—strewn with fountains, decorative buildings, covered walkways, benches, and statuary.

Had he been overly optimistic in expecting to find Hypatia tending to one of the larger flowerbeds now in full bloom? Another hour and it would be as dark as despair.

One more place to look and then he must return home. He passed under a low archway and entered an enclosed garden that had once contained a sunken pool. His then future son-in-law Thomas had stumbled into the pool while creeping around the grounds one night years earlier. Thomas had arrived in Constantinople claiming to be a knight from Bretania. John had been inclined to consider him a fraud. He would never have imagined the big barbaric redhead settling down to the life of an estate manager or fathering John's grandchild. Thinking of Thomas made him think of Europa and Cornelia. He sighed. Waiting for news was like waiting to go into battle, except others were fighting it and he could only observe from a distance.

As John grew older he no longer saw places simply as they were, but also as they had been, as he had seen them through younger eyes, as settings for the events of his life.

The original ornamental pool and fountain were gone, replaced by graveled walkways radiating away from a circular plot in which clipped yews reproduced in miniature the landmarks of the city. A dark-leafed Great Church grew next to a recreated Hippodrome, while nearby the open Chalke Gate of the palace was just tall enough to admit a column of marching rabbits if such a squad had decided to trample through the box-edged beds edging the walkways.

White and purple-red poppies filled the beds, each mass of blooms growing round a yew in a pottery container. Each tree was trained into the shape of an animal. Some were familiar denizens of this world, others had stepped down through the centuries from mythological days to amaze and delight visitors. A bear, a horse, a centaur, a gryphon were among them. The reddish light crept in among the dark shapes, adding long shadows to the advancing twilight.

The garden had been another of Theodora's whims.

Hypatia often worked here and John thought he might find her trimming stray twigs, bringing order to the green menagerie.

She was not there.

John began to walk around the perimeter of the enclosed garden, then stopped. He heard rustling in the foliage, yet saw no one.

He looked around.

There. Crouched behind a plane tree at the edge of the garden. A diminutive figure in green. A triangular, frightened face peeked around the trunk.

"Come here," he ordered.

The girl advanced slowly, hands to mouth, shoulders hunched, as if expecting a beating. She stood hardly as high as John's chest. He found himself looking what seemed a long way down at the top of her auburn hair.

"Excellency?"

"What are you doing here?"

"I was just walking, excellency."

John studied the girl. He recognized her. "Kuria."

She looked at him in amazement. "You know my name?"

"Naturally. You are one of Theodora's closest personal attendants. Have you seen the gardener Hypatia?"

Kuria shook her head and suddenly burst into tears. "Nobody has said a word to me since yesterday," she sobbed. "Where am I to go now my mistress is dead?"

"A new post will be found for you," John reassured her.

"Oh, but I think not," she replied with a flash of venom that surprised him. "I did not want to work for the empress. She only ordered me to serve her because I was from the brothel. She rescued me, she said. She used me as an example of her good works. There will be no other post here for such as me." She snuffled and wiped her pug nose with the back of her hand. "Begging your pardon for saying so, excellency."

It was probably true, John thought. Theodora had taken delight in pointing out her efforts to reform such women, especially when she granted an audience to a representative of a patrician family, someone she could horrify with lurid details.

The girl was right. No one at court would employ her. The girl's grief for herself had overcome her caution, for otherwise she would not have dared to speak to an official in such a fashion.

John decided to abandon his search for Hypatia. Perhaps fate was prodding him to begin the task he had been delaying. In which case, Kuria might well know something useful.

The late empress' attendant followed him obediently to a marble seat positioned to give a good view of the poppy garden.

Kuria confirmed she had attended the empress during her final days. He asked her about Theodora's visitors at that time. Had anyone been to the sickroom frequently?

Kuria's face bunched in concentration. "There was the fat physician, and an old churchman. They both visited every day. The emperor only left the room when they were there. Oh, excellency…" Her voice cracked and tears flowed afresh. "He was devoted to her. He insisted on feeding her himself, though she ate so little and rarely kept it down."

The comment suggested a possibility. "Who brought the empress her meals?"

"Her personal cook. When she took to her room he brought them to the door. One of us attendants took them in and Justinian would feed her, like I said." Kuria dried her wet cheeks with the bright green sleeve of her tunic.

"You say she ate little?"

"Mostly broth."

Poison and soup went well together, John thought. A natural pairing from a demon's kitchen, as many knew to their cost. On the other hand, the imperial couple's personal cooks answered with their lives if there was the slightest suggestion of tampering with their food. He remembered one occasion when Theodora had become ill after eating fish. The unhappy cook was roasted on his own brazier as a lesson to all.

Fish had not been served at the imperial table for some weeks afterwards.

The memory unsettled his stomach. He found himself tasting the swordfish he had consumed earlier. He swallowed hard.

Kuria continued to snuffle. Somewhere in the twilight a bird called but received no answer. As night fell the creatures sculpted from shrubbery solidified into dark menacing forms. Did the wings of the gryphon stir with life or was it only the effect of wind off the sea?

John wondered if the murderer could have paid Theodora's cook enough to risk his life. It was highly unlikely. An imperial cook already lived a life of privilege and luxury in the inner sanctum of the empire. If caught, the consequences would be terrible to contemplate.

"Who else was permitted to visit the empress?" John asked.

"Nobody, really. The empress even refused to see Antonina, her closest friend. She didn't want people to see how she was. All shrunken, her poor face like a skull. And she had times when the pains would grip her and she'd cry out. She didn't want anyone seeing. I think it hurt the emperor even more than it hurt her. His face would turn a ghastly white. Not that I was there all the time, excellency." The girl looked up at him. Her wide frightened eyes gleamed in the dying light.

"You couldn't have been always on duty. But, as far as you know, only the physician and the clergyman—a spiritual advisor, I assume—were regularly admitted. You mentioned attendants. Who were the others?"

"You mean during the last days? Just myself and Vesta. She is lady-in-waiting to Joannina, Lady Antonina's daughter. After Theodora moved Joannina and Anastasius into rooms in her personal quarters Vesta began visiting the empress, reporting on them. Especially when Theodora became too sick to visit the young couple herself. The empress wanted to be assured they were getting on well."

"I understand the empress took a great interest in their betrothal."

"Yes. Toward the end, Vesta spent as much time serving Theodora as serving Joannina. She always brought fruit but the empress could never eat it. We ate it instead. We took turns sitting outside Theodora's door in case something had to be fetched or our mistress needed assistance of an intimate nature."

Vesta. John recalled the name. Hadn't the client who had arrived to see Anatolius been called Vesta? "Describe Vesta."

Kuria's description matched the girl John had glimpsed at Anatolius' house.

John looked across the garden. The sun had disappeared behind the trees. White poppies glimmered as if they retained some fading remnant of the sunlight.

It appeared he would have to look further afield than visitors to the sickroom to find the culprit.

The imperial cook had every reason to hope Theodora continued to live, assuming he had been allowed to live this long. Given Justinian had ordered all the empress' guards executed, the cook was probably dead now as well. As for poor Kuria, about to be set adrift, she had gained nothing but misery by Theodora's demise.

As for Vesta, her mistress Joannina was besotted by Theodora's grandson Anastasius. Yes, "besotted" was the word everyone at the palace used, Cornelia had told him. On the other hand it was common knowledge that Joannina's parents were against the fast-approaching marriage. The last thing Joannina would want was for Theodora, her matchmaker and protector, to die and permit Antonina and Belisarius to have their way.

"Is Vesta fond of her mistress?"

"Oh, yes indeed, excellency. She wanted to be like her in every way. She'd dab Joannina's perfume behind her ears. She thought Anastasius so handsome. She was always saying what a romantic couple he and her mistress made." Kuria buried her face in her hands. "She will be thrown out too, excellency. When her parents take Joannina away from Anastasis, Vesta will be as homeless as I am."

The girl sat on the bench sobbing. John supposed there was nothing more she could tell him. It seemed callous to get up and leave her alone. Yet what could he do to comfort her?

He would have to talk to Vesta and her mistress Joannina. Anatolius had quoted poetry denouncing bad marriages just before Vesta arrived. Was the subject on his mind from a legal perspective? If Antonina and Belisarius wanted to thwart Joannina's marriage they might well have another match in mind for her. A bad one by Joannina's reckoning, no doubt. Perhaps Vesta was fetching legal advice and papers from Anatolius on behalf of Joannina.

Quite aside from that, it seemed clear those best positioned to be used as tools by a murderer all desperately needed the empress to go on living.

Now it was so dark the clipped animals were fading into the gloom. John could still see the bear. Its snarling mouth appeared to be forming a silent laugh. Was it laughing at the impossibility of the task John faced?

The sound of a light step, and a woman appeared through the archway. She carried a basket brimming with greenery. Startled, she glanced at Kuria and then looked up at John.

"Hypatia! I have been looking for you."

Chapter Nine

"It was Anatolius who caused you to leave, wasn't it?" Peter asked.

Hypatia shook her head and a lock of hair, black as a raven's wing, fell across her forehead. She pushed it away with a tawny hand. "No, Peter. I just felt you didn't want my assistance."

Peter levered himself up with his elbow. A cushion from one of the house's virtually unused reception rooms was wedged between his bony back and the wall. "That young man was paying you unwanted attention. Don't think I didn't notice. It was most improper."

"You mean because he's a senator's son and I'm a servant?"

"That's not what I meant exactly, Hypatia. What I meant was that Anatolius is not the sort of man you would, well, get along with. Flighty."

Hypatia couldn't help smiling. Scowling as he was, Peter looked very fierce. His leathery, wrinkled face displayed a finely lined map of his long life. Had he always looked aged? When Hypatia imagined him at twenty, he looked the same as the man before her. His eyes were still as young and lively as they must have been then, she thought. "That was years ago. I'm surprised you remember. It wasn't serious. We both know how Anatolius is about women."

"About attractive young women."

"Why, thank you, Peter." She was sure Peter's face flushed slightly. "What is Anatolius doing now? Still a lawyer?"

"Yes. The master tells me Anatolius is faring well in his profession."

"Not so flighty as he once was then?"

Peter lowered his voice to a whisper. "Between you and me, his business thrives mostly because he used to be Justinian's personal secretary. People come to him because they suppose he might still have the emperor's ear. Not only that, but everyone at court knows he's a good friend of the master and the imperial council the master belongs to hears legal appeals."

"Speaking of which, I intend to stay here as long as you need me, even if Anatolius throws himself at my feet and proposes marriage."

Peter's face sagged. "You don't think he might—"

"Oh, of course not! Here, drink this." She pressed a cup half-filled with brownish-green sludge into his hand. The thick liquid resembled the growth atop a stagnant puddle. "It's a tonic. I make it for Gaius to give his patients."

Peter raised the cup. His nose wrinkled and his lips tightened.

"It isn't hemlock!" Hypatia said.

He managed to imbibe the medicine.

"There, it's not so bad, is it?"

"I'm afraid it is very bad. Very, very bad. But if you say it will help…"

"It will. I'm glad Cornelia is still here. Are they married yet?"

The question seemed to startle Peter. "In the eyes of God, yes."

Hypatia smiled. "It's strange how none of our employer's circle of friends have married. Not Anatolius nor even Captain Felix. Do you suppose it's because they are Mithrans and can't find suitable matches?"

"You know we don't talk about the master's religion, Hypatia."

"I'd only mention it to you, Peter."

"You shouldn't mention it even to me. There are laws against pagan practices. Who can say what danger the master could find himself in?"

"But Justinian must know that—"

"Please. Don't say anything more about it."

The room's single window opened on a vista of the city dominated by the dome of the Great Church. Peter would be able to see it from where he sat propped up against his elegant cushion. Hypatia was not a Christian, but worshiped the gods of her native Egypt. "I understand the master will soon be a grandfather," she said to change the vexed subject.

"That's right. He's awaiting news."

"The child was some time in coming, wasn't it? Europa and Thomas have been married for years."

"We all arrive when God wills it. And depart." Peter lifted a thin arm and moved his hand in the Christians' sign.

"They are still living on the estate owned by Anatolius' uncle?"

"Zeno's estate. Yes. Thomas is still employed as estate manager. I never thought that redheaded rogue would settle down to a regular job."

"He was a military, man wasn't he?"

"Harrumph! He claimed he was a knight. I saw a rogue, plain and simple."

"But things have turned out for the best, as fate would have it."

"Fate? You mean God's will."

Hypatia made no reply. Was it only the Christian's haughty god who didn't consider himself subject to fate? She bent over to straighten Peter's coverlet. "Why don't you let me adjust your cushion so you can lie down? The potion I gave you will make you sleep."

Peter's eyes narrowed. "You said it was a tonic."

"Sleep is the best tonic."

"But I wanted to tell you about what's happened since you worked here last."

"There'll be plenty of time for that."

Grumbling, Peter managed to slip into a prone position, grimacing when he slid his splinted leg further down the bed. "I already mentioned the master is now officially a member of the consistory, although he was always one of the emperor's closest advisors. And you won't be surprised to know he has performed some confidential assignments and had a few close brushes with death while you've been gone."

"Which you will be able to tell me all about in the weeks ahead," Hypatia said, adjusting the cushion.

"I won't be bedridden for weeks, Hypatia. Do you think I won't be able to manage the stairs with a crutch soon or that I can't chop onions sitting down? In a few days I won't need your assistance and you can go back to your flowers and herbs."

"There's no hurry. When our employer spoke to me in the gardens yesterday evening and told me about your accident I agreed to help out. How could I not? I will be here longer than a few days, Peter. Gaius thinks you might be laid up for months."

"Months?" Peter's words slurred and his eyelids drooped.

"Perhaps. Even if it is, I will be here."

"It distresses me to think of you having to care for me that long," Peter mumbled.

Hypatia was pleased to see he did not look distressed.

Chapter Ten

While Peter and Hypatia talked John passed through the cross-emblazoned entrance to the glittering maze of Theodora's private quarters.

He had not lingered at home that morning. After taking a gulp of heavily watered wine and grabbing a chunk of stale bread, he had gone out to continue his investigation.

The sun was rising over the tall cypresses marking the edge of the gardens not far from his house. In the quiet he could hear the faint shouts of laborers drifting up from the imperial harbor as they unloaded a ship. From what part of the empire had it come? What had the crew thought when they were greeted at the docks by word of Theodora's death?

He had awakened to the sounds of Hypatia rattling pots and plates as she cooked and on his way out caught a glimpse of her climbing the stairs to Peter's room. It did not strike him as out of the ordinary. The years since her departure had vanished.

Strange how malleable time and memory could be.

What struck him as unusual was how empty his bed felt. Half-awake, he rolled over and only then remembered, with a pang, that Cornelia was away at Zeno's estate.

After he was so terribly wounded, John came to think of himself as a solitary man. He did not need human companionship in order to exist. What he did not need, he did not want.

What he did not want he did not seek. Was he quite as stoic as he liked to think?

Now and then taking a bite of bread, he marched along the edge of one of the garden terraces and watched the sun spill molten light across the smooth water of the Marmara.

Cornelia would return. Theodora would not return. Justinian was the emperor but he was also a man coming to grips with the fact that he would never see his wife again.

John put off visiting Theodora's quarters for an hour and still his steps slowed as he reluctantly approached their elaborate bronze doors. He rarely entered that part of the palace. The humid atmosphere reeked of exotic perfume and incense. To John it was like breathing the unhealthy miasma of a fetid swamp. The pallid, attenuated eunuchs who flitted everywhere filled him with revulsion.

While she lived, Theodora had made herself less accessible than the emperor, who pretended to a careless affability, willing to meet anyone, any time, at a heartbeat's notice. By contrast, the empress fiercely protected her own realm. It was said even the emperor was not welcome there. But now she was gone, the guards at the doors and in the antechambers beyond seemed almost indifferent to John's passage. Perhaps they were preoccupied with their own fates.

Once past the antechambers John entered a lavishly over-decorated world populated solely by women, eunuchs, and brightly costumed boys—court pages who served mostly, though not entirely, for decoration. A page smirkingly directed John to the rooms Theodora had given to Joannina and Anastasius, deep within the warren.

The girl John had glimpsed at Anatolius' house—Vesta—opened the door at his knock.

Before he could speak, another slender blond girl padded barefoot through an archway leading into the vestibule. She wore nothing but a wisp of a white tunica that swung lightly yet managed to remain clinging to her with each step. "Oh! I was expecting Anastasius."

John introduced himself.

"Naturally I recognize you, Lord Chamberlain." Despite being half-dressed, she regarded him as unselfconsciously as a child. Or, John amended his thought, a much younger child than she actually was.

"Joannina, I wish to speak to your attendant Vesta. Afterwards, I will require a word with you."

"Certainly." The girl spoke as if conferring an honor.

John compared the two young women, mistress and attendant. At first glance Joannina resembled her mother. She had Antonina's strikingly pale hair, the same brilliant blue eyes, the strong chin. A closer look revealed the differences, partly due to age. Less of her smile needed to be painted on. Her skin was not layered to rigidity with powder. But she was naturally slighter of build. Her fingers were long and slim, not plump. Facially she favored her father. She had Belisarius' longer, narrow features, his straight nose and gaunt cheeks.

Vesta was a poor sketch of her mistress although about the same age. Joannina was willowy. Vesta was gangly. Her hair was light, but a mousy brown. Her straight nose was too long, her cheekbones were high but overly prominent. Her strong chin jutted forward a little too far, as did two front teeth when she smiled at her mistress. John had no doubt she avoided smiling as much as possible.

"We will speak outside," he ordered, a precaution ensuring they were less likely to be overheard.

Vesta led him to an interior courtyard filled with a bewildering variety of vegetation registered by John's nonbotanical mind as possessing interesting foliage and bright flowers. At the far end, several tiers of wide steps led down to an ornamental pool. He wondered whether it was meant to evoke the terraced gardens descending to the sea. No doubt this served as a concealed garden for the residents of Theodora's quarters.

He and Vesta sat on a bench beside a marble table shaded by a red and white striped awning. The table was long enough to accommodate a banquet.

Vesta sat very straight as John questioned her about Theodora's final days.

"Only two of us were favored to attend our dear empress. Myself and Kuria."

"You brought Theodora fruit?" John asked, remembering what Kuria had told him.

"I did. The empress couldn't digest it but Joannina—my mistress, that is—she insisted on sending it every day."

"But you and Kuria ate the fruit?"

Vesta bit her lower lip. "What could I do, excellency? Bring her gift back? She would have cried if she knew Theodora was too ill to eat, and it breaks my heart to see my mistress cry."

"How long have you attended Joannina?"

"Years and years. Since we were mere children." The affection in her voice was evident.

"Where were you born, Vesta?"

"Why, Constantinople. My father is in the prefecture." She gave her head a little toss, which perhaps she thought looked haughty. John imagined an aging, petty official, long stalled in his advancement, thrilled for his daughter to get closer to the imperial family than he ever could, if only as a lady in waiting to the daughter of the empress' friend.

"You have been visiting the lawyer Anatolius."

The girl's eyes widened. "Please don't tell my mistress, excellency."

"Your mistress did not send you?"

"Well, yes. But no one is supposed to know. If my mistress finds out someone saw me…"

"You're fond of your mistress?"

"We are very close, Lord Chamberlain."

"She must be concerned about her betrothal now that the empress is gone."

Vesta bit her lip again. "I cannot speak against my mistress' parents. A great lord and lady to be sure. But, oh, she is so vexed, she's beside herself."

"She is afraid her parents will stop her marriage to Anastasius?"

"She's certain they will. It would be a tragedy, excellency. There's never been another love like it. If you saw the two of them together...with Joannina and Anastasius it was love at first sight. She confessed that to me herself. They were made for each other. And he is so handsome. It breaks my heart to think about it."

She pawed at her brimming eyes. John noticed her painted fingernails were badly gnawed. She suddenly burst into a torrent of passionate speech. "Let old dried-up women wag their nasty tongues about my mistress' situation! I wish someone would imprison me with a wealthy and handsome aristocrat!"

John noticed a sparrow had built a nest where the striped awning was attached to one of the marble pillars holding it up. He watched the bird perched on the side of its nest while he gathered his thoughts.

He wasn't surprised that young people might find it romantic to be forced to do what was usually forbidden. At their ages, he had been a wandering mercenary. He had grown up fast after he'd run away from Plato's Academy and his philosophy studies. On the other hand, court youngsters were usually mature beyond their years in the ways of intrigue.

He would have taken his leave of Vesta but Joannina suddenly appeared, dressed in a seagreen stola, her hair coiled at the sides of her head with silver chains. She dismissed Vesta with a nod and the attendant scurried off.

"How can I help you, Lord Chamberlain?" Her voice was supercilious. She gave a toss of her head.

As John began to speak he was interrupted by another voice. Querulous. A man's voice.

"What's the eunuch doing here?"

Joannina turned. "Oh, Anastasius! It's John, Justinian's Lord Chamberlain. You must recognize him." She looked sternly in the direction of the newcomer but John could detect the hint of a smile fighting to escape her frown.

"Is that who it is?" The man who strolled into the shadow of the awning—boy, rather—was exceptionally tall. If not for a pronounced slouch, the no doubt temporary result of recent, too rapid growth, he would have towered over John. His thick hair was sooty black, as black as Anatolius' hair had once been, and his skin had a dusky color which reminded John of Hypatia, but was not as burnished as hers. Like Joannina, he had narrow features and a straight nose, although one that was more pronounced. In fact, he looked like a taller, darker version of his betrothed. He was painfully thin and still moved with youthful awkwardness. John guessed within a couple of years he would fill out and mature into a striking figure.

Already he was a striking figure to his betrothed. Joannina went to his side and raised her head to kiss his cheek, then put her arm around his waist and leaned against him. Anastasius looked down at her fondly, as a child might look at a prized toy. He put his arm around her and let his hand trail downward.

"Why are you dressed like that?" He asked her in the same grating whine he'd just used. "We were supposed to go riding. You promised." He wore a short tunic over leather breeches.

"I didn't expect to have an important visitor." Joannina's gaze darted to John.

Anastasius managed to take his own gaze off Joannina and stared at John as if he hadn't really seen him up until now. "Sorry, sir. I thought you were just...well...there are so many around here...all tall and thin...or short and fat..."

"Now, Anastasius, really," Joannina tutted.

John smiled to himself. It seemed obvious Joannina was not going to tell him anything useful while Anastasius was present to distract her. "Enjoy your ride before the heat sets in for the day."

Joannina beamed with obvious relief. "Why, thank you, Lord Chamberlain."

"We will talk soon," added John.

Her face fell.

John left. He noticed the sparrow busily pecking at its nest, tidying up its grass and twigs, oblivious to the lives and loves and intrigues of the imperial court.

Chapter Eleven

John decided to visit Theodora's sickroom before leaving what had been her quarters. He navigated scurrying crowds of servants, eunuchs, and pages. The empress' residence continued to function under its own momentum, mindlessly, even though its center was gone.

To John's chagrin, Justinian's treasurer Narses was in the sickroom, scratching a list of its contents on a wax tablet. "Justinian has ordered everything loose be packed up," Narses told him. "If you must examine the place, please hurry."

The dwarfish man's fluty tone caused John to bristle. "I'll decide how long I need, Narses."

A sour smile flickered across Narses' face. "As you wish. I do not want to linger here in case Justinian returns. He intends to have the room sealed. I have always been a cautious man, Lord Chamberlain. Since we are conversing in confidence, I will say that, given Justinian appears to have been deranged by Theodora's death, I fear he might decide to entomb anyone remaining in here when it's closed off."

It would be ironic, John thought, if Narses proved to be correct and they were condemned to die in the same tiny room as Theodora had, watched over by the angels painted on the walls.

He did not find it very likely.

He looked around. The dismantled bed was stacked in a corner, its mattress atop it. Neatly folded bed linen lay on the chest of inlaid wood, now sitting against a wall. The marble-topped table stood beside the chest. The gilded icon still hung opposite the spot where Theodora had lain.

"What is in the chest?"

Narses shook his head. "I have not investigated, and since you are here, I'll leave that task to you."

John removed the bed linen and opened the chest. It was half filled with the small bottles he had seen at Theodora's bedside. Wrapped in linen and of varying sizes, the bottles were manufactured of green or blue glass. So far as he could tell, all had been washed. Had any original contents remained, the normal procedure would have been to feed them to dogs taken off the street to gauge the effects.

"You won't find the culprit hiding in there," Narses remarked.

John ignored the comment.

"I have given the matter some thought," Narses continued, "and it is evident anyone near the emperor—need I point out that includes both of us?—is not going to be safe until his desire for revenge has been satisfied. Who knows in which direction he will lash out once his first grief has worn off?"

"I can only attempt to do as ordered," John replied. He was aware of the cloying fragrance Narses used to scent his robes filling the confined space.

"If the empress was poisoned, even if you had a suspect, how can you prove the act? I am going to give you good advice, Lord Chamberlain. Everyone has enemies. Name someone. Anyone. Then let the imperial torturers discover the evidence."

"Enough innocent blood has been spilt because of the empress. I will not add to it."

"It is unwise to speak so freely at any time, and especially at this time."

John continued to unpack the chest. A set of ceramic pots came under scrutiny. These too had been scoured clean.

"Nothing to be learned here in my opinion," Narses commented. "But having done my duty I must hasten back to my office and leave you to continue. I hope you find something useful, for both our sakes. But when you don't, remember my advice."

John gave a curt farewell without looking up. He delved further into the chest. There remained only one last layer, carefully-wrapped bulkier items placed lowest that they might not crush delicate glassware or pots. First out was a large earthenware receptacle, a kind of bowl. A wash basin perhaps. There was also a lidded ceramic jar. It bore the stamp of the imperial kitchens on the bottom. It may have held olives because what appeared to be an olive tree was embossed in its side.

Setting the jar aside, he next removed an alabaster casket decorated with a pastoral motif. Gentle-faced sheep grazed on a hill, guarded by a youthful shepherd. An allegorical scene. The contents of the casket proved to be far removed from the pleasant country setting, for it contained a collection of jewelry. The dull light quenched its glitter as he examined a few pieces: amethysts strung on a finely-worked gold necklace, a pair of crescent earrings supporting three chains of pearls apiece, a set of silver bracelets decorated with cloisonné enameling.

Had Theodora kept the jewelry close at hand to admire or had she insisted on wearing it, deathly ill and all but unrecognizable as she had become?

Free of its wrappings, the final artifact was revealed to be a plain silver bell. No doubt it had been used to summon attendants sitting in the corridor.

John gave the bell an experimental flourish.

As if summoned by its sweet, piercing tone Justinian opened the door and stepped into the room.

Chapter Twelve

As John left the palace grounds and walked along the Mese the image of Justinian's haunted face accompanied him. Had the emperor, passing by the sickroom, opened the door at the summons of the bell? Or had he simply stepped into the room by chance at the instant John had rung it? Was he startled to find John there? Had he expected to see the wife he had buried two days before, still alive, ringing for assistance?

John thought he noticed the emperor's face change when he saw who was in the room. But the transformation occurred so rapidly John could not be sure what had been replaced. Had hope given way to disappointment? Joy to grief? By the time John fully registered Justinian's entrance there was nothing to be seen except the usual tired, flaccid mask.

John was left with the impression that there had been another face an instant before, perhaps not entirely human.

He had to admit that Narses was probably right. The emperor was in such a disturbed state of humors that he could lash out in any direction, including in John's, or, more importantly, in the direction of John's family.

John had excused himself quickly, explaining to the emperor he was on his way to an interview in furtherance of his investigation. It was true. He wanted to speak to a friend and informant of long-time acquaintance about Kuria, the attendant Theodora had plucked from a brothel. There was nothing his friend Madam Isis did not know about the city's brothels.

He could not help but think of her as Madam Isis, though the nature of her establishment had changed within the past year. The building, set in a semicircular courtyard accessible through a nondescript archway, had been one of the best houses in the city, according to both its mistress and such of its patrons who frequented the palace and were wont to brag about their vices.

Now the gilded Eros which had guarded the entrance had been replaced with a gilded cross. Gone from the long, door-lined corridor beyond were the explicit mosaic plaques announcing the services available in each cubicle. The previous summer the place had displayed lewd statuary, colorful wall paintings, and a staff of scantily silk-clad girls. Now it boasted only white-washed walls relieved by a few stern icons.

Of the original luxury there remained only the overstuffed couch in Isis' private apartments, on which John took his accustomed seat, and the polished wood desk where she kept her accounts.

The plump former madam smiled from her chair by the desk. She looked much older without the make-up she had habitually worn and her extravagant silks replaced by white linen robes. "You look a bit uncomfortable John. Does my new vocation bother you? We're friends, remember, from back in our days in Alexandria."

It was an long-standing jest. They had both passed through Alexandria many years before but their paths had never crossed, so far as John recalled. Nevertheless, Isis insisted on regaling John with reminiscences of their meetings there, embroidering her tales with surprising details. John had never decided whether she had confused him with someone else, possessed a better memory, or whether she just automatically employed her former profession's skill for creating a greater intimacy than really existed. Whatever the answer, however, their years of residence in Constantinople had brought about a genuine friendship between them.

"I was surprised to hear about your change of direction," John told her. "How is your new enterprise faring?"

"Very well, John. But why would you be surprised, of all people? First a mercenary, then a slave, and now Lord Chamberlain. Isn't that the way of the world? It isn't like the old days. Today we're free to change our social positions. Justinian was a farmer's son. Theodora was a working girl."

"I understand she was pleased to see her reform efforts succeed so well."

"She gave me her personal commendation."

"Has it helped to pay the bills?"

Isis tapped a naked finger on the codex lying open on her desk. The lack of rings on her wrinkled hands struck John as startling, almost embarrassing, considering the amount of jewelry she had always worn. "My accounts have never been better. Remember my big golden Eros? A private collector gave me a very good price for it, and a bishop donated those angry-looking icons you doubtless noticed."

"I never thought of you as…" He broke off, not wanting to offend.

"As a Christian? I can't blame you, but then again I am not the person you knew last year, let alone all those decades ago in Egypt. We all change. Well, perhaps not you, John." She leaned back in her chair and fixed her gaze on him. "Look at me, my friend. You see what I am now, without paint or gems. An old woman. When I was just another girl working for that dreadful man in a mud brick hovel down a side alley in Alexandria, I was already planning for the future when I would own my own establishment. I accomplished that. Now the time has come to make other plans."

"So the change is a matter of business? You are investing in your soul rather than the goods of the world?"

"I have not given up putting aside a few coins. My refuge owns several shops around the city and I intend to convert this building for similar trade soon."

John asked what her penitents would sell.

"For one thing we do a brisk trade in wonders. Salamander eggs, stone curls of hair from victims of Medusa, strings that once sang in Apollo's harp, that sort of thing. Visitors to the city like to buy them to take home. Currently there's a lot of interest in amulets. We make them here, but you don't need to mention that to anyone."

"What would your kindly bishop think?"

Isis brought her hand up to her mouth and her eyes widened. "Oh, my. You don't think anyone takes our goods seriously, do you? It's all in fun, like reading about Homer's gods, not that I ever had any amusement reading Homer." She let her hand drop and her full, unpainted lips quirked in a smile. "There was one patron who thought it pleasurable for a naked, nubile girl to read to him the battles between the heroes in the Iliad while he—"

John held up a hand. "Please don't give me the details. For all I know it's some official I might need to deal with at court. I'm glad to hear you're doing well, Isis, though I can't believe salamander eggs are as popular as the services your house used to provide."

"Remember, John, shops are less expensive to run. No need to hire doormen and brawny fellows to deal with the results of inflamed passions. No polishing statuary or cleaning floors and bedding. I don't have to buy silks or make-up for my girls. And you can't imagine how much medical care cost me. The pessaries, the procedures to correct mistakes made by my careless employees. Not to mention bribing the urban watch and the magistrates."

"Indeed. And was this why I sometimes saw your girls dressed like penitents begging in front of the Baths of Zeuxippos?"

Isis made a clucking sound of disapproval. "They never begged with my permission! Nor do we beg now. However, I'm happy to say the faithful are inclined to make donations. Imagine when a grand aristocrat or powerful office holder opens his door and sees the poor child he carnally abused now dressed in the garments of a penitent. The same sweet lips those wretched men damned their souls to kiss remind them how to save themselves from the fiery pit. What could be more fitting? Some of them weep with gratitude as they promise to remember my refuge in their wills."

John couldn't help smiling. "And your girls are happy with their new occupations?"

"There you are wrong. Some—the newer ones—complain they have to work too hard and have too little time to themselves. And they miss their silks. The older ones, who have seen what the life can lead to, are happier with the change."

"Which reminds me of what I intended to ask you," John said. "Do you know of a former working girl named Kuria, who became an attendant to Theodora?"

Isis' face hardened. "Yes. Kuria was one of my girls. Theodora noticed her when she visited here to give her official blessing to my refuge. She brought an enormous retinue. They descended on us like an army of shining angels. If you'd sold the clothes off their backs you would have made enough to build a church. When she spotted Kuria she insisted the girl return to the palace with her."

"Why did Theodora single her out?"

"For the same reason many of my patrons singled her out. She has an aristocratic bearing. She was a favorite with a number of men from the palace. One of my more lucrative girls, in fact. But her patrons were so generous to her she became rather spoilt, which always causes difficulties. I was pleased to be rid of her."

An aristocratic bearing? Isis' words did not describe the hunched, sobbing girl John had spoken to in the gardens. But then any of the pampered ladies of the court would disintegrate in tears if suddenly forced to fend for themselves, a task for which none of them was prepared.

"You would not want to take her back?"

"No," Isis replied firmly. "And she knows it. Not an hour before the empress arrived I had decided to discharge her. Do I sound harsh? You know I look after my girls like a mother, John, but she slashed the face of a rival. It was an argument over a favorite patron. It cost me a great deal for medical treatment for her victim, who was left with a bad scar. It happened shortly before I left that life and took my girls with me. The whole story only came out afterwards. If I had known, I would have put her out at once. I never condoned violent behavior. And girls who are prone to jealously over men are jealous about everything. I am sure Kuria would have caused trouble even in our refuge."

John could not imagine the beaten-down girl he had met fighting a rival. It showed how misleading quickly formed impressions could be.

Isis leaned forward and placed a hand on John's knee. "Let's not talk about business. I was just remembering that time in Egypt. The horrible man I worked for insulted me. Do you remember what you did?"

John smiled. "No, I confess I do not. Did I act rashly? Remind me."

◇◇◇

All the way back home John tried to recall the incident Isis had described. How could he forget emptying a jug of scorpions into someone's bed?

It struck him he had a vague recollection of Isis and himself creeping around dark alleys collecting the scorpions. Then again, hadn't she told him that story at length during earlier visits? Didn't the alleys he recalled have the perfumed scent of Isis' private rooms?

Though he could have employed a carriage or a litter or taken a horse from the imperial stables, John usually preferred to walk. Constantinople was not large. He had often been advised that it wasn't safe to traverse the streets without a bodyguard, but having fought from one end of the empire to the other there was nothing in Constantinople that frightened him. Besides, he thought best while on his feet. Walking also gave him the chance to observe the mood of the city. One did not overhear conversations while clattering along in a carriage.

What he observed during this walk was not especially enlightening. The city invariably grew tense when change loomed. People spoke more loudly. They argued. They debated what might happen—was the empire doomed or was it worse than that? The factions did not seem to be out in force, the so-called Greens and Blues, supporters of competing chariot teams, gaudily dressed young men whose increased presence in the street signaled violence to come the way flocks of gulls in the squares announced storms approaching from the sea. That was good news.

The news at home was not so good.

John saw tears in Hypatia's eyes when she opened the door. Was it Peter? Or had there been bad news from Cornelia?

"Gaius has been here," Hypatia said. "He told me Peter isn't doing well. The fall was a blow to his system. He said falls are the beginning of the end for many elderly people."

John felt a rush of relief. For an instant he had steeled himself to hear that he had lost his grandchild or his daughter. Immediately the relief was replaced by guilt, for Peter was also a family member.

Hypatia wiped at her eyes. "He seemed fairly well this morning. We were talking about old times. He was threatening to chop onions in bed. Then he dozed off and slept a long time. He didn't respond when I tried to wake him. I was ready to go and get Gaius when he arrived to see how Peter was."

"When was Gaius here?" John asked her.

"He just left."

"I'll see if I can catch him. Try not to worry about Peter. What's true for many isn't necessarily true for a tough old boot like him."

As the door shut behind him and he hurried across the square, John wished he believed his own reassuring words.

Chapter Thirteen

Vesta, lady-in-waiting to Joannina, plopped down on the bed next to Kuria, former lady-in-waiting to Theodora. "Who do you think I saw just now rushing toward the administrative building? The Lord Chamberlain! I made sure he'd gone by before coming inside. If he was coming to see me again, I didn't want to be found. He makes me nervous. It's almost like talking to the emperor."

"They say he has bags and bags of gold even though he lives like a holy hermit," Kuria replied.

The two young women sat in Kuria's room, a few doors down the hall from Vesta's, deep in the interior of the empress' portion of the palace. The residences allotted to attendants of the most powerful members of the court were luxurious. Without moving from her perch on the end of the bed, Kuria could have touched more silk, silver, gold, perfume, jewelry, and fine glassware than most people in Constantinople would ever possess in their lifetimes.

"The Lord Chamberlain's not only rich, he's awfully tall, like Anastasius," Vesta mused. "I might find him attractive if he were twenty years younger."

"And actually a man."

"Oh, don't be mean!" Vesta giggled. "Anastasius called him a eunuch to his face, can you imagine? I was leaving and overheard."

"If Anastasius doesn't control his tongue he might end up missing an even more important part of his anatomy than the Lord Chamberlain. The part that sits on to of his neck."

The two friends looked strikingly different, Kuria, exceedingly short, had a small pointy face, referred to by the unkind sons of aristocrats as rat-like, while the tall, gangly Vesta possessed features those same spoiled young men mocked as horsey. Kuria wore a stola of dark green to compliment her auburn hair. Vesta was dressed in a garment of the same light blue favored by her mistress Joannina.

"No one is going to harm the empress' grandson!" Vesta said firmly. Suddenly she wrinkled her nose. "Do you know the Lord Chamberlain lives with a woman. Despite being him the way he is. Isn't that the most disgusting thing? And what's the point?"

Kuria gave her a sly look. "What a little innocent you are. There are other things...."

Vesta turned red. "I'm not all that innocent, Kuria. But I'm glad I don't know everything you had to learn."

Kuria's gaze flickered around her sumptuous living quarters, as if she were taking inventory. "It's just as well I learned some skills when I came to this city. I expect I'll be back on the streets before long."

Vesta leaned over and clutched her friend's arm. "Oh, surely you won't go back to the streets?"

"What else? No one but the empress would have a former whore for a lady-in-waiting. Don't fret about me. I'll get along. It was so terrible, when Theodora died. I adored her. I couldn't think straight. I'm afraid I made a spectacle of myself in front of the Lord Chamberlain. Now I've calmed down. I'll think of something."

"You're so brave. I wish I were as brave as you."

"Whatever happens, it won't be that bad. It was a lot worse growing up on the farm. And almost as bad after father sold me to be a city whore."

"How could a man sell his own daughter?"

"Easily, when he's paid enough to buy a donkey."

"How dreadful it must have been."

"Coming to the city wasn't so bad. Father beat me all the time and barely fed me. My first owner in the city beat me too, but he fed me. After a while I escaped and found a new place. Isis fed me and never beat me."

Vesta squeezed Kuria's arm more tightly. "Oh, but I shall miss you if they make you leave the palace. Look, I'll tell father to take you in. We have a huge house. There's plenty of room."

"I'm sure he'd be pleased to have someone like me under his roof."

"He wouldn't know. Father doesn't know about anything except the Praetorian Prefecture or care about anything else."

"Didn't you tell me he's some sort of official there?"

"Yes. Quite important, I suppose, but he wouldn't be connected with the court exactly, except for my service to Joannina. That suits his sense of self-importance. Can you imagine, he's writing a history of the Prefecture. As if it matters. He used to read parts of it to me, all about its regalia, buildings, organization."

"I'd rather be beaten!"

"Listening to him you'd think Romulus and Remus suckled at the teat of some boring old bureaucrat with an account book. He faults Constantine for abandoning Rome."

"There's nothing in Rome these days but Goths and ruins." Kuria laughed. "You've convinced me I would never want to stay at your father's house even if he'd have me."

Vesta drew away from her friend, a look of distress crossed her long face. "I didn't mean to—"

"Anyway, never mind what I'm going to do with myself. What about you? Do you think Antonina is going to let that pair of doves you're looking after continue billing and cooing now that Theodora's gone?"

"The marriage is already scheduled."

"Do you think Antonina cares? It's just as well. You don't want to be a lady-in-waiting forever."

"What do you mean, Kuria? I love working for Joannina."

"Yes, but you really want to find a husband at court, don't you? Isn't that what all ladies-in-waiting want? Well, we've talked about it often enough, haven't we? Not that those of us who are former whores are likely to snag anyone."

"Those of us who are homely aren't likely to find anyone either. Not with all the gorgeous aristocratic women looking for their own men."

"Well, you're not exactly ugly, Vesta. You can make up for homeliness…" Kuria dropped her voice to a whisper. "…in other ways."

"Not if you are innocent." Vesta bit her lip. "Maybe you could teach me what you know. I mean, what it is men like."

Kuria chuckled. "Men aren't particular. It's not like cooking. It doesn't take much skill."

"That can't be true. You said you learned some skills, that they taught you something when you came to the city."

"Mostly we know how to avoid getting pregnant and what draught to take when we got pregnant despite our precautions."

"You've been pregnant?"

"More than once."

"How awful! My poor friend. Just thinking about it…and all the men…different men all the time…" Vesta flushed.

Kuria looked wistful. Her eyes lost their focus, as if they were fixed on something far outside her room in the palace. "There were special men sometimes. They gave me gifts. They told me secrets they wouldn't share with their wives. It wasn't all bad."

She jumped up from the bed, opened a chest at its foot, and rummaged through silks and enameled boxes. She pulled out a rolled sheet of parchment and handed it to Vesta. "Read this."

Vesta unrolled the parchment and her gaze moved across the handwriting.

When she finished the color had drained from her fact, her hands shook, and her features were suffused by a look of utter horror.

Chapter Fourteen

Iohn did not catch up with Gaius but finally tracked him down to his surgery in the administrative complex.

The physician was professionally noncommittal when questioned about the outlook for Peter. The shock of the injury had unbalanced Peter's humors, he said, a serious matter in a septuagenarian. He hoped his concoctions would help restore the balance. The bones had not torn through the skin, so there was less chance of infection. That was a positive aspect to the accident.

The surgery was an airy, whitewashed room brightened by light from windows facing on a wide lawn which ran up to a porticoed structure, another wing of the building where John and Gaius sat. Numerous shelves supported lidded pots alongside jars and bottles containing potions or powdered ingredients. A long bench set under the row of windows held trays of bronze or steel scalpels, probes, bone drills, spathomeles used for mixing and spreading medicinal preparations, hooks, forceps of various sizes, a collection presenting a mute demonstration of the range of treatments a palace physician might be called upon to perform at any time.

They also reminded John of certain instruments to be found in the torture chambers beneath the palace.

Gaius looked as if he had been invited to a chat in those subterranean chambers when John began questioning him further about Theodora. The physician groaned, shook his head sadly, and ran a hand over his perspiration-beaded scalp. "Her death is making a lot of us ill. I have a suitable medication."

He lumbered over to a shelf lined with large jars full of reddish liquid, which turned out to be wine. He poured some into two smaller jars, seated himself, and pushed John's inelegant drinking vessel across the table where they sat. "Administer this as needed. It's a good home remedy for wondering what the empire will come to now that Theodora is dead."

John took a swallow. It set the back of his throat on fire. He coughed.

"My patients need it to be strong, considering some of the procedures I must perform," Gaius explained. "You didn't think I'd keep my office stocked with anything that had no medical purpose, did you?"

John regarded his jar dolefully. "I hope you keep a remedy for this remedy on hand. And to think my taste in wine has been criticized…"

The round table where they sat in a corner of the room could have come from a tavern. It was a table Gaius no doubt felt comfortable using when he talked with his patients, before instructing them to move to the long marble-topped slab in the center of the room. More often than not Gaius would have visited his aristocratic clients at their homes. His surgery was where palace workers who were taken ill or injured would be brought. It was also where those of loftier birth came, surreptitiously, to speak of matters too delicate to be broached at home.

"I know it's being whispered Antonina poisoned Theodora because she will not stop the marriage of that unfortunate young couple," Gaius observed. "Not to mention Antonina's notorious for her potions and practice of magick. After all, what is an old friendship worth compared to getting the result you want? But as I keep telling you, the empress wasted away. It's as simple as that. As you said, if she had been a beggar or a grocer's wife no one would think twice about it. Sad to say, it happens all the time. And, yes, even to empresses. Besides, she was already as good as dead. The disease had poisoned her more horribly than any deadly herb."

"Don't people recover from it, Gaius?"

"Not in my experience."

"Justinian has had two miraculous recoveries, and one was from the plague."

"This was different."

John nodded. "But even supposing Theodora was bound to die soon, I understand Joannina and Anastasius are to be wed before July is over. They've already been betrothed for what? Six months?"

Gaius gave a snort. "What Theodora called betrothed, you mean."

"What I am pointing out is even though Theodora's death was certain and imminent, Antonina would have had good reason to speed its arrival. The same might be true of others."

"Except there was no sign of poisoning," Gaius retorted. "As I have already told you."

"Would any signs have been noticeable given the ravaged state she was in?"

"Possibly not. You might have a point there."

"Did Theodora take any medications aside from those you gave her?"

"Not in my presence, but I'm sure she did. There was always a jumble of bottles and jars at her bedside. Cosmetics, lotions, ointments, and who knows what else. I tried to keep an eye out to ensure there was nothing harmful, but she didn't appreciate my examining her things and she was the empress. I warned Justinian to watch that she wasn't taking too much or this and that I had not prescribed."

John leaned back in his straight-backed wooden chair and sipped Gaius' therapeutic wine carefully. "Tell me this, then. Is there any poison that would mimic the disease Theodora had?"

"Not that I know of."

"Or cause it?"

"I've never heard of one."

"Or make it worse? Something that might not exactly poison but add to the fire that was already consuming her body? Or that might weaken her ability to heal? That might muddle the humors?"

Gaius laughed. "John, you pose questions Galen or Hippocrates himself couldn't answer. This disease she had is little understood. Nothing helps. It has been called the crab. Malignant tumors start to grow under the skin. The swollen blood vessels around the tumor resemble a crab's claws. It devours the body just as crabs scour the flesh of corpses on the sea floor. But these crabs gnaw from within, like demons. And they keep growing, fattening on the flesh and organs of the victim. You know what I've heard? That this monstrous disease was the true child of her union with the King of the Demons."

"If people can believe that Justinian is the King of the Demons I suppose they can believe anything."

Gaius rose, lumbered to his medicine shelf, and refilled his jar. When he sat down again John saw Gaius' hands were shaking. "You can't imagine the torture, John. There were times she would scream until her voice gave out. Dying men on the battlefield roar in agony but their lives bleed away quickly. This disease goes on and on." He took a long drink, swallowed hard. "You question me about poisons, but supposing an enemy wanted to poison her? How could it have been done?"

"You know better than I do, Gaius. The method of administering poison might point to the murderer. What methods might you suggest?"

"There are only so many ways poison could be administered, and I can't see any of them applying in this case. Some methods I've heard about are simply ludicrous and wouldn't work. My favorite is smearing one side of a knife with poison so the meat cut by the contaminated edge is fatal but not that touched by the other side. If that was possible we'd all use our personal blades to cut our meat, but then what if the entire dish was poisoned?

Even so, Theodora did not partake of solid food in the last week, not even mashed fruit and she was very fond of that."

John recalled the fruit Vesta had brought to the sickroom. But the two ladies-in-waiting had eaten it, and they showed no signs of poisoning. Still, it was a possibility. "Could a slow-acting poison be introduced into fruit?"

"There are ways," Gaius admitted. "A tiny hole in an apple can reveal either the presence of a worm, careless handling, or the presence of poison. I've heard of melons being put in a poison bath so they absorb the noxious substance, but that sounds highly improbable to me. And poisoned weapons are all very well but would be impossible to get into that sickroom, what with the guards and attendants and Justinian there all the time. He hardly left her side."

"Do the imperial couple take antidotes regularly?"

"You're thinking of mithridatum, aren't you? Oh yes, that complicated concoction is an imperial tradition, ever since the formula was brought back to Rome. Fifty-four different ingredients, some in minuscule quantities."

"Is it effective?"

Gaius shrugged. "Pliny said that it was a monstrous system of puffing up the medical art and I tend to agree. However, Justinian is convinced he's been poisoned endlessly in the natural course of events, and since he has not died then the mithridatum must be effective."

"Except in Theodora's case."

"Yes. I suppose that's what he thinks." Gaius' pouched eyes narrowed and his broad face reddened to match the color of his bulbous nose. "Unless he suddenly concludes I used the wrong formula, forgot the rhubarb or acacia juice, or didn't prescribe enough, or did so at the wrong intervals. In which case, Mithra help me."

"You said she might have taken medications prepared by someone other than yourself?"

"I'd be surprised if she didn't. Antonina used to make cosmetics for Theodora. I think she had resumed as a gesture of friendship. Not that Theodora had any use for cosmetics in her state. She may have prepared and sent painkillers. The ladies-in-waiting used to bring gifts for the empress from various people. It wasn't any business of mine."

Gaius took another gulp of wine. He licked his lips nervously.

"You couldn't dictate what was brought into Theodora's room, Gaius. No one would expect it of you. Others spent much more time with her than you did."

"Yes, I hope Justinian sees it that way. It's very foolish accepting preparations from people not trained as physicians. Mistakes are easy to make and beyond that, how do they know the person preparing something to be taken or applied hasn't been bribed to poison it? Anyone can obtain poison. It's possible to grow deadly plants anywhere. I have a few in my herb garden here on the palace grounds. I grow them to supply material for the preparations I prescribe. Some plants are like Janus, two-faced. The same ones can be used for good or ill, to kill or cure."

"Indeed."

"Take belladonna, for example. A tiny amount will bring about death, yet it's useful for treating headaches and women's problems. Or how about henbane? A very good painkiller if used in appropriate fashion, but otherwise a person taking too much will soon be beyond the reach of bodily pangs. By all means imbibe a quantity of hemlock if you want to leave the world, yet I also prescribe it to treat disorders of the skin."

"Your garden is accessible to anyone who cared to visit at night to gather certain plants in secret," John observed.

"Yes, it is. Hypatia tends to it. She occasionally makes herbal preparations for me, so she too may well come under suspicion. It's probably best she's under your protection, so far as any of us can protect anyone or ourselves."

John had not considered Hypatia might also be in danger. Was there anyone in the city who was not, one way or another? He scanned the room. "A poisoner wouldn't necessarily have to be an herbalist," he pointed out. "He could steal whatever he needed from your shelves "

"True," Gaius set down his jar. His hand trembled uncontrollably. "And just about everything here could be fatal given in the wrong amount."

"Including your cure for anxiety about the fate of the empire," John tapped Gaius' empty jar.

"Quite right, John. But can you blame me?"

There was a shouted order from the hallway.

"This way!"

Gaius leapt up at the loud thumping of what could only be several men wearing military boots running down the corridor.

An excubitor appeared in the doorway.

He continued past, followed by five others in a hurry.

As their footsteps receded John's gaze turned to Gaius, and to the shelf upon which the physician's hand rested. Gaius' fingertips were almost touching a tiny green glass bottle.

John gave his friend a questioning look.

"For pain," Gaius said.

"It's poison, isn't it?"

"To avoid the pain that can be inflicted by the imperial torturers. I am only too familiar with the unspeakable agony a human body can be made to feel. A devilish hand assisted in creating our flesh. No decent entity would have made it capable of experiencing such pain."

Gaius sat down at the table. "Do you know the terror I've been going through? Remember, I had the knowledge and the opportunity to kill Theodora. I sit here and wait for excubitors to appear and pray they put a sword through me cleanly rather than dragging me down to the torturers. I keep my pain medication near me at all times. A very powerful poison. If they arrested me in this room it would be a corpse they'd be dragging outside."

He reached for his jar of wine but John pushed it out of his reach.

"Try to stay calm, Gaius, and for Mithra's sake, stay away from the wine. You need your wits. Excubitors are always racing about. You can't be going into a panic every time you see an armed man coming in your direction. It's the wine that takes your reason away."

"But I am an obvious suspect and obvious suspects are being—"

"You had no reason to wish Theodora dead and every reason to want to keep her alive. How many years have you treated both the emperor and empress? You could have murdered either long ago. Justinian would have no reason to suspect you."

"What reason did the emperor have to order the silversmith's delivery boy thrown off the seawall this morning? Just because the poor child somehow blundered into the imperial quarters by accident."

John got up as Gaius stood. The physician swayed slightly. His color had changed from red to chalky white. "You've started me thinking, John. All this talk about poisons, and who might have got poison into Theodora's hands. I had not given it enough consideration. But clearly, Antonina has the skill, the personal connection. If Justinian wants a murderer I'd advise him to look in Antonina's direction. She can concoct a poison as well as I can. Expose her as quickly as you can, John, before it's too late for me."

Chapter Fifteen

Manuel, cook for Empress Theodora, locked the storeroom in which were secured victuals and spices for dishes destined for the imperial couple. He nodded a goodnight to the guard stationed at the iron-banded door and went out through the series of long basement vaults that served as the palace kitchens. A skeleton night staff moved through the red shadows cast by the scattered braziers in operation at this late hour. From some distant chamber came a monotonous echoing thump as a servant chopped vegetables—parsnips perhaps—for a soup to be simmered through the night. No, onions. Manuel could distinguish the smell of freshly chopped onion, recognizable even in an atmosphere redolent of banquets past. The sooty whitewashed walls exuded the odor of meats broiled over the years and expensive spices few tongues in this part of the world would ever taste.

The cook was swarthy complexioned or else the smoke through which he moved day after day had soaked into his pores. He was as emaciated as a man who never came within sight of a square meal. When asked how that could be, Manuel joked that in the constant heat from dozens of massive braziers, he continually sweated off the morsels he sampled.

He stopped to speak to Petrus, who took charge during the night. His second-in-command was covered in loose feathers from the chicken he was plucking. One of the slaves should have done the job but Petrus enjoyed plucking and gutting chickens.

"That new assistant hasn't been back?" Manuel asked.

Petrus shook his head. "Just as well. He insisted he knew all about cooking. Always had his nose in one of the pots. I had to keep explaining that he hadn't been hired to cook but to clean and haul supplies off the delivery carts."

"He was good at that. I'd thought he was a bit old for hard physical labor, but you saw the size of him. A powerful fellow."

Petrus blew drifting chicken feathers away from his mouth. "A hard man, I'd say. Not your typical help. I put him down for one of the Praetorian Prefect's men."

"My guess was he actually worked directly for Justinian. I was given to understand he could be trusted because he had worked for highly placed officials."

"A spy?"

Both men knew that the emperor had the kitchens kept under constant surveillance. Some of the guards were known to the staff, others were not. Generally there was a man who reported to the Master of Offices and another employed by the Praetorian Prefect. They kept an eye on both the staff and each other. Usually the emperor had his own spy there to watch everything and everybody else. The watchers were constantly being replaced, making it difficult for them to discover each other and collude. It all made little difference to the functioning of the kitchens, considering the virtual army employed there.

"It isn't a coincidence the man vanished the very day the empress died," Manuel observed.

"No. No coincidence." Petrus slapped the denuded chicken down on the table and picked up a knife. "I think we can safely say the emperor was disappointed in the poor man, whoever he worked for and…well…" Petrus stabbed his blade into the chicken and tore its belly and chest wide open.

"Justinian's gone mad," Manuel said. "He's convinced the empress was poisoned, impossible as that is. He's looking for someone to blame."

"He must think this spy of his missed something important."

"One of the dishwashers didn't show up this morning either. Perhaps he was working for the Master of Offices. I'm sure we'll eventually notice others are gone too."

Petrus reached into the chicken carcass and pulled. A handful of guts came out with a slurping noise. "If Justinian knew who the poisoner was he would have him gutted like this chicken, but more slowly."

"You can't execute someone who doesn't exist. So the watchers pay the price for not spotting someone who was never there. When I delivered the emperor's breakfast I noticed the guards to Theodora's sickroom have been replaced."

Petrus was groping deep inside the dead chicken. Finally his hand emerged, fingers gripping the last, stringy bloody entrails. "At least he doesn't suspect you, Manuel."

The empress' cook grimaced. "I pray he doesn't."

"Don't worry. If Justinian suspected you, do you think you'd still be alive? I'll wager you didn't sleep much last night. Try to catch up on your rest. Come in late. I'll take charge until you feel like coming in." He started sweeping offal from the pile of gutted chickens off the table.

Manuel left to the moist sound of vital organs plopping into a bucket.

He nodded to the sentry at the door. A new man. Had the familiar sentry been reassigned? Or perhaps the question was had he been reassigned to a post in the land of the living or sent to the land of the dead?

He decided to return to his rooms via the brightly torch lit walkway that passed by the Triclinium rather than taking his usual shortcut through the dim gardens. There were so many guards about one might have thought the palace was under siege.

Perhaps it was time for him to retire. How many years had he served the empress? Ever since the previous cook had been—well, it was best to forget the incident of the fish. What would he do now? There were endless banquets to be prepared. Perhaps he might be ordered to take over the cooking for Justinian.

He hoped not. Cooking for the emperor, who was a vegetarian and austere in his tastes, would be like cooking for a peasant farmer. There were those who hated Theodora. Manuel could never understand why. There was no dish too exotic for her palate. She had been a joy to cook for until the last few weeks, when she had been unable to hold down anything but broth. Even so, had she not complimented him on his broth of partridge, venison, and crab?

Yes, he had accumulated enough wealth to retire in luxury. Perhaps he could move to the provinces, run an inn for well-to-do travelers who would be glad to have a good palace style meal during a long journey far from the amenities of the city.

He heard boots thudding along the marble walkway behind him.

Some emergency?

As the footsteps came up beside him they slowed to match his pace.

"Manuel, cook for Empress Theodora?" inquired a gravelly voice.

Two hulking guards, hands on the hilts of their sheathed swords, flanked him. A hollow space as vast as the inside of the Great Church seemed to open up inside Manuel's chest. "Yes?" He wasn't sure how he managed to get the word out.

"You are to accompany us. Orders from Emperor Justinian," said one of the guards. He was practically a youngster. A curl of red hair fell from under his helmet and lay across his unlined forehead.

"What...what is this about?"

"We are here merely to carry out the emperor's orders. Come with us."

Manuel felt a hand on his shoulder. It was all he could do to control his bladder.

They led him down a narrow path into the gardens. Their feet crunched on gravel.

"Justinian desires to see me?"

The guards did not answer.

They passed through a gap in the shrubbery and the bright light illuminating the broad marble walkway and pouring out into the grounds beyond was abruptly blotted out.

Manuel's heart pounded in fits and starts. "Am I...am I under arrest?"

The guards remained silent.

They halted at a patch of dark bare ground surrounded by bushes. Manuel could hear the ratcheting of summer insects in the dark foliage. The sharp odor of dill came to his nostrils. Oddly, as much as Theodora had favored esoteric spices, she had always loved dill.

He heard the whisper of a steel blade slipping from its sheath.

The guards said nothing.

The red-haired youngster slit Manuel like a chicken from belly to breast.

Chapter Sixteen

The sprawling two-story mansion of General Belisarius and his wife Antonina rubbed its polished granite walls up against the southern end of the Hippodrome. It wasn't a salubrious location but then Belisarius wasn't home very often. He was usually camped on some distant border though at present, to hear some tell it, he was on board a ship sailing up and down the Italian coast, shaking his fist at the Goths and waiting for Justinian to send swords and spears.

John guessed when races were in progress the cheers of the crowds must shake the house like thunder. Did the sound remind Antonina that despite her wealth and high position she had come from a family of charioteers? Theodora had accomplished a similar rise to greater power from even lower antecedents, being the daughter of a bear trainer. Perhaps this was the main strand in the bonds of friendship between the two women.

As he climbed the flight of white marble steps, John reflected that even when races were not in progress, Antonina would be reminded of her past by the pervasive smell emanating from the vast stables beneath the track, the same atmosphere in which she had grown up.

He had no desire to speak to Antonina or any reason to suspect her of harming her imperial friend, but her name was on everyone's lips and therefore he considered it prudent to be able to tell Justinian he had questioned the woman. More than that, Gaius had wanted him to speak to her and he could hardly ignore his friend's request even though he didn't expect to discover anything that would make the physician less fearful for his own safety.

At the thud of a knocker shaped like a horse's head the door opened and John was ushered in by a lugubrious servant who escorted him to a room on the far side of an atrium decorated with frescoes of heroic battles from mythology. It was a fitting flourish for the house of a successful general, even if its owner didn't have much opportunity to admire it.

John stepped into the room to which he had been directed and found Theodora staring at him.

A chill prickled the back of his neck, then, in a heartbeat, he realized it was only a painted representation of the empress. She was flanked by attendants in garments almost as rich as her own, though none wore jewelry to rival hers and only she wore a crown. The fresco covered the entire back wall. The room was filled with fragrant lilies and roses in pots and vases.

Antonina reclined on a scarlet upholstered couch beneath a window opened to a garden. "It is a good likeness, is it not, Lord Chamberlain?"

"Indeed."

Antonina's eyes were as blue as a clear morning sky and her hair as pale as the moon in that sky. There were those who claimed she practiced magick and by that means not only controlled her husband but also the hand prints of time. John ascribed her youthful appearance to the lotions and other cosmetic preparations she prepared for herself and other ladies of the court.

If you approached closely enough her age would show, but once you got that close it would be too late.

John sat in an ornately carved but uncomfortable chair facing her, separated from her couch by a low table, acutely aware of Theodora's menacing stare. "A few questions, Antonina," he began. He suddenly realized the window behind her providing a glimpse of an exotic garden, was, like Antonina's complexion, nothing more than cleverly applied paint.

"I know why you are here and will be happy to assist," Antonina replied. "In fact, I can give you information you will find useful." She remained in her reclining position, as if prepared to dine in the old Roman style. Her light blue silk robe were slightly rumpled, showing a trim ankle and smooth muscular calf. She smiled. "I do not have to tell you there are several persons with grievances who might not be amiss to helping our dear empress leave the world."

She glanced at the fresco. "A faithful rendering of the beautiful mosaic in Ravenna, Lord Chamberlain. I was able to obtain the artist's designs. They were costly but well worth the price. The imperial couple could hardly go to Ravenna so their portraits went instead and the mosaicists copied them. Unfortunately the empress looks ill, not that we can wonder at that."

She sighed, theatrically John thought. "I intended it as a gesture of friendship to Theodora but it was completed too late. She will never see it now."

John wondered if a reproduction of the companion Ravenna mosaic of Justinian and his courtiers graced another room and whether Belisarius would approve of these new decorations. Equally, they would serve as a reminder of his taking Ravenna from the Goths, as well as flattering the imperial couple.

As if reading his mind, Antonina said, "No doubt you have heard I was hoping to persuade the empress to intercede with Justinian in the matter of sending more troops and supplies to my husband. It is quite true. Unfortunately, by the time I arrived in Constantinople earlier this month, Theodora was so ill she refused to receive me. As an old friend, it was hurtful even though I believe she was trying to spare me the pain of seeing her as she had become."

Or sparing herself being seen, John thought. "Very few were admitted to her room once she began her final decline," he replied.

"Let us be frank, Lord Chamberlain. I am well aware you suspect me, given I have made it plain I wish to stop the proposed marriage between my daughter and Anastasius. However, since I was not able to visit Theodora, obviously I had no opportunity to do her harm. Then too, even you must agree preventing a marriage is hardly a good reason to arrange for an empress to be poisoned. Particularly since the empress was my closest friend."

"You are of the opinion Theodora was murdered?"

Antonina pursed her lips. "That is Justinian's opinion. Do any of us dare to entertain another?"

"Although you did not visit Theodora you must have sent her gifts. Cosmetics or perhaps something to ease her pain?"

Antonina gave John a frigid smile. "It is customary to send gifts to one's friends. It is hardly a matter of official concern or anything I care to talk about in detail. I am sure my modest offerings were thoroughly examined, as gifts to the imperial couple always are. Since you are looking for the culprit have you considered the Cappadocian?"

"He is imprisoned in Egypt. As he has been for years, since you conspired with Theodora to have him removed from office."

She glared at him. "He can still have eyes and ears and hands here in the capital."

"They would require payment and Justinian was eventually persuaded to strip him of his wealth."

Antonina gave a dismissive wave of her hand. "The Cappadocian's wealth is like the root of a noxious weed. It goes too deep to be pulled up entirely. What I hear is he is free to return and resume his rape of the populace now that the empress is no longer here to protect us."

"I doubt the Cappadocian will have his way with you, Antonina."

She looked as if she was about to spit at him. As John knew, she hated the former Praetorian Prefect, usually derisively referred to as the Cappadocian or more simply as the tax collector.

"I would think you and General Belisarius would welcome the Cappadocian's efficiency in raising revenues," he went on. "Justinian would then have more funds to pursue the war in Italy."

Antonina's eyes sparkled with cold fire. "Let me educate you about how the Cappadocian assisted my husband's soldiers. Bread for an army must be carefully twice baked so it does not spoil for a long time, during shipping, in storage in camp, during marches."

"I am aware of that."

"I forgot. You are from a humble background too." Her expression softened momentarily. "At any rate," she continued, "the method of baking requires extra firewood and extra wages for the bakers, money which otherwise could have been spent by the Cappadocian on luxuries and debauchery. This extravagance, as he saw it, offended him so he had uncooked dough delivered to the basement of the Baths of Achilles where fires continually burn to heat the water. He had the dough placed near this free source of heat until it appeared more or less cooked, then thrown into bags and shipped to Italy. Needless to say, the loaves started to rot before they arrived. My husband tells me you could smell them at the dock where the ship lay moored. Yet there was nothing else to eat. It was in the middle of a summer as hot as this one. Five hundred of my husband's men died. He ordered the armies be furnished bread from the surrounding countryside. At our own expense, Lord Chamberlain."

"It is good to know our soldiers have a champion like yourself."

"You are sarcastic. Doubtless you think I only care about my husband's fortunes."

The cloying odor of the lilies and roses ranged about the room had begun to irritate John. He allowed his gaze to wander, avoiding Theodora and coming to rest in the painted garden outside the painted window behind Antonina's couch. For the first time he noticed, half hidden amongst the elaborately painted leaves, a yellow bird caught in the jaws of a lion.

"I do not see the Cappadocian as a credible suspect," John said.

"If you are looking for a better possibility, consider Justinian's cousin General Germanus. If it weren't for Theodora he would already have been accepted as heir to the throne.

She did everything she could to cripple his career. Now he will thrive."

"At your husband's expense, Antonina. Aren't you afraid he may supplant Belisarius both as Justinian's foremost general and his eventual successor?"

John noticed Antonina's fists clench and quickly relax again. "My husband has no designs on the throne. You remember that was the Cappadocian's undoing. He mistakenly believed Belisarius to be a traitor."

"Yes, and when he went to meet Belisarius you were there with officials from the palace."

"He deserved it for thinking ill of Belisarius. My husband is an honorable man."

"Honorable men are so rare at court, it is dangerous to assume honor in anyone."

She glared at him again. John wondered if her approach to their conversation might be different were he more prone to fall to her artfully preserved charms.

"You are being unfair to me," she said. "Germanus had more to gain by Theodora's death than I did. Why do you insist on turning your suspicions toward me? I know how much you hated the empress. Do you hate her friends too? Which of your enemies will you choose to turn over to the emperor? Everyone is speculating and some are trembling. Am I to suffer for Theodora's sins?"

Antonina got up, kissed her finger, and placed it tenderly against Theodora's painted cheek. "My dear, dear empress. Even in death you are wronged."

She faced John. "You're frowning, Lord Chamberlain. Don't you like my fresco? One of my servants doesn't like it either. She's a superstitious girl, the tedious and stupid sort who insist on finding omens in the shape of spilt wine or the movements of clouds. She will not enter this room for any reason, because she's convinced my beautiful decoration foretold Theodora's death. Were she not so clever at concocting dainty sweetmeats I would dismiss her."

"It is not difficult to be wise after the event, and especially when the event is known to be inevitable a week or two before it occurs," John pointed out.

Antonina gave a grim smile. "Superstitious nonsense, that's all it is. I questioned the stupid child at some length. According to her the attendant shown lifting the curtain is unveiling the afterlife, the imminent departure for which is about to arrive for one of the women represented. Further, it seems the goblet Theodora holds represents an overflowing cup of blessings. The poor girl believes it foretold the blessing of the ending of her agony. There again, for others it may well be a warning we will drain the cup of sorrow. What do you think, Lord Chamberlain? Are there any clues to her murderer to be found in the fresco on the wall of this room?"

John stood. "As much information as you are likely to give me willingly."

Or as much as anyone else at court will, he added to himself.

As he walked out of the mansion into the shadow of the Hippodrome, he wondered who would drain Theodora's cup of sorrow. Not people like Antonina. People like Kuria, cast adrift from palace life with no prospects except returning to a life of selling herself to strangers.

The same people who always drank from imperial cups of sorrow.

If only the painted empress could lift the veil of mist that obscured his vision and reveal the solution he sought.

Chapter Seventeen

Though it had already been a grueling day, John decided to talk to General Germanus, another interview designed largely to satisfy Justinian. If Antonina was pointing an accusative finger at the emperor's cousin others would do the same. However discreetly, once word reached Justinian he would expect to hear John had looked into the matter.

It was not his normal way of conducting an inquiry to be pointed this way and that, but then his inquiries normally revolved around an actual murder rather than one imagined by the emperor.

Or rather one that John feared was imagined by the emperor. He hoped for his own sake and his family's sake that his initial impression was mistaken.

For the time being John intended to interview those he would be expected to interview. Once he had fulfilled that obligation, if nothing had shown up to point him in a specific direction… well, he wasn't certain what he would do.

John was trying to dismiss such doleful thoughts, as well as thoughts of the dinner Hypatia had no doubt prepared by now, when a supercilious doorkeeper informed him that the general was not seeing visitors. John thrust his orders and the attached imperial seal he always carried under the fellow's upturned nose.

The man cringed and explained Germanus was not seeing visitors because he was not at home. He was at the Baths of Zeuxippos.

The baths, between the entrance to the palace and the Hippodrome, was an immense complex of pools, gymnasiums, lecture halls, meeting rooms, and shops. John bought a skewer of grilled swordfish from a vendor who had set up his brazier near the wide stairs leading up to the baths' entrance. The vendor was better at cooking it than John, not nearly as proficient as Peter. When John finished, feeling only slightly less famished, he threw the skewer into the gutter, went up the stairs, and paid an attendant the paltry admission fee.

The atrium was as vast as a public square and packed with people. Some wore elaborately decorated garments, others leather leggings and dirty tunics. Voices echoed hollowly around the towering walls and up into the distant dome. None of the baths were visible but the air was noticeably humid. Corridors led off in all directions. It would have been difficult to locate an individual quickly but it was easy to spot the entourage which accompanied generals wherever they go. John found the contingent in a gallery lined with statues.

There were enough men and arms to have conquered the entire bath complex in less than an hour. They were big men, as broad and muscular as the larger-then-life-size bronze Hercules beside whose pedestal they stood. Germanus was one of the smaller men, wearing a subdued rust-colored dalmatic rather than a leather cuirass. In his early forties, Germanus was, like Justinian, a nephew of the late Emperor Justin. Unlike Justinian, his appearance betrayed his peasant origins. He had a blocky build, powerful, sloping shoulders, a thick neck. His dark hair and beard were trimmed almost to a stubble.

As John approached, Germanus grinned, displaying square ivory-hued teeth. The big men surrounding him did not grin. They stared. Scarred fists tightened on spears and swords.

"Lord Chamberlain! I've been expecting you. The palace is buzzing over your inquiries and I know some busy bees have aimed their stingers at me. The question is, who sent you?"

"You'll understand I can't answer that, general."

Germanus' grin broadened. "Not that it matters. I can guess." He glanced around at his scowling bodyguards. "You will understand why my men are surly and wary. There are those who can't believe I intend to wait my turn to take the throne and just might want to stop me from doing so."

"It's common knowledge Justinian intends you to succeed him, even though he did not make it official while Theodora was alive."

"Considering her hatred for me and my family, can we be surprised? You'll doubtless agree I wouldn't have any reason to kill Theodora. She might influence the emperor while he's alive but she could hardly influence him to deny me the throne when he was dead."

"She might have convinced him to anoint a new heir before he died."

Germanus laughed. "I wasn't looking that far ahead. It doesn't matter now. I'm happy for my whole family, Lord Chamberlain. My daughter Justina and her husband can return to Constantinople. They've been living on one of my estates in Bithynia, near the hot springs. My son-in-law feared for his life when it was rumored Theodora ordered Antonina to have him killed merely for marrying against her imperial wishes."

"Was there any particular reason Theodora objected to the marriage?"

"Spite, Lord Chamberlain. That was all. My sons still aren't married. Justina defied her. She was eighteen. How much longer could she wait?"

Theodora had a penchant for interfering with marriages. John wondered if Cornelia was right, that interference in personal relationships was more likely to result in retaliation than political, religious, or financial meddling. When power or money was at stake people acted with a clear view of Theodora's enormous power. When the issue was personal, passions reigned.

He was reminded of Europa, who had never been far from his mind lately. It irked him to have to remain in the city, chasing shadows, when he should be beside his daughter.

Germanus strolled away from the bronze Hercules and his retinue flowed with him. John remained at his side.

The gallery featured a mismatched collection of bronze figures: pagan gods, philosophers, military men, anonymous Greeks who had been famous enough to immortalize in a long distant era.

"It's not as impressive as when I was a boy," Germanus said. "Before the mob burned the baths down during the Nika riots, there were some magnificent works here."

"I remember."

"One day the whole imperial school was herded over here to hear Christodorus perform his poem about the statues. A tiny, shriveled-up Egyptian with lungs like one of Justinian's heralds. He took us from statue to statue, thundering out his descriptions of each. The bronze was silent. He kept telling us that. Then he would help the mute bronze out by imagining what Homer or Sappho or Apollo was thinking. As if he had any way of knowing. We would have been just as happy if he was silent. We were only interested in the heroes, or at least the boys were. Pretending to battle Achilles. Hiding behind Ulysses."

It was hard to imagine the burly, dark-bearded man as a child. It was easier to imagine him battling Achilles. He differed from his imperial cousin in that he was actually a military man. He had fought on the battlefield, had his horse killed under him on one occasion, and nearly died himself. A true soldier emperor in the Roman tradition.

"It was not the educational experience your tutors desired," John observed.

"No, but I'm certain Christodorus received a fee. Poets have to earn a living somehow." Germanus stopped in front of a bronze Aphrodite. "This is the only statue rescued from the ruins, and not entirely intact. Years after that performance I looked the verse up. 'Her breasts were bare but her robes were gathered around her rounded thighs.' A true enough description, but now she has only a single breast. The goddess of love turned into an Amazon warrior!"

The restorers had done their best to repair the statue. Perhaps they had honestly mistaken her for an Amazon.

Germanus' smile faded for the first time. He ran a hand over his cropped beard. "Such genius and centuries of art annihilated in a day by the ignorant rabble, all of whom together could not create even the kerchief that binds Aphrodite's hair. There is no justice in the world, Lord Chamberlain."

"There is a little justice in the world, Germanus."

The general's hulking guards shifted their grips on their weapons, shuffled their feet, looking bored. They appeared to John the type of men who would not be fully engaged by anything except violence.

Germanus smiled again. "I have fought my whole life to gain justice for my family. Here I am, descended from a royal line, and myself and my children are told to stand aside for whores and bastards bred from a bear keeper."

"But no longer."

"No. However, don't think I'm only concerned with justice for myself…" He trailed off abruptly. "Lord Chamberlain, every single person you approach will single out an enemy as a potential suspect. Therefore I wish to stress Artabanes isn't my enemy."

"General Artabanes?"

"A fine commander. The opposite of his predecessor. Justinian should never have sent Areobindus to Libya. He was a senator, not a military man. And a coward to boot. I'm sure you know the story."

John did indeed. Areobindus had surrendered himself and his wife Praejecta to the rebels. Artabanes arrived, restored order, and rescued Praejecta, but not before Areobindus had been assassinated.

"Are you telling me Artabanes acted against Theodora?"

Germanus' thick lips tightened. "As good as, Lord Chamberlain. A month ago he visited me at my house, supposedly to discuss the situation in Libya. But before long the conversation turned to the imperial couple. They were both worthless in his opinion. He claimed he wasn't alone in saying so. On the other hand, I was as close a relative to the old emperor Justin as Justinian, and more fit to rule being a military man and not a self-styled theologian, a soft fellow who took orders from his wife. If only I had been older at the time of Justin's death, and so on.'"

John pointed out such talk was tantamount to treason.

"That's what I told him. But he took no notice. He said he knew I was a fair-minded man. Everyone knew I was fair-minded. Otherwise some treacherous senators would have already begged me to put Justinian out of the way."

"He wanted to gauge your interest in deposing Justinian?"

"What else? He told me Justinian didn't even try to rule. He sat up all night without any guards, just decrepit old priests, studying the holy books. In effect he explained to me exactly when and where the emperor could be assassinated and how simple it would be."

John looked around at the bodyguards. They gave no evidence of listening but had doubtless taken interest in the entire conversation. How might they feel about serving an emperor rather than a general?

"He hated Theodora even more," Germanus continued. "He hated them both. Murdering her would be a blow against Justinian. It would weaken him."

"People with grievances like to talk about revenge, even when they know they can't take it."

"In Libya, Artabanes personally stabbed a tyrant in the tyrant's own banqueting hall. He's a courageous man."

John questioned Germanus further but having delivered his prepared speech the general remained affable but effectively as silent as the bronzes. Christodorus might have ventured to guess what he was thinking.

John did not and took his leave.

Chapter Eighteen

As John walked toward the Chalke Gate he formed the impression he was being followed.

It was a sense an inhabitant of the palace soon developed.

He turned and went through an archway leading to the square of the Augustaion in front of the Great Church.

His pursuer had no intention of merely following. A towering, granite column of a man—the largest of Germanus' guards—overtook him and spoke. "Lord Chamberlain."

John stopped. "There was something your employer forgot to tell me?"

"That's right. He is worried about your safety."

"I appreciate that."

Passersby streamed around the two men as if they were two rocks in a river.

"A high official should not be walking around alone, Lord Chamberlain. You never know who might be lurking around the next corner. Especially when you start asking powerful people the wrong questions."

"Is that what Germanus said?"

"An intelligent man like you can deduce the answer." The guard turned and plowed his way back through the crowd.

The man's words puzzled John. He had been threatened too many times to be concerned about threats to himself. What he worried about was Cornelia and his daughter and grandchild.

He followed the retreating guard out through the archway. He would have preferred to return home to see if there had been any word from Cornelia, but after talking to Germanus he knew there was one more stop to make.

He had seen the sun rising over the palace gardens as he began the day's investigations, and before he was done he would see it drop below the rooftops of the city toward which it was falling even now, stretching the shadows of buildings, statuary, pillars and pedestrians and stray dogs in the direction of the Sea of Marmara as if the shadows intended to drown themselves in the dark waters as night closed in.

◇◇◇

Germanus stamped into the atrium of his house, cursing effusively. The servant who had met John at the door earlier shrank away.

"You never should have told him I was at the Zeuxippos baths," Germanus thundered.

The servant had simply offered the usual report on who had called at the house and the general had started shouting.

"But what else was I to do?" The servant's voice quavered. "He was acting under Justinian's orders. He showed me the seal."

"Next time tell him you don't know where I've gone. Or that I'm off hunting in the Cypress Forest. Send him up the Bosporos looking for me. Tell him I've set sail for Egypt!"

"I tried to get rid of him as quickly as possible. I didn't want him to run into—"

"No, certainly not! And what about our other visitor?"

"Gone to see the lawyer."

"Again? What good will that do? I hope the lawyer knows enough to keep his mouth shut. I don't like all this running around. Too much risk of being seen."

The servant was visibly trembling and Germanus softened his tone. "You did well to keep the Lord Chamberlain out. No one is to get past the atrium, and if possible not even that far. Maybe you should say my cook has the plague."

The huge guard who had spoken to John loomed in the entranceway.

"You had a word with him?" Germanus asked.

"Yes. I would have preferred to show him some steel to make the point clearer."

"The Lord Chamberlain's no fool. Steel isn't necessary. Yet. Come with me."

The two men made their way down a long many-doored hallway decorated with wall paintings and through the storage areas at the back of the house to a walled courtyard in which laborers were unloading sacks and crates from the back of a cart. An archway in the high wall opened onto a narrow alley. Two sentries were posted by the archway.

Germanus looked up and down the alley, which came to a dead end a short distance from the archway. "I want you to make sure that anyone coming in by the back way isn't being followed," he instructed the towering guard beside him. "Put someone out on the street to watch whoever approaches. Disguise him as a vendor or a beggar. And keep an eye out for people lurking around."

"You think the house is being watched?"

"I hope not. I don't like being visited by high officials carrying out imperial investigations."

"There's nothing you've done that anyone could prove was illegal."

"Since when does the emperor have to prove anything? The less he knows the better."

Chapter Nineteen

Peter was awakened by the banging of a door.

He turned his head to look at the window. Movement was difficult. His skull seemed to weigh as much as the dome of the Great Church. In the darkening sky above the dome he could make out a star.

Had the master returned home?

Peter thought about stars. Some said they were angels but there was nothing angelic about those cold, hard, sharp points of light. They were jewels on a rich man's robe, caught in the church lights during a night vigil.

The pain in his broken leg waxed and waned like the unseen moon. A throbbing pain, as deep and intense as pain could possibly be. It brought tears to his eyes.

It wasn't time for him to die. He must remain to see the master through this latest trial. He didn't like to think about him going around the palace, questioning powerful people, any one of whom would not suffer for having him killed if it suited them. The master was a powerful man himself, but an outsider. Not to mention a Mithran. What would the Lord think about Peter having spent so many years serving a Mithran?

"Please, Lord," Peter muttered. "Keep the master safe. His beliefs may be wrong but you should know him by his works, if you don't mind me saying so."

A noise interrupted his thoughts. Or had it awakened him? What had he heard?

"Hypatia?" He was startled at how weak his voice sounded. There was no answer.

He had the impression Hypatia had opened the door a crack, peered in at him, and shut the door. It might have been his imagination. The girl was always underfoot. He ought to make it plain to Lady Anna that Hypatia was not to interfere in his kitchen. Her duty was to grow the herbs Peter needed. She was not a cook. It would not do for her to be in the way while he was standing watch on the pot boiling over the hot coals.

No. That had been years ago. Both he and Hypatia had been Lady Anna's slaves before her death freed them and they came to work for John.

The potions Gaius had given him were making Peter light-headed.

"How can I manage in such a state? What was the scoundrel thinking of? Does he imagine I can lie around like the idle aristocrats he treats?"

He closed his eyes.

He remembered a young servant he used to meet at the back of a garden at the house he worked in years ago. He could feel the soft flesh of her rounded arms and her warm breath.

She would be an old woman now. He felt a sadness deeper even than the agony in his leg. What kind of a world was it where such beauty withered away?

Peter had never known a woman for long. For much of his life he had been on the move, as a camp cook, constantly on the march, as a servant moving from one household to another. He had always thought that some day he would find himself in the right situation and the right woman would present herself. But it had never happened. And without ever being aware of it, he had finally stopping thinking about it.

Now he was an old man and it was too late.

"Too late," he whispered. Yet there was nothing one could miss in life that meant anything compared to the glories waiting in heaven. "I have always served you, Lord, to the best of my ability."

Peter felt himself drifting. His bed might have been floating on the Marmara. How long had he been in bed? He was useless, and just when the master needed him. The least he could do was make him a decent meal. Hypatia would insist on overspicing the dishes.

His leg didn't pain him as much. He shifted, experimentally, and found his body no longer felt as inert and heavy. He pushed the coverlet down, took a breath, and swung his legs over the side of the bed. The splinted leg stuck straight out, which made it awkward when he stood, bracing himself against the wall with one hand.

He hobbled toward the door. Obviously Gaius had overreacted. Peter was perfectly able to put weight on the supposedly broken leg.

He was standing next to his cooking brazier before he knew it.

"Let's see," he clucked to himself. "A dish needing only one pot. I can't be standing too long. What's on hand?"

He found several eggs lined up on the windowsill and a basket under the table containing a cabbage. The wine jug was full and neither the master nor Hypatia had eaten any of the cheese intended for breakfast.

He sang a hymn. His voice was the creaking of a cart wheel.

"Why do you veil your faces?
"Let your hearts be uplifted!
"For Christ, Christ has arisen!
"Glorious and gleaming,
"Christ, Christ is born
"Of He who gave light."

Wasn't the master's god, Mithra, the lord of light?
It was something to consider.
But first the evening meal must be prepared.

He chopped happily at the cabbage and tossed its shredded remains into the large pot simmering over the glowing coals. He splashed in some wine, added cheese and eggs, and leftover scraps of the swordfish that had caused so much trouble. He took a clove or two from the string of garlic hanging from a ceiling hook and tossed them into the now bubbling mixture.

Then he was back in bed, once again feeling the warm breath of the long ago servant girl as they sat together in the cool grass behind a hedge.

Or rather, it was Hypatia's warm breath, her face bent down close to his. But it had been the servant girl's lips touching his cheek, not Hypatia's. Surely.

"What are you looking so glum about, Hypatia?" Peter asked, but she drew away as if she hadn't heard.

He hadn't managed to speak. He made a determined effort.

This time she heard. "Peter, you were so still I was worried. What are you saying?"

"The evening meal. I started it. It's on the brazier."

"What do you mean? I've just been in the kitchen, and there's nothing…" Her voice trailed off. "Oh, I see. Yes. Thank you, Peter."

She turned and left the room and Peter could hear her sobbing for some reason in the hallway.

Chapter Twenty

It was twilight by the time John reached Artabane's house, a one story villa in the classic Roman style, not far from the northern wall of the Great Palace.

"Close enough so the Great Whore could keep an eye on me," Artabanes explained in slurred tones when John noted the convenient proximity.

The Armenian was a lean, sinewy man, clean-shaven. If he'd been sober he would have been handsome. Now his deep set eyes were bloodshot, his finely chiseled features flushed, his narrow lips slack.

The dignified, gray-haired servant who answered the door had been turning John away because his employer was too ill to see anyone when Artabanes came lurching across the atrium, as if engaged in a slow corybantic dance, utterly intoxicated.

"John? John the Eunuch, isn't it?" Artabanes said heartily. "Pay no attention to my servant's lack of manners. Welcome. I was just out in the garden communing with nature."

"That part of nature which grows on vines," muttered the servant.

John raised an eyebrow at the disrespectful remark.

"He is a difficult master, sir," the servant said. "He'll forget everything said before he's in bed tonight, if not sooner. If he manages to make it to the bed for a change."

Artabanes stumbled forward and grasped John's arm. "Let me show you the way to the garden." Leaning heavily on John, he pointed toward the left side of the atrium. "This side, please."

John saw the tiled floor was bisected by a broad black marble stripe leading from the street door, across the atrium, and into the garden beyond.

Artabanes noticed where John directed his gaze. "That's the border, Lord Chamberlain. Beyond lies enemy territory."

"Enemy?"

"The bitch. My former wife. The harpy Theodora forced me to live with. I may be imprisoned here but I won't live with her except in disharmony. I divided the house in two. She stays on her side, I stay on mine."

Once the entrance to the garden was reached, the symbolic frontier continued with a knee-high hedge that crossed the open space and then reverted to a black marble stripe when the green barrier reached the edge of the portico on the far side. The height of the hedge gave an indication of how long Artabanes and his wife had lived under these peculiar circumstances.

"Do the servants have access to both sides of the house?"

"I caught one of hers stealing a fig from my tree. I had the villain scourged. Does that answer your question? Her servants are forbidden to speak to mine or to me."

John reflected that there were worse penalties for straying across borders. "Who announces guests when your wife has visitors?"

"My former wife, you mean? The servant who let you in, Augustine, is our ambassador. He handles diplomatic missions when necessary."

"Indeed."

"Here, sit down." Artabanes collapsed onto a bench, forgetting to let go of John's arm and nearly pulling the Lord Chamberlain down on top of him. John freed his arm and positioned himself as far away from Artabanes as possible, which proved to be not far enough to escape the miasma of sour wine the man emanated.

"Not that she has many visitors," muttered Artabanes. "Why would she? She's not from Constantinople. She was happy enough to stay in Armenia, until I made a name for myself, until she realized I might suddenly have a few more coins than her suitors. I'll wager that surprised her. Then she was on the trot to Constantinople, weeping and wailing to the Great Whore. The Lesser Whore, that's what my former wife is."

"Theodora decreed you were not divorced under Roman law," John pointed out.

"Roman law! I repudiated the bitch. That's the way we do it in Armenia. Repudiate and be damned!" Artabanes spat. "While I'm off spilling my blood on the battlefield, back home half the nobility is spilling its seed into her. What's Roman law have to say about that?"

He reached under the bench and pulled out a jug of wine, lifted it to his lips, and drank. John was thankful his host didn't offer him any. He could hear a few bees buzzing in the gathering darkness. Like John they were putting in a very long day.

Artabanes belched. "So the empress ordered me to share this miserable excuse for a house with the bitch. But what can I do? She sentenced me to years of torture is what it amounted to. Don't feel sorry for me. You're suspected too, Lord Chamberlain. She made no secret of her enmity toward you. It's a miracle you're still alive."

Artabanes might be preposterously intoxicated but he was not entirely without sense.

"Until Justinian is satisfied we're all liable to be executed," John observed

"We both have reason to wish the Great Whore gone. I wish my cursed wife was gone!" He gestured wildly with his jug, splashing wine on his tunic. "I shall renounce her for a second time tomorrow and leave the city and be a soldier again!"

"I would advise against it, Artabanes. The empress hasn't been dead long. Justinian might be inclined to enforce her wish you live with your wife."

The general hiccuped and turned bloodshot eyes to John. "I know why you're here. Oh, yes. But note this well. Theodora gave me an excellent defense by her own actions. Even if I managed to murder the entire court without being suspected I still could not marry the woman I love above all others. It's too late. She's married Praejecta off. Married her to the son of one of those plotters executed after the Nika riots. My beautiful treasure handed over to a traitor's son."

He lifted the jug to his mouth again, found it empty, and flung it clumsily into his wife's half of the garden.

"Then again, I might kill my beloved's husband," he continued, bleary eyes brightening. "The idea has crossed my mind once or twice, I confess. Yes. A blade between the ribs. The soldier's way. None of this poisoning business. That's for women and eunuchs. But sssh, don't say it too loudly. Spies, you know. Spies everywhere. Might give the bitch ideas."

"I am told you tried to convey some ideas to General Germanus. Treasonous ideas. About how he would make a better emperor than Justinian."

"Who could argue with that?"

"The emperor's Lord Chamberlain might. Did you in fact visit Germanus?"

"Yes. We have both served in Libya."

"And did you hint that you might be interested in seeing Justinian replaced? I had the impression Germanus considered you quite capable of having murdered Theodora. To weaken Justinian's will."

Artabanes reached under the bench, produced another jug, and lifted it to his lips. Wine dribbled down his chin. "I don't recall saying anything. Then again, I don't remember half of what I say these days. Thankfully."

"Because you are perpetually intoxicated."

"Praise the Lord for the fruit of Bacchus." Artabanes waved the jug and emitted another belch.

John decided it was quite possible a man in Artabanes' state might say things he didn't mean and fail to remember what he

said. Artabanes seemed too intoxicated to be properly inter-
rogated. On the other hand, his wine-liberated ramblings supported his innocence, at least at first impression. Unless it was
all for show. Still, revenge was said to be as sweet as honey and
if Artabanes could not have the wife he wanted, perhaps he felt
it only fitting Justinian should lose Theodora.

"I won't trouble you further," John said and started to rise.

Artabanes grabbed his sleeve and pulled him back onto the
bench. "You see a drunken fool," he said thickly. "This is what
the imperial couple has done to me. I am a brave man, Lord
Chamberlain. A hero. Who was it saved Libya from the rebels?"

"I am certain Justinian appreciates—"

"Let me tell you how it was. Let me tell you. We were invited
to a banquet by the tyrant. His name was Gontharis. Imagine
the scene. He sat right beside me, exactly as you are. So then,
Lord Chamberlain, imagine you are the tyrant. A merry tyrant,
gorging yourself, offering choice morsels to the guards who stand
behind you. Let us suppose those shrubs there are the guards.
The tyrant is drinking. He is very drunk. Perhaps not as drunk
as I am right now, but drunk enough."

"Yes. I have heard—"

Artabanes plunged ahead, slurring his words. "Suddenly, as
planned, one of my men rushes into the hall. Straight at the tyrant
he runs, sword bared. A servant shouts a warning. The tyrant turns.
'What is this? What did you say?' He cups a hand to his ear."

Artabanes pushed himself to his feet, made a wide slashing
motion with his arm. John ducked his head to avoid being hit.

"The sword comes down. Slices a flap of scalp and cuts off
two fingers. One of the fingers splashes into my wine. But the
tyrant leaps to his feet. Leaps, Lord Chamberlain! I must show
you! Stand up. Stand up."

John got up reluctantly. Artabanes reached inside his own
tunic and brought out his hand with the index and forefinger
pointing straight out.

"I draw my dagger. A two-edged dagger. A wicked thing.
Death to the tyrant! Blood's spewing from the stumps of his

severed fingers. He can hardly see because that gory scrap of loose scalp is flopping in his face. I don't hesitate. I lunge with the dagger. Plunge it into the beast's side. Up to the hilt."

He took a tottering step and shot his hand forward, poking John's side painfully with his stiff fingers.

"The tyrant falls!" Artabanes sounded jubilant.

John took a step away but did not fall.

Artabanes face was a fiery red, sweat beaded on his smooth, broad forehead. He smelled like a tavern. "Then we take care of the guards."

He started lashing his invisible dagger at the shrubbery. Leaves flew like green flesh. Artabanes reeled forward, banged his knee on the bench, and tumbled across it and into the foliage, where he thrashed around in panic before finally ending up on his back.

He lay there in the embrace of the branches and looked up at John. "It was wonderful. I was a warrior then, Lord Chamberlain, and look what I've become."

John helped him to his feet, grimacing at the wine fumes which seemed to be seeping from the man's every pore.

"So is it any wonder Praejecta fell in love with me as soon as I unlocked the door to her room?" Artabanes raved on. "I was still soaked in blood. Her rescuer, the avenger of her cowardly husband. She was mine. She is mine, by right! She gave herself to me willingly. Eagerly. A toast to Fortuna for arranging the Great Whore's long agony!" Artabanes raised his hand and realized he was holding neither cup nor jug. "Ah, well. I just wish her torment had lasted as long as my miserable marriage."

A breeze wandered into the garden and was strangled by the stifling heat. Snatches of song passed them, carried on a tantalizing smell of frying onion.

"I suppose your kitchen is cut in half too?"

"Oh yes. Yes, it is. But, you know, onions cut in one side still make eyes on the other side water. That's how it goes, isn't it? Just how it always goes."

Artabanes wandered away abruptly.

John decided it was his opportunity to escape. Perhaps his thoughts would march in better order if he was somewhere cooler.

Somewhere along the coast perhaps.

He could go to Zeno's estate and surprise Cornelia and the others.

If it weren't for this hopeless investigation. He could not leave the city with Justinian likely to summon him at any time.

Since he had to stay, a long walk round the city would be helpful in ordering his thoughts, as it had been on numerous occasions.

John left quietly, while Artabanes urinated across the border.

Chapter Twenty-one

A flash of white hurtled from the open doorway straight at John's face. He put his hand up just in time and the object smacked against his palm. His fingers curled over a smooth surface. When he opened his hand he saw he was holding an unbroken egg.

He went into the inn wedged between the towering walls of the Hippodrome and the looming fortresslike Baths of Zeuxippos. The scale of the world changed as he stepped out of the darkness into a brightly lit room where smoke hung against a low ceiling.

Laughter greeted him.

It was Felix and Gaius, sitting at a table near the entrance.

"You've still got a fighter's reflexes, John," Felix called out.

John made himself smile in greeting and sat on a stool next to the two. He seldom stopped for a cup of wine so near to the palace. He preferred places where he was less likely to run into, or be observed by, members of the imperial court. That usually didn't apply to friends, but John would have preferred this evening to have a quick, solitary drink before hurrying home to find out what news there was, if any. The more troubled he was, the less John wanted company.

The place was unpleasantly noisy. At the counter the bald proprietor was arguing with a short man dressed in the mud-spattered garments of a laborer.

"You fool!" the proprietor yelled, waving a ladle. "I shall outlive the lot of you put together!"

The man he addressed ignored this prophecy, leaned forward, plucked another egg from a basin on the counter, and sent it winging out the door.

John looked at the egg he had caught.

"Hard-boiled," Felix explained with a grin.

Gaius leaned forward to be heard more easily against the background noise and breathed into John's face. The physician smelled as if his insides were fermenting, almost as nauseating as Artabanes. Obviously he had not stopped drinking since John had visited his surgery in the early afternoon. "You see," Gaius said, "the fellow who owns this excellent inn is known as Alba. He has strange humors at times and will only eat white food. Hence his nickname. His real name is...is...do you know what is it, Felix?"

"Nobody knows," Felix replied. "But his name is white and so is his diet."

"Not healthy," Gaius lamented. He shook his head sorrowfully. His words were thick.

"And tedious," Felix agreed. "A man can't exist by eating only white food. The very thought of carrots and parsnips and eggs and fish must choke the throat after a few years. Look at what's it done to Alba. Every last hair on his scalp has fled in disgust."

Another egg flew out the doorway.

The proprietor stepped around his counter, grasped the egg-thrower by the neck, and propelled him into the street, helped along with a boot in the laborer's ample rear. Patrons raucously praised the entertainment. Wiping his hands on his grubby tunic, the proprietor came over to the trio. "Wine for you, sirs?" he addressed John and Felix. "Gaius, I know you'll have more."

John nodded. After spending dawn to dusk listening to aristocrats describe their enemies as potential murderers, he needed a drink. He presented the egg to the proprietor, who took it and began polishing the shell on his tunic as he walked back to the counter for wine.

"Alba's a patient of mine," Gaius told John. "We trade services. I get free wine, he gets free treatment. Now there's a good deal for me, wouldn't you say? I've been trying to persuade him to eat other foods, but he insists that good health and balanced humors are only obtainable by dining on white dishes."

"With white food on them," Felix put in.

"You see that bowl of black olives on the counter?" Gaius said. "I brought them myself this morning. I'm hoping he'll be tempted to try one. If Felix leaves any for him, that is."

"Dangerous to tamper with a man's favorites," Felix observed. "Especially food. So I thought I'd remove temptation." Suddenly Felix's voice sounded much too loud.

It was because the room had grown quiet.

An excubitor, clad in a leather cuirass and carrying a lance, filled the doorway. A curl of fiery red hair stuck out beneath his helmet.

Felix jumped to his feet, strode over to the excubitor, and exchanged a few words before returning to the table.

"I have to go. Justinian wants to see me. Immediately."

John gave him a questioning look.

"No idea what it's about. Except it's urgent."

"Maybe he's had a sudden whim to have somebody executed," Gaius mumbled.

As soon as Felix vanished with the messenger the room exploded into an uproar as every drinker offered his conjecture about what new disaster the red-haired excubitor's visit might foretell. A couple of customers got up and departed, muttering about trouble being on the way.

"I haven't seen much of Felix lately" John said to Gaius. "Justinian is keeping him busy. The emperor's afraid Theodora's death might give someone an opportunity to do away with him too."

"Theodora, there was a woman!" The speaker was the proprietor, who had arrived at their table with a wine jug and cup for John. "Oh, I could tell many a tale about her. I knew her when she was a young woman, still working in the theater. Many's the time she's dropped in for a cup of wine after performances."

"And borrowed the upstairs room for another sort of performance!" a patron sitting nearby declared.

The proprietor winked at John and set the jug down. He had peeled the egg and began to munch on it. "She has a couple of sisters," he said between bites. "Both made good marriages with Theodora's assistance. In those days they were not as well-dressed—"

"Undressed, you mean," the patron interrupted.

The comment unlocked a torrent of reminiscences about the late empress, many of which involved Theodora's famous act in which geese pecked grain from her private parts.

It seemed that most of the male population of Constantinople of a suitable age had had some acquaintance of the empress in her youth. In fact, to judge from the ages of the storytellers, she had debauched more than a few babies in their cradles.

"I'm amazed the palace cooks dare offer roast goose for imperial meals," Alba remarked. "Though I suppose nobody would be so stupid as to snigger or mention grain shipments from Egypt during an imperial banquet."

"Not within Theodora's hearing," John told him. "At the far end of the table, that's another story."

Alba went away chuckling. The next time he regaled his patrons with stories about Theodora he would no doubt tell them he had it on good authority, from a high official, that the empress was derided right under her nose by lascivious court wits.

"Speaking of roast fowl," said Gaius. "Theodora's cook has vanished. Everyone thinks he's been executed, but there's no reason to suspect him. The kitchen has more guards watching it than the Persian frontier. Not even Croesus could pay anyone enough to attempt to poison either of the imperial couple, given there's not enough gold in the world to buy an easy death once you're in the hands of the torturers. And in these cases, the servants are first to be taken underground."

Gaius hid his face in his cup again.

John knew from experience there was no point arguing with the physician about his drinking. The best he could do would be to persuade him to leave and escort him safely back to the palace, luckily only a stone's throw from the inn, but a long and perilous journey for a man alone and in Gaius' present state.

Alba's customers had begun trading stories about Theodora, and one man was describing for Alba's particular attention what he had heard from a servant he knew. "A parsnip, he said it was. At a private party years ago. He could hardly forget it, though fortunately for him Theodora had forgotten him. Since I heard about her act I've refused to eat parsnips."

"All the more for me, then, and better health as a result. But still the woman had courage."

"Oh, I don't know. It wasn't a very large parsnip."

"Forget the parsnip! I'm talking about the riots." Alba finished peeling the shell from another egg and carefully excavated the yolk. "Everyone knows Justinian was all for fleeing but she insisted on staying."

"A pity," someone at the back of the room remarked. "But there again, what if someone like the Cappadocian had taken power after they fled? Eggs and taxes would cost five times what they do now for a start!"

Alba gulped down the last piece of egg before replying. "Yes, a nasty piece of work, the Cappadocian. Give him half a chance and he'll take all you've got and your daughter and wife as well."

"Not even half a chance!" said the man at the back of the room. "He'd squeeze us for taxes as if we were grapes in a wine press and keep most for himself. As for the women, he's been known to boast making free with them is part of his job. Keeps the populace cowed, so it's easier to collect what's owed. You have to admit Theodora getting rid of him to that Egyptian monastery was about the only good deed she did."

John was reminded of the demonic tollgate keepers with whom Theodora would be required to negotiate, using the coin of good deeds to ascend while fending off attacks meant to tumble her to a dark fate.

"Well, what about that refuge she set up for former whores?" Alba asked.

"Left all the more business for her!" came the near simultaneous reply from three men.

"A toast to Theodora!" one cried, waving his wine cup and baptizing his companions. "May Theodora be kept warm by lusty demons for eternity! And may Alba's parsnip never freeze!"

Gaius reached for his cup, missed and knocked it over. Luckily there was only a drop of wine left in it. His face was flushed. His bulbous nose glowed like the dome of the Great Church.

"It's time to go," John told him, getting to his feet.

"No, I...I don't want to leave..."

"I'll accompany you, Gaius."

Gaius put his reddened face in his hands. "I confess I'm afraid, John. Especially in the early hours of the day. You've heard that saying about Theodora some wit put about a year or so back? The one that says meet her at dawn, you'll have reason to mourn? It's hard to keep your mind on the job when all the time you're expecting a tap on the shoulder."

"You've served the emperor and empress for years, Gaius. Justinian trusts you without question. Otherwise he wouldn't have appointed you to treat Theodora."

"He'd be all the angrier if he thought I'd betrayed his trust. It would be the torturers for certain and not simply a kindly blade or a noose." Gaius sniffled. "I wish I had stayed at Samsun's Hospice. Things were so much easier. I treated the poor, who thanked their Lord they were being treated at all. I was doing some good in this benighted city and I had plenty of time to earn a bit by treating a few wealthy clients who appreciated my services. I should never have been enticed to change my practice, to work for the imperial couple."

"When the imperial couple requests one's services it is hard to refuse. Besides which, you did your best for the empress."

"It's true. Yes. But if Justinian believes Theodora was poisoned...if he suspected the cook of poisoning her...I...I was in a far better position to poison her than the cook. I explained to him that I was administering the smallest effective doses. There was never a bottle large enough to hold a harmful does in the sickroom. I made sure of it. But what if I made a mistake or Justinian thinks I did? I'm always listening for the knock on my door. When that excubitor arrived looking for Felix my first thought—" He began to blubber.

"Never mind," John told him, taking him by the elbow. "No one is going to come knocking at your door tonight. Justinian should be getting over his shock by now and coming to his senses."

Should be, John thought as he helped Gaius stagger out into the growing darkness, but probably hasn't.

Chapter Twenty-two

John sat at the kitchen table while Hypatia ladled the stew she had kept simmering onto his plate. He had discarded his cloak and changed into a clean linen tunic. The hour was very late.

Hypatia carried the pot back to the brazier and set it down with a crash. "I'm not surprised Gaius threw up on you, master. He'd been drinking when he arrived to see Peter judging from the smell of him, and it was only the middle of the day. How can he treat patients if he's drunk all the time?"

"You say Peter's no better?"

Hypatia's lips tightened for a moment. "No. He's wandering in his mind. He's under the impression he came down here and prepared dinner."

"Let's hope he doesn't try. I won't need you again tonight, Hypatia. I'm going to try to get some sleep."

She went down the hall, climbed the stairs to Peter's room, and cracked the door open quietly. His window let in the faint glow the city gave off even in the depths of the night, barely enough to show the rise and fall of the sheet covering the sleeping form in the bed.

Did she dare ask the Lord Chamberlain to find a more reliable physician?

She was a servant. It wasn't her place to suggest any such thing. Besides, Gaius was John's friend. But should she let Peter die just because she was a servant?

She went back downstairs. The house was large and felt empty. Why did the Lord Chamberlain choose to live this way?

No wonder Peter seemed glad to have her company.

Hypatia stepped out into the dark garden, into the smell of foliage and damp earth. Night insects chirped, hidden in the black leaves. She took a narrow flagstone path in the direction of the burbling that filled the quiet space. Some light-footed creature rustled away through the bushes.

Hypatia lowered herself on the bench by an eroded fountain. She could make out faint reflections in the gently bubbling water. In the square of night overhead a few stars blinked in the humid air.

In even such a tiny patch of nature she found respite from the brutal world of humankind. No matter what miseries men visited upon each other the insects would continue to chirp and the wild creatures would go on their nightly forays.

The Lord Chamberlain had been distressed by the lack of news from Cornelia. Hypatia could see it plainly in his face, which was unusual. He normally masked his emotions.

He had said he intended to sleep but Hypatia knew he would sit up drinking wine in his study and talking to the mosaic girl on the wall.

He would be better off if he stopped talking to bits of colored glass, came downstairs, and listened to the sounds of his garden. Cornelia had probably told him as much. It was good she was living here now. The Lord Chamberlain was not as solitary as he had been when Hypatia had first worked for him. People shouldn't be alone.

A breeze, chilled by the darkness, made Hypatia blink. She had been dozing off on the bench, lulled by the fountain's music.

She pushed herself to her feet, walked wearily back inside, guided by a single torch beneath the peristyle, and tiptoed up the stairs and down the hallway.

As she'd expected, a line of lamplight showed under the closed door of John's study. She knew Peter had sometimes stood outside the door long enough to hear John muttering to himself, or rather, as he imagined, to Zoe, the mosaic girl. She hurried past, preferring not to hear, and climbed the stairs to the servants' quarters.

Her room was next to Peter's. She lay down on her pallet, then realized she should check on him before she slept.

She must have been more exhausted than she imagined. The next thing she knew she was waking to a sharp banging noise.

Had a crate fallen off a cart passing by outside?

Shouts.

From downstairs.

More banging. Knocking.

Someone at the house door.

She leapt up and scrambled down the stairs, still half asleep. John's study was dark.

She heard footsteps, more voices.

By the time she reached the atrium there was only silence inside.

From outside came the rattle of wheels and the clatter of hooves on cobbles. The sound was coming through the front door, standing open.

A carriage vanished around the corner of the excubitors' barracks across the square.

She slammed the door, and went up the stairs two at a time.

The kitchen was just as empty. So was the study and John's room.

"Master," she called. "Lord Chamberlain."

There was no reply.

Chapter Twenty-three

Joannina loosened the top of her light blue tunica, dabbed more perfume between her breasts, and settled down on the couch to wait for Anastasius.

She had dismissed Vesta for the night, after pressing upon her a silver chain she considered too heavy for her own delicate neck but which suited her lady-in-waiting. It pleased Joannina's vanity that Vesta made every effort to emulate her and Joannina was determined to turn the girl into a suitable match for some handsome courtier. Not that the plain-looking Vesta had any chance of catching a man such as Joannina's Anastasius, but then that match had been made by the empress herself.

On second thought, Joannina got off the couch and padded barefoot around the room snuffing out all the lamps except for one in a far corner. Anastasius preferred to have the lights blazing but she felt more comfortable with a softer ambiance.

Except for the diaphanous tunica and too much perfume she wore only tiny silver earrings in the shape of sea shells. Anastasius, she knew, liked her to keep on a bit of jewelry.

She was partial to silver jewelry. It suited her pale skin.

Skin the color of moonlight, Anastasius had told her.

It would have been better if he had left it at that and hadn't elaborated by telling her she was more glorious than the heavens because the heavens boasted only one, rather than two silvery moons. And even then the words might have struck Joannina as more poetical if the poet's hands hadn't been so busy with the celestial orbs.

Where was he anyway? He hadn't seemed himself since the Lord Chamberlain's visit. He'd been short-tempered. He had done nothing during their ride that morning except complain about how much he was sweating. When they'd returned he'd changed his clothes and gone off without telling her what he was planning to do. Which was rare. Perhaps he intended to surprise her with a present, to make up for his bad mood.

At least he wouldn't stumble home intoxicated as men did, she had heard. He put more water in his wine than anyone she'd ever seen and he never drank except at meals. In that way, he was only a step removed from the abstemious emperor.

Anastasius was, she thought dreamily, the ideal husband, except that he wasn't quite her husband yet.

"Well," she murmured to herself, "in the eyes of the Lord we are man and wife, and that's all that truly matters."

She liked to hear herself say that. Unfortunately, unless they were legally married and beyond the interference of her parents, it was unlikely they'd be allowed to continue living together.

If only Theodora had lived a few weeks more, she would have ensured the ceremony was held as scheduled and no one would have dared to come between the two young lovers.

Joannina had been terrified when the empress first suggested that Joannina and her grandson marry. The young girl was awed by Anastasius. Tall and regal with his thick mane of glossy black hair, he was a familiar figure at court, bantering easily with his few equals, withering inferiors in the heat of his disdain. Everyone deferred to him despite his youth. It was not surprising, considering he was Theodora's grandson.

Nevertheless, Joannina's parents had not approved. Her mother had been apoplectic judging from her letters. But what could her parents do? They were in Italy. Joannina thought they should have been pleased to see their family allied with Theodora's. For one thing, it would block the ascension of General

Germanus over Joannina's father Belisarius once and for all. She had been aware of their rivalry practically before she could talk. But no, her mother insisted Theodora was just trying to get her hands on Belisarius' family's fortune. As if the empress needed anyone else's miserable fortune.

And what right did her faithless slut of a mother have to interfere in the authentic pure love shared by Joannina and Anastasius?

Joannina was hardly more than a child, but a child has eyes and ears. She had observed the men who came and went when her father was absent. And there was the one who was her step-brother. How vile.

Yet there were those who disapproved when Theodora ordered Joannina and Anastasius to live together in the same rooms in the empress' part of the palace. People whispered. Most of the girls Joannina's age who whispered were envious. They could only wish the empress would force them to share a bedroom with the most handsome young man at court, and a member of the imperial family no less.

Not that Theodora had exerted any force, despite what gossips claimed. Except for forcing the two into common living arrangements.

Once Joannina had made a blushing and stammering Vesta tell her exactly what the ladies-in-waiting and other attendants were gossiping.

"Oh, your ladyship…I'd rather not say…but…oh…they claim Theodora came here herself and instructed you both to go into… into…the bedroom and…and disrobe. And then…oh…must I? Then she told you both exactly what to do and even helped…"

Joannina had laughed. "What nonsense! Theodora has hardly been well enough to move around on her own since Anastasius and I have been living here. She has never visited. It was nothing like that. Nothing like that at all."

She did not tell Vesta what it had been like. That the haughty and handsome Anastasius had been absolutely terrified to do what his grandmother had made clear he must do.

That had done more than anything to endear him to Joannina.

Thinking about it, Joannina began to grow impatient. Where was he?

Despite her annoyance, she started drifting off to sleep on the couch. When he stamped into the sitting room he startled her.

She saw he was empty-handed, hadn't brought anything for her. "What's the matter, dearest? Where have you been so late?"

Joannina felt she had a wifely duty to assuage his anger, but when in the past she had tried soothing words or put her arms around him, it had just stoked his fury.

"I've been out and about asking questions." He flopped down on the couch next to her, yanked off his malodorous boots, and threw them across the room. "I don't like it! I don't like it at all! Someone's going to pay. I'll have my revenge, you wait and see. Vengeance will be mine!"

He sounded more petulant than vengeful.

Joannina pulled herself into a sitting position and leaned over Anastasius who was slouched on his spine with his long legs stretched out on the floor. "What are you talking about? Vengeance for what?"

"For the murder of my grandmother. It's not just a rumor. It's true. She was murdered. Justinian has ordered that eunuch of his to find the culprit. I didn't believe it, but now I have it on good authority. He spent the whole day visiting people who are under suspicion."

"Vesta and ourselves are under suspicion?"

"And Germanus, not to mention your mother."

"That's silly. Mother was Theodora's friend."

"Maybe. But it's very convenient for your mother that the empress died before our marriage, isn't it?"

Joannina drew away from him. "You don't think my mother killed your grandmother, do you?"

Anastasius said nothing but frowned furiously.

Joannina frowned back. "You can't be thinking of taking vengeance on mother!"

"Well, no. The eunuch visited Artabanes. That's who I suspect."

"Why Artabanes?"

"Because Theodora arranged for his…uh…marital relations, just like she did ours, but the opposite, don't you see?"

Joannina tentatively put her hand on his narrow shoulder. "What do you mean?"

"She arranged for us to stay together. She also arranged for Artabanes to stay with his wife. See. Artabanes wanted to marry Praejecta, just like we want to marry each other. But in Artabanes' case, she stopped the marriage and forced him to live with his wife, while in our case, though we aren't married, she made us live together so we can be married. It's almost exactly the same except different."

Joannina ventured to let her hand run down Anastasius' arm. "I see, now that you explain it so clearly."

"So Artabanes wanted revenge on Theodora for spoiling his marriage plans. That would make anyone want revenge."

"But it isn't your job to take revenge on anyone, Anastasius. And certainly not on Artabanes. We barely know the man."

"It it weren't for him there would be no way your parents could stop our being married!"

"Your grandmother was very ill," Joannina pointed out.

Anastasius slid lower on the couch. "But she wouldn't have died before she saw to it we were married if not for—"

"You sound as if you care more about our marriage than your grandmother!"

Anastasius turned toward Joannina and put his hand out. She moved slightly and the hand brushed her shoulder. "You know I care about you more than anything in the world, Joannina, my little sparrow."

"Now that's the Anastasius I love." She kissed his forehead and her hand went to his belt. "Let the Lord Chamberlain worry about vengeance."

Chapter Twenty-four

The carriage was utterly dark. The windows had been covered.

John had caught only a glimpse of the conveyance as he was thrown roughly inside it. It was an imperial carriage in poor repair, nothing the emperor would ride in, and had been relegated to other uses.

He tried the door. Not surprisingly, it was locked. He couldn't see his hand or anything else. Except that he could feel his breath going in and out he might already have been a disembodied phantom.

The carriage had an unpleasant sour smell. The smell of fear, perhaps, from previous passengers.

At least half a dozen excubitors had come to the house. They hammered on the door loudly enough to wake him in the study where he had dozed off in his chair. Once he confronted them they had become taciturn about their mission and John's destination.

"Emperor's orders! That's all you need to know!" their apparent leader barked when John tried to question him.

John recognized the man by the unruly red hair spilling from underneath his helmet.

He was the excubitor who had summoned Felix from the tavern for an urgent meeting with Justinian.

A meeting to order John's arrest?

There had been no use resisting. John had not tucked the blade he usually carried into the tunic he had intended to wear to bed. It didn't matter. A single man, even properly armed, would have no chance against so many trained soldiers.

He fought the only worthwhile battle left, the battle to maintain his dignity.

After so many years of imperial service, was his life going to end like so many others—like the guards outside Theodora's sickroom, like the imperial cook—unexpectedly, at the whim of the emperor?

Everyone at court heard stories of people spirited away to be summarily executed on Justinian's orders. Sometimes acquaintances or family members. And then they wondered what would it feel like? How would they react when they were roused from sleep and told they had less than a hour to live, if they were lucky? If they were lucky enough, that is, to be killed simply and cleanly and not taken down to the torturers first.

But however close the victim had been to a particular person, it was like hearing about someone killed by lightning or a runaway cart. An acknowledged possibility, but never something you really imagined would happen to yourself.

John stared into the blackness that pressed in on him like dark water. He feared deep water. Now he fought off the feeling he was drowning. He kept his lips tightly pressed together as if the darkness might get in and choke off his breath.

He didn't know what time it was. How long had he dozed before waking? It might be the middle of the night or nearly dawn.

One wouldn't have expected the emperor to schedule a meeting for either time.

He wished he had heard from Cornelia.

The carriage wheels creaked. John was jolted continually. He couldn't tell where he was being taken. At least the carriage had not been moving downhill, which would indicate that the destination was the docks or some lonely stretch of sea wall beyond which the hungry waters waited for the emperor's offerings.

Instead, the carriage was going uphill. It slowed, turned, came to a halt.

"Mithra!" John muttered.

The door swung open. Powerful arms pulled him into the night and dragged him along before he had a chance to get his bearings.

Abruptly he was released.

He stood amidst massive sarcophagi illuminated by torches in curving walls.

Was this some kind of horrible jest on Justinian's part?

John realized he had been brought to Constantine's mausoleum behind the Church of the Holy Apostles. Around him lay emperors, who having lived in the purple slept for eternity enclosed in the imperial color. Purple porphyry folded angular arms about Constantine, Theodosius, and other departed rulers. Although Zeno lay under dark green Thessalonian stone, veined in white.

Thinking of the emperor reminded John of Anatolius' uncle Zeno, on whose estate John's family was currently living.

A hand shoved him forward.

He moved through a haze of incense, its sweet perfume foretelling the gardens of heaven.

He might have been dreaming.

An excubitor stood on each side of him. He could see the steel of their drawn swords glinting.

Light flashed from the mausoleum's gem-studded gold fittings, icons glittered in lamplight glowing from silver dove-shaped lamps suspended on long chains from the frescoed roof, reflected in marble walls.

They passed out of Constantine's burial place and into the mausoleum Justinian had only recently had completed.

The excubitor with the red hair stopped and clamped a hand on John's shoulder. "Far enough!"

The guards at John's side moved away.

A prickling sensation ran from the nape of John's neck down his back.

Where would the steel penetrate?

He remembered well the feel of a blade cutting through flesh.

He had endured the pain before and he would endure it one last time.

◇◇◇

Hypatia stood in the dark kitchen, trying to overcome her fear. The clatter of the carriage moving away across the square still seemed to reverberate through the house,

The Lord Chamberlain may have been called away on business, she told herself. Though it was before dawn, it would not have been impossible. Affairs of the empire did not keep regular hours.

But he would never have left the door open or gone without leaving word with her.

Would he?

Then again, he had been working too hard. He was exhausted. It was plain in his gaunt features.

What about the raised voices? Had they only sounded overly loud and angry because they had startled her in the middle of the night?

She told herself not to leap to conclusions. The Lord Chamberlain did not explain his comings and goings to her.

Perhaps he would return soon.

She preferred not to think the worst.

She pulled a chair up to the table, sat down, and waited.

Chapter Twenty-five

John waited to die in Justinian's mausoleum.

But the sudden pressure he felt against the middle of his back was not sharp steel but flesh. One of his guards gave him a shove.

John took three stumbling steps forward before he saw the emperor kneeling by Theodora's sarcophagus.

How horrified the empress would be if she could see the emperor kneeling in the presence of one of his subjects.

Justinian got to his feet. At those times John had seen him since Theodora's death his demeanor had been so stolid John had wondered if he really was a demon exhibiting a false face to the world as many believed. Now, however, very human tears glistened on his gaunt cheeks. Justinian's face had grown so thin it resembled the skulls of Timothy, Luke, and Andrew, three of the most sacred treasures held in the Church of the Holy Apostles. The impression had scarcely formed in John's thoughts when Justinian smiled wanly in his direction.

"I shall be laid to rest next to the empress in due course," the emperor remarked in an even tone. "But I feel as if I were already entombed. I feel like Emperor Zeno. The story goes that he was locked in his tomb while still alive and called from his darkness for three days before his voice fell silent forever."

Justinian patted Theodora's sarcophagus fondly, as one might caress the head of a child.

John fought to reorient himself. Mention of the former emperor inevitably reminded John of Cornelia and his daughter Europa at the estate of Anatolius' uncle Zeno.

"It is a beautiful creation, excellency," he replied automatically. The color was strangely appropriate. For Theodora was enclosed not in the purple of imperial majesty but by reddish-brown, as if the stone had taken on the hue of her murderous nature.

"Sardian stone," Justinian said. "I commissioned it three years ago, never expecting...she was only forty-five at the time and..." He stopped and for an instant John thought the emperor's voice would break and he would begin to sob. If he had been about to do so, he controlled himself. Instead he traced a finger along the top of one of the the fluted columns carved on each corner of the sarcophagus. John saw the finger trembled.

John, himself, was trembling, the effects of his stressful journey. He hoped it didn't show.

"Look here, Lord Chamberlain," Justinian said. "See how the doves circle the heads of lambs, indicating her nature. And there at the end, and on the lid, the olive wreathes enclosing crosses."

John said nothing. He found it impossible to imagine that even the man who had been married to her could have believed Theodora's nature to be reminiscent of doves and lambs and olive wreaths.

Perhaps least of all the man who had been married to her.

And the emperor knew how Theodora had hated John. Did he expect to convince John now of his wife's saintliness? Or did he have something else in mind?

"I did everything in my power to help her," Justinian went on. "But what did it come to in the end? It is commonly said I have the power of life and death over every person in the empire, but in truth I have only the power of death. It's not a great matter, since death is certain anyway. And what can I do now, to serve the empress in death? I promised to allow those heretics she sheltered in the Hormisdas Palace to remain there. I will do so, but would it not be better if there were no heretics?"

His gaze fastened on John. Did Justinian know his Lord Chamberlain was a Mithran, a heretic? Did he care?

"You have always done your best to mediate between the opposing factions, excellency," John said.

Justinian looked at the sarcophagus. "Yes. Without success. It is even more urgent now that this wretched matter of the Three Chapters be resolved. What do you think of the Three Chapters, John?"

The Three Chapters was the name by which the current religious controversy had come to be called, due to the fact it revolved around three writings by long dead churchmen which some deemed to be heretical. John couldn't believe Justinian had had him abducted from his home and driven to this mausoleum in the middle of the night to discuss religion. "I lack your expertise in theology, excellency," John replied.

"It is a knotty problem," Justinian acknowledged. "Countless tomes written debating the nature of Christ. Over years of study I have come to the conclusion that it is all exceedingly simple. Nestorianism, you see, is the opposite of Monophysitism. Nestorius claimed that Christ had two natures, human and divine, both distinct, while the monophysites believe that Christ had only a single nature, his human nature being absorbed into his divinity."

John felt dazed. During the long carriage ride he had steeled himself for death, but instead he found himself listening to an arcane lecture. He struggled to recall what he knew of church councils. "Did not the Council of Chalcedon condemn both as heretical?"

"Yes. The fathers ruled that Christ has two indivisible natures in one person. He was both fully human and fully divine. Having given the matter much thought, and as God's representative on earth, I came to the conclusion that two indivisible natures are not necessarily different from a single nature in which a second nature has been subsumed."

"A matter of words."

"Nothing more. When I summoned Pope Vigilius to Constantinople I discovered he had never read the passages he was defending, for he does not read Greek. He knew only what he had been told. After I had them translated for him, he saw they were heresy and agreed with me that they should be condemned. If more churchmen spoke both Greek and Latin, as you do, Lord Chamberlain, perhaps this misunderstanding would never have arisen."

It was true that John spoke several languages. It was a useful skill. Justinian and those closest to him were Latin speakers, while the rest of Constantinople spoke Greek or the various languages from the far flung parts of the empire from which they had come. Over the years John had become so used to alternating between languages according to whom he was speaking that he hardly noticed changing back and forth.

"I recall that Vigilius issued his pronouncement condemning the Three Chapters at Easter," John said. "So you have all but brought about a reconciliation between the monophysites and the Orthodox church."

Justinian nodded, then looking to where his wife lay, frowned. "Theodora was pleased. But now Vigilius is wavering. Cursed man! The churchmen in the west, in Italy, are horrified. They say a repudiation of the Three Chapters amounts to heresy."

John had managed to control the fear he had felt while locked in the carriage, on his way to his execution as he had imagined. Now, however, he felt a new chill. What sort of man would choose the side of his wife's tomb as the place to ramble on about the current religious dispute? Perhaps the tears on his cheeks were as false as the human face he wore.

Or perhaps Justinian was not a demon, but simply insane.

Justinian continued talking. Was this the sort of thing that ran through his mind when he sat up at night, poring over holy books?

John allowed his attention to wander. However the disputants wished to slice up Christ's nature it made no difference to the world, except insofar as it affected the empire.

"This is a Christian empire," Justinian was saying. "If the church is not united, the empire is not united."

"I can see that, excellency."

"Why are you looking so grim?" the emperor asked. "Do you suppose I intend to have you dispatched to the next world, with my praises of Theodora the last earthly sounds you hear?"

John had put the idea out of his mind. Now that Justinian had mentioned it he felt himself tensing again.

Suddenly he could feel the presence of Theodora. He was acutely aware her remains lay within the stone tomb beside which he stood. She was now nothing but lifeless flesh and bone. Yet she was not truly gone. Not from the city or the empire or John's life.

"I require a report on your investigation," Justinian said. "I do not care to leave my wife's side. If I alarmed you…well, perhaps you will be spurred to greater efforts to find her murderer. What progress have you made?"

What progress? For some reason John's thoughts turned to his visit to the inn. Making the acquaintance of a man who ate only white foods could hardly be called progress. It seemed to sum up his accomplishments so far.

Nevertheless, he recited the list of those he had visited, leaving out the former madam Isis. "Joannina's lady-in-waiting Vesta, Theodora's physician Gaius, Antonina, generals Germanus and Artabanes."

Justinian's face remained expressionless. He gave no hint of whether he considered this an acceptable effort or not.

When John had finished the emperor merely nodded. "Thank you, Lord Chamberlain. When you are ready your escort will take you home. But first you might want to visit the vigil being held for the late empress." He started to turn away, paused. "I suspect some of those present are not true believers." He glanced at John with a slight smile.

Again John wondered if Justinian suspected or knew John would have to be counted among those devoted to another god should a roll call be made by suddenly appearing angels.

"Speak to Vigilius. He is in attendance," Justinian added.

Was he asking John to investigate the pope?

The emperor turned his back and John walked out into the night. Although the sky overhead was black it had begun to gray in the east, revealing the city's ragged horizon of tenement and mansion roofs, domes and monuments, and not far away, mounting above all, the long shadow of the Aqueduct of Valens.

John was surprised to be alive.

Chapter Twenty-six

After hours of darkness Hypatia realized that the kitchen was filled with gray, predawn light.

Had she dozed off, waiting for the Lord Chamberlain to return?

If so, she surely would have awakened if he had come in.

She went down the hall anyway, looked through the open door of his bedroom, into his study.

He had not returned.

Maybe he really had been dragged off, like so many others in the past few days, to be…

She tried to put that fear out of her mind.

What should she do? She was a servant. The only court official she could possibly approach for help was the Lord Chamberlain.

Anatolius! John's friend. He knew Hypatia. He was a lawyer now but had worked in the palace for years. And his house was not far away.

She raced downstairs, took the key from the hook beside the entrance, and went outside, pulling the heavy door shut behind her.

The gray light in the sky wasn't yet filtering down into the city. The square was a black lake, the far side marked by a single torch outside the excubitors' barracks. She waded out into the darkness, wondering if she would be able to find her way.

By the time she emerged from the Chalke Gate the streets had brightened enough for her to make out and avoid the shadowy forms of carts on their way out of the city after making nighttime deliveries. Gulls and feral dogs were out in force, scavenging before the thoroughfares became crowded.

She made a wrong turn down a malodorous alley, but no ruffians laid in wait.

Finally she recognized the entrance to the short, alley-like passage leading to Anatolius' home. The burly gatekeeper narrowed his eyes as she approached.

"I've come from the Lord Chamberlain's house," she said. "I'm his servant Hypatia. Anatolius knows me."

The gatekeeper made a noncommittal grunt, walked back and into the massive villa the high wall enclosed, emerged quickly, and swung the gate open.

She could see him smile to himself and shake his head as she went past. He couldn't help but be aware of his employer's proclivities.

Anatolius himself met her at the entrance. He was dressed as if he had already been up and working though he looked rumpled and tired.

He led her across the atrium but stopped short of his office. Shadows clustered in corners and gray fingers of light pried through shutters.

Anatolius wearily rubbed his unshaven face as he listened to Hypatia's account of the unseen morning visitors. "You're right to be worried," he said. "I'll go to the palace. Someone there will know what's going on. Little stays secret there for long."

Hypatia shivered involuntarily although the atrium was warm.

"Probably it's nothing to be concerned about," Anatolius added. His tone didn't sound convincing.

His office door was partly open and Hypatia thought she glimpsed movement inside.

"I'm sure you don't want to leave Peter alone too long," Anatolius went on. "I'll let you know what I find out but most likely

John will be home before I hear anything." Anatolius placed his hand lightly on her arm as if to usher her on her way.

Hypatia realized she had been staring toward the office. She was certain someone was in there.

""Will you be able to help the master?"

"Oh, I'm sure there will be no need. Nevertheless, I will look into the matter."

"Thank you, sir."

She had the feeling he wanted to get her out of the house.

Chapter Twenty-seven

John left the mausoleum and walked around to the front of the church, gathering his thoughts. Light streaming from many windows illuminated armed guards positioned in the porticoes on each side of the marble-walled building. The golden domes on the roof reminded John of eggs but what would hatch from those architectural look-alikes sitting atop the arms of the cross-shaped structure and over their central intersection could not be fathomed.

A crowd of worshipers issued from the entrance. The vigil must have ended.

John made his way against the tide into the well-lit interior where knots of people still lingered. He did not need to seek out Vigilius. Vigilius found him.

"Lord Chamberlain, I have been hoping to have a word with you."

Except for his sumptuous ecclesiastical robes Pope Vigilius was not an impressive figure. He was short. His features looked squashed together. His nose curved down toward a prim mouth as if it were reaching for the neatly trimmed white beard that thrust straight out from the chin. His narrow forehead slanted back into a vast expanse of shining scalp bordered by a bushy growth of dark hair halfway down the back of the head.

Had he been told John would be there?

John gave him a formal greeting. "How may I be of service?"

"I was hoping you might intercede with the emperor for me, Lord Chamberlain. You are a member of the consistory, are you not?"

John acknowledged it was true.

Vigilius indicated he wished to speak where they would not be easily overheard. He led John to the front of the nave where a row of marble columns twice a man's height and surmounted by an architrave barred the laity from the sanctuary beyond. Waist high slabs of marble between the columns were engraved with crosses and the monograms of the emperor and empress. The architrave bore depictions of the twelve apostles. Stands in front of the columns displayed icons and reliquaries. Vigilius halted in front of an elaborate silver-barred cage in which an eroded, broken stone column was displayed like one of the exotic beasts in Theodora's menagerie.

"It is the column of flagellation to which our Lord was tied when he was scourged," Vigilius said needlessly, seeing where John's gaze had drifted.

John continued his survey of the nave. No one was taking special notice of their conversation. Most of the assembly looked as if they would much rather be in bed. However, for those at court it was important to be seen participating in official mourning.

"What is it that concerns you?" John asked stiffly. He did not like the prospect of becoming involved in church affairs. Religious disputants were less inclined to reason and compromise than statesmen or generals.

"You know I have been imprisoned here in the city for more than a year?"

"Imprisoned is too harsh a word. My understanding is that Justinian has decided that you and Patriarch Menas should come to an agreement before you leave and the chance for agreement is lost."

Vigilius frowned, pulling his nose even further toward his beard. "I was arrested—that is the word—arrested—while celebrating the feast of St. Cecilia. In the middle of the service I was dragged away to a waiting ship!"

"What is it you want? Surely the emperor is willing to speak to the pope?"

"He will speak to me but he will not necessarily listen. His wife poisoned his mind against me. Theodora, with her heretical views is behind the trouble. She was the one who insisted I be held here and broken, forced to accede to her wishes."

"You're talking about the Three Chapters," John said wearily. "You already acceded to her wishes by condemning them, did you not?"

"I said I had come to my own independent conclusion and that being the case I can change my opinion."

"Which you intend to do, particularly now that Theodora is dead."

Vigilius didn't argue the point. "I hope the emperor will soften his views now that Theodora is gone. Her passing may have been the hand of God. A blessing, allowing Justinian to see the error of his ways and return to the orthodox church."

"Justinian considers his own beliefs to be orthodox. He has been trying to convince all the religious factions to admit that their beliefs are not so different as they seem to think."

"Not different? To imagine that Christ had only one nature—"

John raised his hand. He had already heard too much about the nature of a god in whom he did not believe. "I am not a theologian. I would think you and Patriarch Menas should resolve this matter and then approach Justinian together."

A clergyman does not spit on the floor of a church but Vigilius looked very near to doing so. "Menas is Theodora's creature!"

"How can that be? He supplanted her protegé Anthimus in the patriarchate."

"Menas is malleable. He's changed his views."

"Malleability is a virtue Theodora much admired, but I think it was you who changed your views, not Menas," John replied. "That is why Theodora hated you more than Menas. She knew that Menas was orthodox. He was made patriarch against her will. You, on the other hand, were chosen by her to do her bidding. You betrayed her."

"You insult me, Lord Chamberlain."

"I am only telling the truth. I was here when Pope Agapetus died during his visit. I am well aware how Theodora arranged for you to replace him as pope after you promised to support the monophysite cause."

Vigilius reddened. "How can you...do you believe—"

"You were expected to be another Anthimus for her," John went on, paying no attention to the sputtering Vigilius, "but as pope rather than patriarch. Unlike Anthimus you were not going to be deposed and vanish from the face of the earth. At the time of your appointment you were nothing more than a deacon. You owed your elevation entirely to Theodora, but once you were safely back in Rome you reneged on the agreement. I cannot fathom your theology but I am very familiar with political blade in the back."

"But—"

John shook his head and continued in a weary voice. "What did you expect from Theodora after that? You are fortunate to still be alive."

He was almost surprised by the harshness he heard in his own voice. The way Vigilius stood, hunched and tense, a pained expression on his face, he might well have been imagining he was tied to the column behind him, being flagellated. Perhaps that was the way he viewed his sojourn in Constantinople, a long flagellation by the emperor, to be followed by a hideous death on a cross.

John reminded himself Justinian had directed him to talk to Vigilius. The pope might benefit from Theodora's death or so it had been whispered during Theodora's long illness. After all, Justinian had spent years trying to find some doctrine to which the pope in the west and the orthodox patriarch and less than orthodox monophysites in the east could all agree. The empress had been a staunch monophysite. Now that she was gone, Justinian might not care so much about placating the monophysites.

If their concerns were put aside, Vigilius could probably find common ground with Menas and return to Rome. Nevertheless, John had a hard time envisioning the pope as a murder suspect.

"You refuse to intercede?" Vigilius was saying. His voice had risen to a whine.

John released his breath slowly. "I will speak to the emperor. I will see how he feels about the matter at the appropriate time. Theodora's death has made him all the more determined to see her wishes carried out. You might consider that. Clearly Justinian considers his position a compromise. He believes he is being accommodating. If you could see it as a compromise too, rather than a capitulation, you could be on a ship back to Rome tomorrow."

John did not add he found the whole question of how many natures Christ had and how much they were stirred up together of less practical consequence of how many eggs and how much stirring was called for in one of Peter's recipes. He realized, however, that to some, for unfathomable reasons, they were of grave import.

Vigilius looked at the floor, then up at John. He remained silent, as if debating whether to say more. "Very well, Lord Chamberlain. I will be grateful if you have a word with the emperor," he finally replied.

He moved off, not looking grateful in the least, walking carefully, as if his bent back under the heavy robes had been scourged.

Chapter Twenty-eight

It was time for John to leave. He walked toward the aisle, passing the reliquaries housing the skulls of saints Andrew, Luke, and Timothy. The reliquaries resembled miniature churches dipped in gold and encrusted with gems. The flames of their surrounding candles made them flash and glitter and twinkle so the gaze could not fix upon their surfaces but was constantly drawn away by the moving light, as a glowing soul might draw the attention from a physical body.

"Lord Chamberlain, I noticed you speaking with Vigilius."

The long-bearded, narrow face of Patriarch Menas loomed in John's path.

"We exchanged pleasantries."

"The pope did not look very pleased, but then he rarely does. I see you are admiring our relics. Some day you should let me show you everything we have here. Relics of John Chrysostom and countless other saints and martyrs. The bones of the three apostles are buried beneath us. They were discovered in three wooden coffins when excavations for this rebuilt church were under way. It was the Lord's way of blessing Theodora's enterprise."

"I was present at the ceremony when she laid the cornerstone," John replied.

The endless ceremonies he had attended blurred into a soporific cloud of glittering tedium but he could not help recalling the empress in her finery, playing the part of a mason on a brutally cold windy day, managing to splash mud over both herself and the emperor while the assembled officials and courtiers desperately tried to stifle their laughter for the good of their necks.

"She did more than lay the cornerstone," Menas said. "As it happened there hadn't been sufficient money allocated for construction. The three apostles appeared to Theodora in a dream and instructed her to go to the shore by the city gate, where she would find twelves jars filled with gold buried. She did so and in fact there were jars of gold coins bearing the likenesses of the apostles."

The picture of the empress digging in the mud on the beach almost made John smile. "Do you believe that legend, Patriarch Menas?"

"It is a story the common people enjoy, Lord Chamberlain."

"And so perhaps you thought I would enjoy it also?"

Menas reddened. "I meant no insult."

"Indeed. What did you wish to speak about?"

"Pope Vigilius. I hope he has not been slandering me?"

"Why would he do so?"

"It is no secret we are at odds over the Three Chapters." Menas gave John a bleak smile. "I sometimes wish I had remained head of Samsun's Hospice. I felt I was truly serving the Lord there, ministering to the poor. I would be happy to be doing that today. What greater work is there than alleviating the suffering of our fellow men?"

John had no intention of recounting to Menas his conversation with Vigilius. "You are worried what people might think now that Theodora is dead?"

"You mean because I replaced that favorite of hers, Anthimus, as patriarch, people might suppose I was somehow involved with her demise?"

"You are the one who mentioned slander."

"It was more than a decade since I was appointed. And it wasn't as if I sought the position. Pope Agapetus asked me to take it. If Theodora had a grievance with anyone it was with

Agapetus. As for Theodora and I, we reconciled long since, even if her views were less than orthodox."

"That hardly needs to be said. At any rate, Vigilius told me as much."

"So he was being honest for once." Menas shook his head vehemently, causing his long beard to tremble. "A troublesome man. When he first arrived he cut me off from the table of the Lord for four months. I wish Justinian would send him back to Rome."

"You can hardly blame him for being unhappy. He was after all abducted from church forcibly and transported here." John was remembering his own recent abduction.

"Abducted? Rescued, you mean. The populace was so disgusted they threw stones at his ship as it sailed off. He had no business becoming pope in the first place. Theodora sent him to Rome with a fortune in gold and orders to Belisarius to install him on the papal throne."

"Do you think Vigilius would have sought to harm the empress?"

"Physically, you mean? I know what is being said but I would never accuse him of murder."

"Tell me, did you visit Theodora while she was ill? She must have sought spiritual guidance. She wouldn't have allowed Vigilius to offer it, but she might have accepted comfort from you as patriarch."

"She seldom summoned me after she took to her sickbed, Lord Chamberlain. She did not seem interested on receiving clergymen, or at least I was never informed of her asking to see one."

"Odd behavior, I would say," John offered.

"Very unusual. Perhaps she regretted her heretical leanings or maybe she took comfort from Justinian. He is after all God's representative on earth."

They continued to speak for a short time. Menas appeared satisfied Vigilius had said nothing to John which might cause Menas trouble, and John managed to avoid being drawn into further theological discussions.

Both being satisfied, they went their separate ways, John back to the house he had not expected to see again.

Chapter Twenty-nine

Hypatia thanked Anatolius and left his house. She was sure there had been someone observing her from the office. Who could possibly be there on business at this hour?

As she left, she saw the gatekeeper grinning to himself. Anatolius must have been entertaining a woman when Hypatia arrived. That was it. The gatekeeper suspected there had been trouble.

She came out of the passage and started across the small forum from which it led. In the forum's center a statue of an emperor or some lesser forgotten luminary appeared to be wading in a fountain basin.

When she reached the corner of the street leading in the direction of the palace she paused.

A sudden impulse caused her to look back.

It wasn't her business who Anatolius chose to entertain. Peter was more important than Anatolius' love affairs.

But why had Anatolius been anxious for Hypatia to leave? What did he care whether John's servant caught a glimpse of his lady friend?

As she stood in the shadows a figure emerged from the passage.

A woman dressed in a bright blue stola.

Vesta.

Joannina's lady-in-waiting glanced around and then walked toward Hypatia.

Hypatia backed quickly into a doorway.

Vesta appeared to be in a hurry. She went by with her eyes down, so close Hypatia could smell her perfume. If she noticed a form in the shadowy doorway she must have taken it for a drowsing beggar.

Hypatia waited long enough to be certain Vesta was well on her way and then set off at a brisk pace for the palace.

She did not have time to ponder why Anatolius apparently had not wanted her to see Joannina's lady-in-waiting. Having done what she could for John, her thoughts turned to Peter.

If Gaius were fit to treat the empress surely he was qualified to care for an elderly servant? But physicians were not always mindful enough of their patients' comfort. Surely it wouldn't interfere with Peter's treatment if she made a potion to relieve pain. She could collect the necessary ingredients from Gaius' herb garden on the way back.

Once on the palace grounds she took the wide path used by carters and others to ferry supplies to the kitchens. Now the sun had risen further, and shadows cast by lines of trees barred the path. Through the trees could be glimpsed the vegetable beds where Hypatia spent much of her time cultivating those needed for culinary purposes.

At its far end the path forked, one side leading to the kitchen buildings and the other to an open space where carts unloaded boxes of eggs, slabs of fly-encrusted meat, barrels of fish, sacks of flour, crates of fruit, and other supplies. Passing through the vegetable garden beyond would bring her out on a walkway providing a short cut to Gaius' herb garden. It was a familiar route for Hypatia, who often took it when returning from an early morning visit to the market, but wished to pick fresher herbs for sauces or stews than those offered in the city.

She again thought of Peter left alone and quickened her step, ignoring the jests of three burly men carrying amphorae into the back door of the kitchens. She soon reached a large grove of pine trees shading a marble statue of Poseidon guarding a fish pond. Created to resemble an open space in a wood, the shrubby glade featured patches of ferns and wild flowers clustered here and there among moss-covered boulders. Poseidon's fish, ornamental rather than destined to be served at the imperial table, lived in a rocky, shadow-dappled pool fed by a trickling stream.

A flicker of movement caught Hypatia's eye as she passed the entrance to the grove.

Vesta was visible just behind Poseidon, working in a tall patch of foxgloves alive with the humming of bees going to and fro between the flowers' purple fingers. Vesta kept looking around, furtively, as she stooped to collect foxglove leaves she put into a small bag.

When she first arrived at the Great Palace, Hypatia had been surprised the showy flowers were permitted to flourish on the grounds. They were praised by physicians for treating affectations of the heart, but she knew the purple spikes were also the source of a deadly poison and thus perhaps not the wisest choice of plantings in a court whose members would kill to advance a step in the hierarchy or eliminate a rival for an obscure imperial post.

Recollection of poison reminded Hypatia of John's seemingly impossible task of finding Theodora's poisoner, if indeed such a person existed.

Was the poison Justinian believed had been used to murder Theodora been brewed with these or other examples of the beautiful if deadly plant?

And to what purpose would Vesta put the material she was secretly gathering?

Intrigued, Hypatia hid behind a nearby summerhouse until Vesta emerged from the grove, and followed her a second time through the rapidly growing crowds in the city's thoroughfares.

Vesta's destination lay in the shadow of the Hippodrome.

Antonina's house.

Chapter Thirty

John found his house door locked. He knocked, waited, and tried again. There was no response.

He looked up at the second story window of his study. The diamond-shaped panes showed only muddled reflections.

He raised his fist to pound harder, then paused to think. If Hypatia were there she would have answered. She must have gone out, and Peter wouldn't be able to navigate the stairs even if he could hear John's knock up on the third floor.

It would be best if Peter didn't hear because if he did, he might foolishly attempt to get out of bed.

What could have prompted Hypatia to leave Peter alone?

The answer was obvious. She assumed John was in danger, having been abducted in the middle of the night, and had gone to seek help.

Should he look for her at the Urban Prefect's offices?

She would hardly have sought the assistance of the prefect's night watch. They worked in concert with the excubitors and it had been excubitors who carried John off.

He doubted she had seen his captors but if by good fortune she had glimpsed the carriage surely she would have recognized it as an imperial vehicle.

Therefore, he reasoned, she would seek help from someone outside the palace.

Who did Hypatia know in the city who could help?

Anatolius. Who else? John's friend, who had at one time paid her unwanted attention.

John strode back across the square in the direction from which he'd just arrived.

The sun rose higher, measuring its power in shadows fingering rooftops and statues. Already it was warm, heralding another stifling day. Carts carrying crates of produce and squawking chickens rattled through streets coming alive with artisans hurrying to their work and beggars rolling out of sheltered corners to begin scratching out a hopeless existence for another day.

John took a shortcut, little more than a crevice between buildings. He was sorry almost as soon as he emerged from it when he was hailed by a man scrubbing the entrance to a business selling costly linen, wool, and similar cloths.

"You are abroad early, sir. A worker like myself, no doubt? Times are hard for those who labor to earn an honest crust."

The man sat back on his heels. "It's not just outrageous taxes. When do you think Justinian will authorize measures to protect merchants from beggars using our doorsteps as lavatories?"

John was reminded of Artabanes urinating across his hedge frontier. Before he could answer, the shop owner, evidently a man happy to pass the time of day with anyone who would listen, continued.

"Every morning I have to scrub my steps. The ladies don't want to buy in a place smelling of—well—it reminds me of a certain landowner one of my cousins works for. This landowner, you'd know him if I mentioned his name, very well-known he is, he's so rich he has a servant whose only task is to keep his master's collection of statues cleansed of bird droppings. And yet he only collects damaged statues! You know, missing a limb or damaged in the casting. What's the use in buying such statues, I ask you, sir? They're fit only to melt down for the value of the copper."

John agreed that it was quite puzzling and hurried on before the fellow could bring up Theodora's death and point out a rival who sold cloth colored with poisonous dyes.

It occurred to him that the peculiar collector might feel he was sheltering those poor, injured images. At times he found himself reacting to a statue he passed as if it were alive. Feeling sorry, for example, for the long-forgotten dignitary who stood year after year in the forum near Anatolius' house, alone and unrecognized though he had been a great man once. Could a statue retain some part of the living man? If a dessicated piece of bone could harbor the essence of a saint, why not?

His thoughts uncharacteristically wandering, he almost failed to see the figure emerging from the entry of the passage to Anatolius' house.

It was Vesta, walking quickly with her gaze on the ground.

John stepped back and positioned himself behind the unfortunate statue standing forlornly in the fountain's basin. The marble man could have used the assistance of the benefactor of statuary. The less than artful modifications made by the weather and gulls made it hard to tell whether he was a general or a poet.

John waited until Vesta's slim figure vanished down the street before continuing on his way.

When he had seen Vesta at Anatolius' not long before, Anatolius' comment had indicated the fair-haired lady-in-waiting was a client. However, it seemed a strange hour to be conducting business, and with a girl practically young enough to be a daughter.

Anatolius greeted him effusively.

"John! So you are well after all! Hypatia must be relieved."

"She was here?"

"Yes. Didn't you meet her on your way?"

John shook his head. "I took a shortcut."

"She was frantic. Something about you being dragged out into the night. I was just about to rush off to the palace to see what I could find out."

John gave a brief account of the night's events, leaving out the fear he had felt.

"You best be getting home, John. Who knows what Hypatia will do when she gets back and finds you're still absent?"

"Hypatia is a sensible woman. I'm sure she realizes she's done what she could. Although I missed her, I did see Vesta leaving," John added after a short pause.

Anatolius shook his head tiredly. "I'm overwhelmed with work, John. Vesta was here again yesterday. I stressed I couldn't see her today because of a number of important appointments. So what does she do? She turns up on my doorstep before dawn, or as she put it in advance of my first appointment."

"Is she consulting you on behalf of her mistress?"

"What else? The girl is a devoted servant but I wish she wouldn't harass me endlessly. I've told her repeatedly there is nothing I can do to help a couple living together illicitly and without the approval of the girl's parents."

He paused and rubbed his red-rimmed eyes. "Since Anastasius is Theodora's grandson he'll doubtless avoid prosecution. I've stressed that more than once to Vesta, not to mention pointing out the young couple should be grateful for the protection Theodora extends them from the grave."

"A strange notion," John observed.

"Yes. Well, I shouldn't detain you."

John was struck with the unsettling impression that Anatolius was concealing something. Was his friend really so tired or was he trying to mask his nervousness? Did he seem overly anxious for John to return home?

Perhaps Anatolius sensed John's doubts. He smiled ruefully. "I must be getting old, John. The young ladies visit my house only for advice these days."

"You mentioned that the last time I saw Vesta here."

"Did I?"

In the old days a young lady who insisted on visiting Anatolius with regularity would most certainly have found herself subject to his attentions. Not that Vesta was a beauty. She was still just a ungainly girl.

"At least I have saved you going to the palace to try and save me," John said. "I'd best be on my way."

"Wait, my friend. I'm afraid I might have given you the wrong impression. I didn't mean to be rude. Stay a little while. Have a cup of wine. You look as if you need one."

"But Hypatia—"

"As you say, she's sensible. She was much calmer by the time she left. I'll have the wine brought. You don't have to worry about Hypatia."

Chapter Thirty-one

Hypatia peered toward Antonina's house, into which Vesta had just vanished.

Why would Vesta be taking foxglove from the palace garden to Antonina? She would have to tell the Lord Chamberlain, when she saw him.

She tried to assure herself she would see him soon.

There was Peter to think about now, though.

She started back to the palace, hurrying, avoiding knots of idlers lounging against the walls of the Hippodrome and stepping carefully to avoid rotting straw and vegetable matter scattered along the way.

She passed by the Palace of Antiochus with its distinctive domed hexagonal entrance hall and turned onto the Mese. A one-legged beggar seated on a pile of rags near the intersection shook his walking stick at her. "Charity, lady, for the love of heaven," he rasped.

Preoccupied with concern for Peter and having nothing to give anyway Hypatia barely noticed the man. She hurried past with a shake of her head. She hoped Peter would not panic when he realized she was gone. She hoped in particular that he would not try to get out of bed.

A footstep sounded behind her. Before she could swing around or shriek, a hand clamped over her mouth and she was dragged through an open doorway. It happened so quickly it was unlikely any passersby had noticed, even more unlikely that strangers would come to her aid.

"Charity, lady, for the love of heaven," leered the beggar she had ignored. His tone sounded quite different and he was suddenly spry and two-legged.

Hypatia bit his hand. Her attacker yanked it away and as she started to scream smacked her face hard with his other hand. She fell to the ground, stunned. By the time she regained her senses the hand was clamped over her mouth again. The air smelled of ashes. From the little she could see in the dimness they were inside a fire gutted store.

The erstwhile cripple bent over her. "Maybe I should let you shout, lady. There's plenty who would like to share in your charity! After all, what is one more man? Or a couple of men?" He tore a strip of cloth from the hem of her tunic, stuffed it roughly into her mouth, and rolled her onto her back.

Half choking, Hypatia stared up at him. How could she have allowed her attention to wander while out on the streets by herself? A child would have known better. If only she could go back to the point when she had watched Vesta emerge from Anatolius' house. She should never have followed her. She would be home now, tending to Peter. She forced herself not to think of it. Whatever happened, she would not plead with her assailant.

"Not going to struggle?" The beggar sounded disappointed. "Perhaps a little encouragement…?" His hands closed around her neck.

Then, as if mad with rage, he screamed.

◇◇◇

As John started down the Mese on his way home, he told himself he had lingered too long with Anatolius. Talking about current events over a cup of wine, Anatolius had seemed less wary, more himself. Even so, John sensed an unusual undercurrent. Was his old friend trying too hard to appear himself? Did he speak too lightly and at too much length? Did he smile too broadly? Or was it that John was exhausted and overly suspicious?

He would never have registered the familiar sight of a beggar emerging from the side of the Hippodrome and settling down in front of a row of vacant shops if Hypatia had not appeared almost immediately from the same direction.

He increased his pace to catch up with her. He saw the beggar hold out his hand as she passed where he squatted on his rags.

Then John saw the beggar leap to his feet, nimbly, despite the walking stick he'd displayed.

As the assailant dragged Hypatia into a fire-gutted shop, John sprinted toward them.

He heard Hypatia scream.

He increased his pace and dodged around two laborers on their way to work. A ragged woman jumped out of his path and stared incredulously after the tall, lean man racing as if pursued by demons.

Finally he burst into the burnt-out building. It took an instant for his eyes to adjust to the dimness. Then he saw the beggar kneeling over Hypatia, his hands around her neck.

John stepped forward before the beggar realized he was there and reaching around the man's face dug his fingers into the eye sockets.

The attacked man shrieked. Twisted away. Elbowed John in the stomach. Though he must have been half blinded, he stumbled out onto the Mese and ran, weaving back and forth.

John didn't bother to pursue him. He helped Hypatia to her feet instead.

"I'm all right, master," She assured him, brushing ashes off her torn tunic. Her voice quavered.

It was sheer good fortune John had happened to be on hand to save her from assault. He did not like having to rely on fortune.

"I thought I would never see you again, master. I thought they had come to..." Her voice quavered.

"The emperor had a sudden urge to discuss theology," John replied. Already the night had taken on the quality of half recalled nightmare, a confused jumble of horror and incongruity, in which the incongruities were somehow as terrifying as the obvious threats.

They walked slowly down the Mese. When Hypatia regained her composure she recounted her visit to Anatolius.

John listened with increasing concern and bemusement. That Vesta had gone directly from Anatolius' house to the palace gardens and then to Antonina's house suggested the possibility of connections, not only between Vesta and those she had visited, but between Antonina and Anatolius.

In addition, the man who attacked Hypatia had been unusually quick and strong for a beggar.

"Are you certain you weren't observed by anyone at Antonina's house?" John asked Hypatia.

"I didn't see any guards posted outside," she said.

That she hadn't noticed any guards didn't mean no one was watching. Or she could have been followed, even as she was following Vesta. Unaccompanied women were frequently assaulted in the streets. It struck John as strange Hypatia should just happen to be attacked after seeing Vesta visit Antonina. He thought of how Germanus had sent one of his guards to subtly threaten John after being questioned.

Yet he could see no way that Antonina could have ordered such an attack, so quickly, even if someone had spotted Hypatia lingering outside the house.

No, John decided, there had probably been no connection. He was trying so hard to find connections where there were none—to find a link between Theodora's death and someone at court—that he was beginning to see them where nothing existed.

He left Hypatia at his house.

As much as he would have liked to visit Peter, and have a bite to eat and a rest, he had other business to attend to first.

Chapter Thirty-two

Vesta greeted him at Joannina's rooms in the womens' quarters.

She must have left Antonina's house shortly after Hypatia had turned around and headed back home.

"Lord Chamberlain! I shall fetch my mistress at once."

"After I speak with you, Vesta. I am told you picked foxglove leaves from the palace gardens and took them to Antonina."

The attendant looked at him like a frightened child. Again he noted the mousy brown hair, the overly long nose, the protrudent front teeth. John found it hard to imagine Anatolius carrying on an affair with this homely, half-formed adolescent despite the apparent evidence.

"It's true that I delivered them to Lady Antonina. She uses foxglove in her herbal preparations."

"What sort of preparations?"

"All kinds. It's a common ingredient. It's often used for love potions." She blushed.

"Your mistress and her mother are estranged. She doesn't approve of your mistress' liaison with Anastasius."

"Oh, excellency. It's more than an affair. Empress Theodora intended them to marry and they will marry unless—"

"Unless Antonina prevents it. So how is it you are permitted to assist Antonina and go back and forth between the two households?"

"My mistress is trying to mend things between them."

Not to mention using you to spy on Antonia, John thought.

Vesta bit her lip. "It's been tiring. So many extra chores. And sometimes it's been terrifying. I have to be out in the city at night, unattended. Because, you see, the ladies don't want anyone to know they are availing themselves of Lady Antonina's services."

"Services such as love potions?"

"Yes. I suppose that might be it. Lady Antonina never reveals to me what the ladies have ordered."

John, thinking of Hypatia's recent observations, accepted the truth of this part at least of Vesta's statements. "Did Antonina have you take anything to Theodora during her illness?"

Vesta looked distressed. "She gave me packages for the empress. I don't know what was in them."

"Did Theodora instruct you to ask Antonina for potions?"

Vesta shook her head. "No. I have delivered notes back and forth."

"You have been kept busy, Vesta. And in addition to everything else, you continue to seek out legal advice at odd hours?"

Vesta flushed. "Yes."

"Nothing else? You didn't deliver potions or packages to Anatolius? Gray heads sometimes need them, although a girl your age might not realize that."

Vesta's face reddened further.

John looked around as he heard quiet footsteps.

Joannina appeared in the atrium. "You may go now, Vesta," she said and then turning to John went on, "I take it you have established my lady-in-waiting has an acceptable reason to be visiting my mother?"

John smothered his irritation as Vesta hastened away.

"I heard part of your conversation, Lord Chamberlain," Joannina said. "My mother did concoct potions and cosmetics for Theodora at one time or another. After she returned to

Constantinople, I believe she resumed the practice. For a very short time. If mother wanted to poison the empress, she had opportunities. But she and Theodora were very close friends."

Joannina was smiling, but her blue eyes looked as hard as glittering gems. "My mother and I have our differences, but, based on Vesta's reports, my impression is lately mother's main interest was persuading the empress to advise Justinian to send more aid to my father. Not in thwarting Theodora concerning my marriage."

"Indeed," John replied. He noted Joannina did not bother to protest that her mother was incapable of murder.

Joannina's eyes suddenly filled with tears. "Now the empress is no longer able to insist Anastasius marries me, what will happen to us?"

Her air of confidence evaporated. She resembled the young girl she was. A girl who was afraid.

"Is Anastasius here?"

Joannina paused. "No. He's gone out. Why? Why do you ask?"

"I wish to talk to him. He has an interest in the situation."

"Yes, the same interest as mine, Lord Chamberlain. But bear in mind he surely wouldn't have killed his own grandmother, even if she were opposed to us marrying. Her death was a double loss for him. I have no idea where he went and I can't imagine what he could tell you that would be of any assistance."

John took his leave. No one was telling him the entire truth. Of that he was certain. But to what extent they were lying, and about what, or what exactly they might not be telling him, he could not fathom.

He needed to take a different approach.

Chapter Thirty-three

Anastasius left his carriage and guards waiting conspicuously outside Artabane's house and stalked to its door, doing his best to project an air of menace.

A gray-haired servant looked him up and down, projecting an irritating lack of respect, let alone fear. "Your name?"

"Anastasius"

The servant looked unimpressed. "For whom are you calling?"

"Artabanes of course!"

"You are on the wrong side then, sir, please step this way." The servant inexplicably gestured to the left of a line of black marble running down the middle of the atrium. Anastasius stamped through the door, stepping on the black marble.

"Please, sir." The servant inclined his head and nodded at the offending foot. "That is enemy territory."

The old man must be losing his wits, thought Anastasius. He moved his foot and followed the man along the left side of the black strip, into the garden, and down a path beside a knee-high hedge.

Artabanes was sharing a bench with a collection of wine jugs and cups. He pushed himself up from his seat, swaying and blinking.

"Anastasius wishes to speak with you," announced the servant before bowing slightly and departing with a faint sniff of disdain.

During the short ride from the palace Anastasius had been stoking a blaze of anger. He had vowed to Joannina that he would take revenge on the man whose actions had thwarted their marriage, or else see to it that Artabanes atoned for it by aiding the young couple. However, as soon as he was out of sight of Joannina, the idea of confronting a powerful elder terrified him.

Truthfully, he feared confrontations. To face them he had to work himself into a blinding fury, but the sight of this skinny little man, badly shaven and utterly inebriated, quickly quenched the flames. Anastasius had envisioned himself shouting demands and threats. Now he could barely remember what he intended to say.

Artabanes peered foggily at him. "Anastasius? You are Theodora's grandson, aren't you? My commiserations. That is to say, on your grandmother. Your grandmother's...uh...passing..."

"Yes...well...so...so, you deny everything then?" Anastasius recalled part of the speech he had planned, but it didn't make as much sense as it had earlier when his imagined Artabanes played his role better.

Losing the fight to keep his balance, Artabanes took a staggering step backwards. His legs hit the bench and he sat down abruptly, knocking three empty cups into the bushes. "Please have a seat," he said thickly.

Not only was the bench crowded with cups and jugs, but it also looked coated with what, at best, might be half-dried wine. "No, thank you! You deny everything, I take it?"

"Deny? What do I deny?"

Artabanes' refusal to play his role began to get Anastasius angry again. "Murdering my grandmother!"

Artabanes stared at him with bloodshot eyes. He picked up a cup, noticed it was empty, tossed it away, picked up another, and slurped some wine. "What do you mean, I murdered your grandmother? Are you intoxicated, son?"

"You're asking me whether I'm drunk?"

"Are you?"

The general was as mad as his servant, thought Anastasius.

"One as young as yourself should not become involved with Bacchus," Artabanes went on. "However, since you have already been drinking, please have some wine." He gestured toward a large blue glass jug.

"No, thank you."

Artabanes narrowed his eyes. "Perhaps you are too young to—"

Anastasius grabbed the jug and picked up a wine glass that didn't look too soiled. He poured himself a drink and gulped it down. He might as well have swallowed fire. No water had been added. Once he had managed to avoid choking, however, he had a second cup.

"Now," said Artabanes. "What is this about my murdering your grandmother? If I was the sort to resort to murder I would have killed her before she forced me to occupy this wretched house with my so-called wife and married off my beloved to another man. It's a little late now."

"You wanted vengeance. People do want vengeance. As a matter of honor."

"Let me guess, that is why you are here. To avenge your grandmother."

Anastasius, who was finishing another cup of wine, made a conscious effort to stand up straight. "That is correct, sir." The wine was helping him regain his resolve.

"A fine sentiment, son. It's good to see a youngster with some spine. But alas, your anger at me is misplaced."

"I don't understand. Do you mean that after everything my grandmother did to you...well, not that I wished you'd killed her..."

"No, aside from how much I am sure you loved your grandmother, there is that matter of your marriage to...what is her name...Belisarius' girl."

"Joannina."

"Yes. Joannina. That marriage is not likely to occur now, is it? Any more than my marriage to Praejecta did. Your grandmother was forever meddling, one way and another. Assisting you, thwarting me." He paused and his gaunt features tightened as he looked down into his cup. "There is some deep ironic philosophical lesson in our situations, son, though I have no idea what it might be."

Anastasius licked his lips. He felt warm inside from the wine and its fumes seemed to be rising into his head. He didn't care for the way Artabanes kept calling him "son," particularly since it had never been made clear to him by what lineage, exactly, Theodora considered him her grandson.

"Yes," he finally said with some difficulty. "Our situations are exactly the same but just the opposite. But, you see, the irony is if they weren't exactly the same they couldn't be opposite, so they are more the same than they are different. If you see what I mean."

Artabanes nodded gravely. "You are a born philosopher, son."

"But look, sir. I'm glad you didn't harm grandmother, but the emperor could have overruled her, couldn't he?"

"In such an affair? Unlikely."

"Yet he could have. But he is weak. He even allowed grandmother to tell him which general should have command in Italy. She never liked Germanus, the emperor's own cousin, and he listened to her."

"Everyone who has a grievance against the emperor imagines that Germanus would be an improvement."

"Wouldn't he be?"

"Why ask me?"

Anastasius was distracted by women's voices. He looked over the low hedge toward the front of the garden and saw a well-dressed woman in her thirties accompanied by a companion who had the air of being an attendant. The woman had dark hair and tawny skin. Anastasius thought she must have been attractive in her youth. The two women came down the path on the other side of the hedge.

Artabanes went on speaking, giving no sign that he noticed them. "You aren't going to ask me to ally myself with Germanus in a plot against the emperor, are you? Every young, ambitious hothead in the capital is talking like that. It's all it is, talk. Do you hear what I'm saying, son? Don't pay attention to them. That's enemy territory. We take no notice of what goes on over there."

"Your wife?"

Artabanes gave a grunt of disgust. "I have no wife."

The women strolled past, hardly an arm's breadth away, chattering on about certain flowers which were beginning to bloom. Anastasius and Artabanes might as well not have been there.

Anastasius drank more wine. He realized hitherto he had been adding too much water to his wine. It was much tastier undiluted. It wasn't surprising Artabanes would possess a store of very good wine. He was, after all, a general.

"It would suit you if Germanus took over, wouldn't it? He'd banish Belisarius and Antonina. Then you and…uh…whatever her name is…could get married as Theodora planned. Without you having to kill your intended's mother. They don't like their mothers being killed."

Anastasius studied the receding backs of the women over the top of his cup. It was rather humorous. He had to keep blinking or else he saw four women. He wondered how Artabanes had seen his intentions so clearly. He had thought it rather subtle. A way to remove Antonina's influence, but not in a manner that would turn Joannina against him.

Artabanes struggled to his feet and clapped a hand on Anastasius' shoulder, in either a show of companionship or simply to support himself. Before Anastasius knew what was happening Artabanes was refilling his cup from the jug he held.

Anastasius had begun to feel dizzy. Joannina wouldn't want him drinking so much. She'd be angry if he arrived home inebriated. Well, he told himself, how dare she? It wasn't up to her to tell him how much to drink. He was a man, wasn't he? What business was it of hers?

He poured more wine down his throat.

"It's not that I couldn't slay the tyrant," Artabanes was saying. "I've slain tyrants in my time. Gontharis for one. Let me tell you about Gontharis. We were at a banquet. Gontharis was drinking. He was drunk. You, son, pretend you're the tyrant."

◇◇◇

John was on the way to the administrative complex when he heard his name called.

He turned to see a young woman running in his direction. Her robes—much too heavy and lavish for exertion—were disordered and her hair flew in all directions. At first he mistook her for Vesta, then he realized it was the girl's mistress, Joannina.

She stopped beside him, gasping, hand held up to her heaving chest. "Lord Chamberlain! Thank goodness I caught you!"

"Is there some trouble?"

"It's Anastasius. He visited Artabanes and the general tried to poison him."

Having seen the sorry shape Artabanes had been in the previous day John found it difficult to imagine him having the ability, let alone the presence of mind, to attempt poisoning a visitor. "What makes you think Anastasius was poisoned, Joannina?"

"He told me so, after his bodyguards carried him home."

"Carried him home?"

"He couldn't stand up. He was horribly ill."

"Did he by any chance smell of wine?" John asked, recalling that wine was a poison very much present at Artabanes' villa.

"That's what the poison was concealed in, obviously," said Joannina.

"Do you think Anastasius is in danger?"

"No, he's recovering. He told me it was lucky he only had a sip of the poisoned wine. If he'd drunk a whole cup…" Her lips began to tremble and she broke off. "I don't want to think about it. You must have Artabanes arrested immediately!"

"What were Anastasius' bodyguards doing while Artabanes was poisoning his wine?"

"They were waiting outside with the carriage."

"So he was able to walk out to the carriage?"

"No. They told me they heard shouting from inside the house. The sounds of fighting. So they raced in. What about Artabanes? Aren't you going to have him arrested?"

Joannina's voice had risen to a screech and passersby gave the pair curious looks.

"Did the bodyguards say anything more?"

"They told me they ran into the garden and saw Artabanes attacking Anastasius."

"It seems odd. Why would he do that if he had poisoned him?"

"Because the man is demented. He was swinging a stick and shouting 'You're dead, Gontharis I stabbed you in the heart!' Demented, obviously!"

John recalled Artabanes reenactment of his killing the Libyan tyrant Gontharis "I see," he replied. "And Anastasius was unable to fight back?"

"Only because his own stick had broken. And then he fell down and his bodyguards had to carry him home. Artabanes will no doubt claim Anastasius attacked him. People were supposed to think he had killed Anastasius with a stick in self defense, to cover up the fact he'd poisoned him."

John's opinion was that such a plan was beyond Artabanes. He made polite noises about looking into the matter further. Joannina began to calm down. Did she truly believe Anastasius wasn't simply inebriated? "Why did Anastasius go to see Artabanes in the first place?"

"He didn't tell me, Lord Chamberlain. I didn't know he had gone there until the bodyguards carried him in and put him on the couch."

"You shouldn't be away from Anastasius too long. Go home and take care of him. I don't believe Artabanes is dangerous."

He managed to send her away slightly mollified and continued on his way, quickening his pace to make up for lost time.

Chapter Thirty-four

John caught Felix leaving his office in the administrative building. The excubitor captain looked annoyed when John asked that guards be posted secretly to keep a watch on Anatolius' house. "Do you suspect your friends now, John?"

"I'm not interested in Anatolius, but in who might be seeking his legal advice."

"I don't know if I can spare the men, John. Since Theodora died you'd think Justinian was fighting a war in the city, ordering guards here and there, usually for no reason I can see." He ran a big hand through his bushy beard. A patch of white bristles had recently appeared in its center, like the first snow of the year glimpsed at the very peaks of distant mountains.

"I'll find some men somewhere," he went on. "I wish it were a war. With a real enemy we could come to grips with. How are excubitors supposed to defeat phantoms in Justinian's mind? I wish I'd made my career in the army. I'd be a general now, rather than the leader of a bunch of bodyguards."

"The Captain of the Excubitors ranks above most generals," John reminded him. "If you really would prefer a military command, you might yet have the chance. Now that Theodora is gone, Germanus might take over from Belisarius. Justinian has always wanted—"

"And what makes you think Germanus would favor me? I don't know the man. And, now, I need to go. Urgent business. All the emperor's business is urgent these days. I will see that Anatolius' house is kept under watch but I can't believe you would try to catch him at something he shouldn't be doing."

"If he is doing anything he shouldn't, or being tempted to, it would be better if I caught him at it before the emperor does."

Felix grunted. "I suppose so."

Then John was looking at his friend's broad back receding down the corridor.

He seemed as impatient to get away from John as Anatolius had been. John thought of Peter, sick, and Cornelia gone to Zeno's estate and silent. Theodora's death had shaken John's whole world.

Why should he be surprised that the world changed? That people grew older and died? Why did he notice the gray in Anatolius' hair and the white in Felix's beard? What did those details tell him that he didn't already know? How much time did people spend making meaningless observations that only confirmed what they already knew?

They weren't observations but distractions, just as his interviews of the previous day had been. What had he learned except that most of the court had reason to want Theodora dead? If he interviewed everyone who wanted Theodora dead he would need to talk to most of the population of Constantinople just for a start.

What was more important than motive was how Justinian's theoretical murderer had reached the empress. The question was not merely who had access but who had access to those who had access. The lady-in-waiting Vesta, for example, was in contact with Antonina, Joannina, Anastasius, and, unfortunately, Anatolius.

Thinking about Vesta reminded John of the other young woman who had served Theodora, the girl the empress had plucked from Isis' brothel, Kuria.

He thought he should talk to Isis again. The former madam had remembered Kuria as being a favorite of courtiers.

Now that a day had passed—a day that felt more like a week—perhaps Isis would be able to remember more about her former employee.

Chapter Thirty-five

John's route to Isis' house for penitents took him through a nondescript square bounded on one side by a porticoed warehouse. As he approached it, the heap of gaudily hued rags piled in one corner moved. A dainty hand waved a greeting.

"Pulcheria!" John replied.

The beggar turned the good side of her face toward her visitor. It was an attractive face. Middle-aged now. Like everyone else John knew she was showing her age. Or at least one side of her face was attractive. The other side, ruined when a dissatisfied client had thrown a burning lamp at her years before, had not aged at all. It was still a melted mass of flesh, the visage of a demon caught in the act of changing into human form.

"You are enjoying our warm weather, Pulcheria?"

"Oh, yes. Those of us who live outdoors prefer the heat. But it has been so hot lately that people are staying inside, and so I have had fewer coins tossed my way. If you had a job for me, I would be pleased."

Before John could reply there was a loud hiss. A mangy feline resembling a worn-out sack on three twisted sticks wobbled out from the sheltering rags, hissed at John again, and wandered away with all the grace of half a spider.

Pulcheria looked fondly after the cat. "Poor Tripod. He's feeling his age in all three of his legs."

"I am amazed he is still with you."

"Oh, he's tough. Nearly twenty now as near as I can tell. Thank the Lord. I know he can't go on forever, but I try not to think about it. We all need a companion. I can almost feel sorry for the emperor."

"I noticed you in the crowd watching Theodora's funeral procession."

"We must all pay our respects to our rulers whatever our stations in life."

A generous attitude, John thought, for a woman who had been forced to make a living as a prostitute until disfigurement turned her into a street beggar. She showed no signs of bitterness. He saw she still bound her dark hair with countless colored ribbons, matching the wild arrangement of brilliant rags which formed her clothing.

They spoke for a while, then John pressed several coins of a denomination rarely glimpsed by beggars into her hand. He turned as if to leave, paused, exchanged a few more words with her, and added another coin. Finally he continued on his way.

John shouldn't have been startled to see Isis poring over the Christians' holy book at her desk, but he was and admitted as much. "I realize people don't believe I could possibly take religion seriously, but I do," Isis told him. "It is my business to take it seriously. Would you care for one of these honey cakes?"

John shook his head. Although he had hardly eaten all day, his empty stomach rebelled at the idea of the rich, sweet cakes which were normally favorites. He sat on the couch.

Isis wiped a few crumbs from her white linen robe. "Christ was a troublemaker. I never knew that. Patriarch Menas would not have liked him very much."

"You think not?"

"Would the patriarch like me if I walked into the Great Church and started telling him he had got his religion all wrong? It seems to me he was just asking for trouble."

"My understanding is that he was well aware of the danger and knew what was coming."

"Have you made a study of it, John? After all, Justinian is always immersed in church controversies."

"I take an interest in religions. They are too important to the empire to ignore. I'm not a theologian. Justinian looks elsewhere for advice on theology."

Isis licked honey off her fingers. "A haughty sort, this Christ, or so I originally felt. Arrogant. Demanding. But a brave man and at times gentle. Reading the story for myself is giving me quite a different impression of him."

John sighed. "Man? Or God? Or both?"

"What do you mean? Oh, I know. What do they call it, the Three Chapters argument? I haven't got to the part yet where they explain all that." She gave him a playful smile.

She was just bantering as always. He carefully broached the subject of Kuria.

"That wretched girl! Did I look fierce when you reminded me of her yesterday? I must learn forgiveness."

"Do you recall any of those men you said were attracted to her? Officials, patricians?"

"I don't know, John. So many girls and so many men. I tried not to notice the men, or remember them. And the girls...you'd think I would remember. Maybe it's my age. I only recalled Kuria because she wounded one of my girls."

It was understandable, John told himself. Though a visit to the brothel might have been a memorable experience for each individual, for Isis it was simply a business. Would a vendor remember who she'd sold a couple of melons to years earlier? And as for clients from the imperial court...most of the court had probably crept past the gilded Eros that once stood outside Isis' hospitable door, if they hadn't slunk in through the back door instead.

He wanted to believe Isis was not concealing anything from him as everyone else seemed to be doing.

"Why do you suppose you remembered her having aristocratic clients at all, Isis? Did something we talked about bring it to mind? Was it someone you might have associated with Theodora or Justinian? Or with me?"

"With you, John?"

"I deal with many people at court. I thought perhaps there might be a connection to be discovered. Talking to me might set a spark of memory flickering."

Isis pursed her lips. "A friend of yours perhaps? That big bear Felix."

John stiffened. "Felix was visiting Kuria?"

"He wanted to marry her."

John leaned back into the cushions with a sigh of relief. "No, no, Isis. That was poor Berta many years ago. She was the girl who was murdered."

Isis made the Christian sign. "Yes, you're right, John. It must have been Berta I was thinking about. Poor child. It just seemed as if it was more recently your friend was in here doting over her...strange how muddled the past gets."

"The more important events always stay close to us, Isis. The less important recede. Berta was involved with violence as Kuria was, although Berta was the victim. That might be why you mixed up the two."

"Yes, probably." Isis looked alarmed. "I wonder if my mind is going to fade away as I get old? I can't afford that to happen. I've always taken care of myself."

"We all become a little forgetful as we get older, Isis."

Later, on his way home, John remembered his consoling words to Isis.

He had never forgotten anything. And there were so many things he wished he could forget.

Chapter Thirty-six

Hypatia met John as he came up the stairs. Except for bruising on her neck she showed no ill effects from her recent frightening encounter.

He asked if there had been word from Cornelia. "No." She hesitated, then added, "If I may say so, it's barely been three days. Babies don't keep appointments, master. They arrive when they feel like it."

John reflected again on what Isis had said about the past becoming muddled. It seemed to him as if Cornelia had departed a week before Theodora's death, not two days afterwards.

"Hypatia, if you need to take the rest of the day off—"

"Oh, no, master. I'm fine. I have to keep an eye on Peter."

"And how is Peter?" The puffiness around her dark eyes showed she had been crying.

"Worse. I managed to get some of the potion I made down him. It seems to have helped the pain but I think he's drifting away. I've propped him up against a pillow so he could breath more easily. He's been asking for you."

John went up to the servant's room slowly and with trepidation. Peter would never normally ask to see him. He would not consider it his place to make requests of his employer.

Peter was motionless, head slightly elevated, eyes shut. It would have been impossible to tell he was breathing except for the faint erratic, whistling that issued from his dry, slightly parted lips.

"Is that you, master?"

"Yes, Peter. Hypatia said you wished to see me."

The old man's eyes fluttered open. "I am sorry to trouble you, master."

John pulled a stool to the side of the bed and sat down. He saw laid on the bedside table the coin from Derbe which Peter had found in Isauria during his military days, a lucky coin or so he claimed, because it came from a city visited by Saint Paul. Beside it, on a leather thong, lay the Egyptian amulet Hypatia had given him years before when she had worked for John. And then there was the wooden cross above the bed.

All equally ineffective.

"It's no trouble, Peter. How are you feeling? Hypatia tells me she made a potion for you."

"A lovely girl, master, even if hopeless at cooking." Peter lapsed into silence. His creased face was gray, inert and heavy as if eternity had already begun to insinuate itself into his flesh.

From the open window came the clump of boots on cobbles. Excubitors were returning to the barracks. Or leaving. A gull screeched and others returned the shrill call.

John did not have words of comfort for his long-time companion. Christians were quick to assure the sick and bereaved they would pray for them. It came automatically, provided them with comfort. Not that John had ever known such prayers to alter fate. Was that surprising? Even the gods of Olympus had been subject to fate. Why not the Christians' god?

John's own Mithra was not a god who would look kindly on pleas that he alter the natural course of life. It was up to the Mithran to deal with life, whatever that might entail, to survive uncomplainingly, to serve.

Peter spoke at last. "Don't trouble yourself over me, master. If my time has come, I'm ready. Only I'm sorry it has to be now, with your grandchild not yet arrived, and when Hypatia has just returned." He fell silent for a heartbeat, his eyes turned toward the blank plaster of the ceiling. "Do you know," he resumed. "I was dreaming just now of my mother. I was a very small child and she was telling me the story of Tobit. It is my favorite because it was the first story my mother told me. Tobit went to sleep by the side of the house and was blinded by bird droppings. That got my attention."

"Yes, it would."

"Tobit's son—just a boy—goes on a long journey. His dog accompanies him. I liked that. And the angel Raphael is his guide, except he doesn't know his companion is an angel until the end. They battle a giant fish and drive away a demon. My mother didn't tell me it was a demon of lust, though."

"It is the kind of story a boy would like."

"I became a Christian right away. It sounded exciting. I didn't like the story about the crucifixion at all. I couldn't help imagining how it would feel to have nails pounded through my hands. And the idea of a dead body rising and walking out of a cave—that kept me awake."

"Your mother was wise to start with Tobit."

John's own faith—or at least his adherence to the strict, soldierly ethic of Mithraism—had come to him as an adult, following the drowning of his friend Julius, and had strengthened during his enslavement and castration by Persians.

When they had served together as mercenaries, he had resisted Julius' efforts to teach him about Mithra. After John had suffered, the words of his dead companion returned to him, and he realized he had not truly heard them before. Thus had Julius spoken from the dead.

Mithraism was a religion of endurance and acceptance. If John had not run away from his philosophy studies to become a mercenary he might have become a stoic rather than a Mithran.

He studied Peter uneasily. He shared John's stoicism and his tendency to keep his thoughts to himself—particularly his darker thoughts. It was unlike Peter to speak of such personal matters.

"Master, would you…would you open the chest at the foot of my bed? I can't reach it. You'll find a sandalwood box there."

It sat in a corner of the chest, pushed down beside neatly folded garments. The box held a flat, terracotta flask no longer than John's thumb. There were handles on each side of the tiny artifact. Engraved into its oval center was a simple picture of a man, with a camel on each side.

"It is the Saint Menas flask I brought back from Egypt," Peter said. "It contains holy oil from the lamp that burns outside the saint's tomb."

John thought it ironic that the current patriarch, who did not strike him as a saint but rather just another of the powerful men who ruled the empire, should share his name with a holy man. "Do you want me to set it on the table beside your coin and amulet, or do you want to hold it?"

"If you would open it for me, please, master? There's a bit of wax over the neck. If I had enough strength to lift my arms I would do it myself. They say Constantine's daughter was cured by holy waters from beside the saint's tomb. I have saved the flask for years. Now, I feel, it might be time to use it."

John scraped off the wax and held the flask tentatively between thumb and forefinger. What did one do with holy oil?

"Could you place a drop on my forehead, master? I know I should not be asking you, but…"

"It's little enough to ask, Peter."

John turned his hand and a drop of oil ran out onto the tip of his finger. There was nothing mysterious about it. It was simply a drop of lamp oil. He dabbed a bit onto Peter's parchment dry forehead.

"If you could draw another across that one…"

John did so, uncomfortably aware he was mimicking the sign of the Christians.

He put the flask down, propped it upright against the amulet in case oil remained inside.

Peter let his eyes close. His breath whistled in and out, more regularly now.

Had he gone to sleep?

John rose quietly and went out. He didn't care to wait.

He was half afraid Peter would next be asking that he pray for him.

Chapter Thirty-seven

When he reached the bottom of the stairs leading down from the servant's quarters, John paused. He was exhausted. After a day of investigations, followed by a largely sleepless night and then being dragged out to his interview with Justinian, he felt as if he were carrying the dome of the Great Church on his shoulders.

He went into his bedroom and lay down to take a brief rest before deciding what to do next.

He opened his eyes to total darkness.

It took him a little while for his eyes to adjust and grope for the lamp and striker on the bedside table. Hypatia must have closed the shutters to keep out the dust stirred up in the square by the constant comings and goings of the excubitors.

What time was it? He checked the clock in the corner. The water in the basin had sunk to the eighth hour of the night.

Dawn was four hours away, even if they were the shorter hours of summer, but now John was awake he decided to take a walk.

John was familiar enough with the layout of paths and gardens to make his way around the palace grounds by the vast dome of starlight. He usually untangled problems while he walked, but tonight, though he turned his thoughts toward the various matters bedeviling him, his peregrinations did not seem to help.

Perhaps he should seek assistance elsewhere.

He left the path and plunged into a sculpture garden where ghostly white figures depicting mythological figures stood in consecutive circles, as if poised to dance with each other. Pan blew his pipes opposite a stately Minerva, Zeus stared haughtily at that troublemaker Eros, the lame god Vulcan leered at Venus, at whose narrow feet a bold and exceedingly stupid lover had left a bunch of now fading roses.

John walked on, leaving behind ordered flower beds and groves. Passing by a chapel he was misted by wind-blown spray from the fountain set beside its entrance.

As he moved further away from the more cultivated areas he took a nearly invisible track between flowering shrubbery nearly twice his height. Beyond lay an artfully designed wild area planted for the delight of those who enjoyed less formal gardens.

John had long regarded the wild area as a useful place for those inclined to plot ill will, since it boasted numerous hiding spots and was well away from the more traveled parts of the grounds.

His footfalls deadened by moss, he soon approached the low buildings housing the imperial storerooms adjacent to the kitchens.

A guard nodded to him in recognition. Perhaps the man wondered what the Lord Chamberlain was doing prowling around the palace in the middle of the night, but it was not his place to ask.

John passed through a shadowy alcove which seemed to have been constructed of stacked amphorae, went through a side door, and entered the rear portion of the kitchens. Here and there unquenched embers in long braziers sent ghostly, shifting fingers of dim orange light up plaster walls and into the rafters. The light glittered off enormous copper pans hanging from the walls like shields. It sparkled on multi-colored glass bottles crowding shelves and tables, reflected dully from myriads of earthenware jars filled with everything from spices and olives to honey and nuts.

Someone coughed nearby.

John peered through the brick archways opening into the middle portion of the kitchens and saw the vague silhouette of a man moving past tables and braziers and storage shelves.

He had only a brief glimpse of the figure before it passed through a doorway and was gone.

It was enough. He recognized Justinian.

Rumor had it the emperor never slept. That he wandered the buildings and grounds of the palace at night, often without his head.

At least the emperor had not discarded his head this time.

It had been impossible to tell whether his face had relaxed into the demonic aspect certain people swore they had glimpsed as he passed by.

John knew for a fact that the emperor kept strange hours but then, tonight at least, so did John.

At the far end of the room a shadowy figure guarded an obscure door which looked as if it might conceal a cupboard. The man, dressed in laborer's garments, issued a challenge, "How was he born?"

"From a rock," John responded, referring to Mithra.

The man opened the door and stood aside. There was no formal gesture of acknowledgment to one of superior rank, for in Mithra all were equal and this entrance was one of two ways to reach the hidden underground temple dedicated to John's god.

John made his way through a network of subterranean corridors and chambers, his footsteps echoing on stone floors. Some doors stood open to reveal piles of amphorae containing wine, sacks of grain, barrels holding the pungent fish sauce known as garum, and similar comestibles stored against those occasions when one or another was late in arriving from various parts of the empire.

Penetrating to the deeper parts of the labyrinth John finally arrived at a stout wooden door.

Behind lay the mithraeum, the temple to Mithra, a long, narrow, pillared room lit by torches set in brackets on roughly dressed stone walls. Above, a ceiling encrusted with shards of pottery suggested a cave.

John descended a short flight of steps and bowed his head briefly to the altar at the far end of the room.

He held the high rank of Runner of the Sun. The honor of the post he offered to Mithra, being content to remain at that level since he could not devote the amount of time to religious matters that would be required if he rose higher, not least because in an officially Christian court Mithrans were proscribed and subject to harsh penalties if discovered.

That a temple, albeit a secret one, could be built on the very grounds of the palace was a testament to the courage and fellowship of the anonymous men who created it. He had heard its sacred statues and beautifully chiseled marble bas relief had been brought openly to the palace in large crates the cart drivers claimed held special items to decorate Theodora's quarters and therefore had not been opened and inspected.

It was amusing to think Theodora, a supporter of monophysite heretics to the chagrin of the orthodox, had been an unwitting accomplice of pagans whose views even she would have disapproved.

Here, John hoped, he might find some inspiration in solving his task.

His gaze had, as always, been drawn to the sacred scene depicted in the bas relief behind the altar. The shifting shadows thrown by the fire burning on the altar animated its depiction of Mithra slaying the Great Bull.

As Lord of Light, Mithra was honored thrice daily by prayers offered by the Father, the priest in charge of the temple.

On this occasion, however, John had arrived as a brief ceremony was concluding with a final prayer.

"...fallen far away defending the frontier and even now ascending to thy realm of light though buried without the appropriate rites for one who loved and served thee. Grant that he be found worthy of living in thy radiance," the Father intoned.

Three men ranged behind the Father responded as one with John and the Father.

"Lord of Light, we beseech thee!"

The five Mithrans bowed to the altar before the trio of men took their seats on a bench and waited in silence as the Father greeted John.

"As you heard, we have lost another adept, John. A brave man, one advancing rapidly in the ranks." The Father was about John's age, a familiar face at court though considerably outranked by John. "We are losing others too. Lately many are neglecting their religious duties."

"Have you seen Felix recently? Of course, he's been rushed off his feet since Theodora died."

"I'm afraid he's one who has fallen away. I haven't seen him for months. I intended to ask you where he's been."

John exchanged a few more words with the Father and then sat on a bench in the quietness of the sacred place.

He had hoped to compose his mind, to think about the problems he faced. But the absence of Felix from his usual place of worship had given him yet another matter to worry about.

Chapter Thirty-eight

"The captain hasn't been in this morning," a clerk told John. "He may be inspecting the barracks."

"I expected him to have left word for me."

The clerk, a thin, pallid creature and clearly not a military man, pawed through scrolls on Felix's desk. "I'm sorry, Lord Chamberlain. There's nothing but routine paperwork here."

Early morning sun slanted across the paved courtyard visible through the window. The plaster walls were bare except for one of the official crosses installed all over the administrative complex. It was not a salubrious office, but then Felix never spent much time behind a desk.

John went into the corridor. Clerks and minor officials were wandering into their offices, blinking sleepily.

He had spent a long time meditating in the mithraeum and then had come straight here, to see what information had been gleaned during the night by the watch Felix had put on Anatolius' house. The fact that Felix had not been waiting for him, had left no word, seemed to indicate no one of interest had been seen entering or leaving the house, but John would have preferred to have been told that was the case. Apparently Felix had not thought it necessary.

He left the palace and found Pulcheria in her usual spot. She had moved from the shadows to sit in a patch of sunlight and her multicolored rags resembled a wild, formless mosaic, the perfect adornment for a church of some sect whose views would make even the most blasphemous of heretics flush with disapproval. Tripod the three-legged cat peeked from behind her, a lurking demon glaring malevolently at John as he hunkered down to talk to Pulcheria.

"What of the assignments I gave you? Have you learned anything yet?"

"About the one matter, nothing yet," Pulcheria replied. "But as to the more pressing question, concerning your friend—"

"So you were able to observe Anatolius' house last night as I asked? Did you see anything?"

Pulcheria divided the last of the fish on which she was breakfasting, ate one bit, and gave the other to the cat. She looked slyly at John with the good side of her face. "Oh yes, Lord Chamberlain. I followed your instructions. Your largesse will buy me many a fine meal, but I think you will find it was money well spent."

"Did you see that young servant I described to you? Did she arrive early and spend the night as I expected?"

Pulcheria wiped greasy fingers daintily on her colored rags. "No. Your friend was not up to his usual antics, not last night at least. I hired an acquaintance of mine to help me. The poor fellow is lacking a leg but his eyesight is excellent. I set him to watch the front entrance and he says he didn't see anybody unusual going in."

"Is this acquaintance reliable?"

"Certainly, Lord Chamberlain. He is a former military man. Unfortunately, he squanders his pension on wine."

It was not necessarily a description that would have led John to consider a man reliable. However, he made no comment. Pulcheria had always been very reliable. He would trust her judgment.

"I thought if anyone wanted to come to the house unobserved they wouldn't go to the front door," Pulcheria continued. "So I found a cozy space with a clear view of the back of the house."

"Did you notice any excubitors watching?"

"No. They must have concealed themselves well."

"As they should have," John said. It surprised him that excubitors, even without their uniforms, could have hidden themselves from a street beggar. And what could she have noticed that they had not?

"I settled down quite comfortably before sunset," Pulcheria went on. "I'm not particular where I wait when I am keeping watch." The undamaged side of her mouth lifted in a laugh. "A couple of men came and went before dusk. One delivered a crate. Another brought a big sack full of cheese. I could smell it when he walked by. I had to grab Tripod by the scruff of his neck to keep him from leaping out. He is very fond of cheese."

"But eventually you saw a suspicious visitor?" John prompted, aware Pulcheria was enjoying drawing her story out.

"Oh, very suspicious, Lord Chamberlain! But many hours passed first. Several drunken faction members wandered by quarreling about their racing teams, pushing and shoving one another. After they'd gone I found a nummus one had dropped. Well, then, it was nearer to dawn than sunset when a visitor arrived. The house guards looked practically asleep at the back gate, but they raised their lances until they saw who he was, then they ushered him in, most obsequiously."

"A man," John said, trying to hurry her along.

"A big man, yes. Powerful once, but gone to fat. Looked middle aged. His head was tonsured and he wore a burlap garment. Surely he was a monk or cleric to judge by his looks most would say? But I knew better, Lord Chamberlain. I recognized the scoundrel. It was that vile tax collector, John the Cappadocian."

For an instant John looked at Pulcheria without speaking. "Are you certain?"

"The gate is well lit by wall torches. They revealed his obscene face clearly. He is more bloated than he was before being exiled. He is quite deserving now of the nickname given that rapacious protegé he appointed to rob the provinces—Flabby-jaw. Yes, the visitor was definitely the Cappadocian."

John was silent, absorbing the information.

"You are perhaps doubtful I would recognize him?" Pulcheria asked. "But don't forget, in the profession I practiced before my accident forced me to beg on the streets, I knew many high officials very well, and knew other girls who knew other high officials. Girls who had loose tongues. What I could have discovered for you in those days would have much more valuable than what I can observe now!"

She sighed. "I made a better living then. But the Cappadocian…to think of him revolts me even now. He would hire a dozen girls at once and have them lie down naked in his private room. Then he would eat delicacies off their bodies, gorging himself until he vomited into a golden basin. He wasn't satisfied until he sated every one of his horrid appetites, preferably all at the same time. He would watch an enemy being tortured while the poor girls performed certain services for him as best they could manage while trying to ignore the victim's pitiful screams. Why, I heard he had girls come to his bed clothed only in golden jewelry and a thick coating of fish sauce!"

"Very little surprises me after years of hearing court gossip."

Pulcheria cackled and glanced at her cat. "You'd like fish sauce, wouldn't you, Tripod?"

John pushed himself to his feet.

"It seems to me some people aren't human, Lord Chamberlain."

John gave Pulcheria quizzical look.

"Seeing that evil creature gave me a fright. It made me think. People all appear to be the same flesh and blood, and maybe they are. But the same jar can contain wine or poison. Do you think there's something different inside a creature like the Cappadocian than in you or I? Perhaps such things should not be called people just because they look like people on the outside?"

"Some call such people demons," John said. "Or monsters, like the person who harmed you."

Pulcheria ran a delicate white hand down the scarred ruin that made up one side of her face. "The man who threw the burning lamp at me wasn't a monster, Lord Chamberlain, just a drunken fool."

John pressed another coin on her and she did not protest.

He left the square, walking slowly.

He was almost sorry he had hired Pulcheria. It wasn't right to spy on a friend, was it?

But John had merely wanted to explain Anatolius' odd behavior. He had expected to learn Anatolius had resumed his old ways with women, that he had taken the young lady-in-waiting for a mistress, the sort of backsliding not uncommon with middle-aged men who were noticing the gray in their hair. He had never expected to implicate him in...in what?

There could not be any innocent explanation for the appadocian's secret presence in Constantinople when he was supposed to be in exile in Egypt.

Reluctantly, he turned in the direction of Anatolius' house.

Chapter Thirty-nine

That's done, Kuria thought, and so now for the next step. She set off down the Mese, having left the palace for the last time. She felt more confident than she had in days.

When she had returned to her room earlier after a stroll in the gardens, she found it sealed up, the door boarded shut.

There was irony in her being barred from her own room. Like most of the attendants, she rarely closed her door, let alone locked it. In this part of the palace there was no need. When they were not on call the young women spent as much time in each other's rooms as their own.

The eunuch who oversaw the quarters for the ladies-in-waiting would not arrange for Kuria to be let back in, even to collect a few precious belongings. He claimed to have had the orders from the Master of Offices.

She asked if she might return for some things later when the room was cleared out.

The eunuch laughed. Everything inside was to be burnt.

Kuria felt a momentary pang of regret she had not chosen to go to the gardens later. If she had been present when the Master of Offices' men arrived, she might at least have salvaged one particular item.

Perhaps it had been wise to go to the gardens early. For all she knew, they might have thrown her out of the palace bodily. She supposed, eventually, someone would do so. A bureaucrat in a warren in the administration building had probably forgotten to sign all the required documents.

So she had been deprived of a place to stay before being officially evicted.

There was no point in waiting.

After the shock of Theodora's death had worn off, she had made plans. She had done what needed to be done in the palace, and now she had taken the first step on the way to her new life outside the palace.

Although she had lost almost everything, it was some consolation that she happened to be wearing her favorite dark green stola. It was no coincidence she practically coruscated in the morning sun, thanks to her jewelry. She'd prudently worn every piece she owned every day since the empress died.

Besides, she needed to look attractive for what she had to do.

She needed to make it plain that she was a lady now.

Kuria was not a beauty, but when she put her mind to it she was able to project an air of assurance that indicated a much higher station than she held.

A pair of laborers, judging by their dusty breeches and stained tunics, moved aside deferentially as she strode along.

Good, Kuria thought.

She was almost there.

She was prepared.

But it was also necessary for her to find a little of the young whore she'd been, to apply a dab of that garish makeup. Enough to say that she was a lady, but willing to be a bit more exciting than most ladies.

She passed the Hippodrome and crossed the street that ran along the side of the racecourse. She didn't glance at the one-legged beggar sitting on a pile of rags near the intersection.

She never knew he was there until he was dragging her through the doorway of a vacant shop.

Chapter Forty

Instead of looking John in the eye, Anatolius stared down at the skull depicted on his desk top. "How could I turn him away, John? My father knew the Cappadocian well. You remember how much father wanted me to take up the legal profession. How could I refuse legal aid to one of his closest associates?"

John had broached the subject as soon as he set foot in the study.

"I am amazed Senator Aurelius would have allied himself with a man like John the Cappadocian," John replied, keeping his voice level. He couldn't help thinking of the Cappadocian's escapades as described by Pulcheria. Nor could he see Anatolius' staid, respectable, and happily married father engaging in such behavior or even wanting to be associated with a man suspected of such outrages.

Anatolius finally looked up. "That's unfair, John. I know what people say about the Cappadocian. My father had a different view. He used to tell me people hated the man because of his reforms, because they didn't like change."

John wondered if he were, in fact, being unfair. He was angry that his friend had concealed the presence of the Cappadocian in the capital from him. "I admit I never dealt with the man. His reputation is unsavory."

"I have no opinion on his reputation for licentiousness, if that's what you mean. Mostly rumors, no doubt. My father worked with him in a purely official capacity. He respected what he did as Praetorian Prefect. Before he took over, the prefecture had become an empire unto itself, paralyzed in tradition like so many bureaucracies," Anatolius replied. "There are those who devote themselves to writing histories of bureaucracies—the prefecture, the Master of Offices. They have a ready audience in their fellow civil servants. A clerk might spend his time poring over the the accounts of estates, adding up taxable goats and sheep, but at the end of the day he wants to read he is a valiant soldier, battling for the empire in an institution stretching back to the age of Augustus."

He paused. "The Cappadocian had the temerity to imagine that the prefecture was supposed to function for the benefit of the emperor rather than for the benefit of its bureaucrats. Naturally, he was resented and hated. The civil servants didn't care about doing things more efficiently. They loathed having to use Greek rather than Latin, for example."

"You sound as if you are preparing to be a Cicero for your client, Anatolius. It is commonly said the Cappadocian was guilty of endless financial depredations. How do you defend him against that charge?"

"He merely enforced the tax laws others refused to enforce. If the rates are onerous, well, it is the doing of the emperor."

"You should have told me he was in the city."

"Why? It is my job to represent clients who come to me for legal advice. Do you tell me about every private discussion you have with the emperor?"

"His being in the city might well have a bearing on my investigations. He was one of Theodora's bitterest enemies. Everyone knows that. He's an obvious suspect in her murder."

"But you said you do not believe the empress was murdered."

"At the time I thought the Cappadocian was safely confined in Egypt."

Anatolius' expression was unreadable. Apparently the flighty and emotional young poet of the past had learned some lawyerly skills.

John asked bluntly what, exactly, Anatolius was doing on behalf of the Cappadocian.

"In general, he wants me to investigate whether he can reclaim certain properties confiscated when he was exiled. He thinks it might be possible because Justinian did allow him to maintain considerable wealth in Egypt despite being disgraced. It is his opinion it was only on account of Theodora's animosity that he was deprived of office. I can't go into specifics."

"In other words, he heard of Theodora's illness, decided she would soon leave the world, and decided he should get a head start on returning to his former prominence?"

"He hasn't said as much, but I gather that's correct. You know what a favorite he is with Justinian. As soon as the emperor conquers his grief he'll be issuing orders for the Cappadocian's return."

"How long has he been back in the capital?"

"He didn't tell me."

"When did you first see him?"

Anatolius met John's gaze. "You know I should not discuss a client."

"He was here before Theodora's death? That would make him an obvious suspect, as I have already pointed out."

"I am representing him in land dealings, straining my eyes over dusty documents. I have had no reason to question him about other matters."

"Both he and you are aware there are other matters involved, not least the fact he is in the city illegally, otherwise he wouldn't be creeping in your back gate in the middle of the night. Whatever the Cappadocian might be up to, you will naturally be implicated. Justinian won't care whether you were serving as the man's lawyer or not."

"You can't think I am working against the emperor?"

"I would prefer not to think so, Anatolius. Where is the Cappadocian staying when he is not here seeking your aid?"

"I cannot say."

"Does that mean you won't say, or that he hasn't told you?"

"It isn't my business to know where he's living."

"Spoken like a true lawyer."

"I'm surprised, John. You're a man of principle. I thought you would understand I have my own duties as a lawyer."

"We also have duties as friends, Anatolius. Your association with the Cappadocian puts you in grave danger. And yes, before you say it, if I fail to find a murderer for Justinian, I am in danger too."

Anatolius started to reply, stopped. His gaze wandered from John's face, fell to the skull in the desk top. He pushed an opened codex over the leering face. "So you intend to offer up the hated Cappadocian as a sacrificial lamb?"

"That's not what I meant," John snapped with evident anger.

"I apologize, John." Anatolius paused. "We shouldn't argue over this matter. We both have our duties. I will arrange for you to speak with the Cappadocian. Will that suffice? Perhaps he will see fit to tell you things he has not told me or that I am not at liberty to reveal. But not here. Not at my house. I will make arrangements. Come back tomorrow and—"

"No. Today, Anatolius. I will speak with the Cappadocian today."

"I can't guarantee that my client…" Anatolius stopped and shook his head wearily. "All right, John. I will see what I can do. Come back after midday."

◇◇◇

The sun was a blinding orb of molten glass as John walked slowly and pensively back home. The streets throbbed with heat, all surfaces—the pavements, columns, bronze statues, brick edifices, and John's skin—blazed with it.

Felix and Anatolius had both lied to him.

His two oldest friends.

Felix had either concealed the fact one of his watchmen had spotted the Cappadocian, or he had lied about sending watchmen. Did Felix know Anatolius had been meeting the Cappadocian and yet had not told John?

And what was the real reason Felix had not been seen at the mithraeum for so long? Were Vesta's visits to Anatolius truly about legal matters? If the men had lied to John about the Cappadocian how could he expect them to be telling the truth about anything else?

Had he got anywhere at all with his investigation? Had he learned anything beyond the obvious fact that numerous powerful people might have wanted the empress dead?

Artabanes would have seen it as revenge for Theodora foiling the marriage he desired. Antonina, on the other hand, could save her daughter Joannina from the marriage Theodora had been forcing upon her. With Theodora's interference gone, Germanus might finally be elevated to the level of power he was arguably entitled to as Justinian's cousin. And now there was the Cappadocian, who would not only revel in the death of his imperial persecutor but also, perhaps, be allowed to return to power.

He had at least confirmed that very few had had access to the empress—ladies-in-waiting, clergymen, a physician—none of whom appeared to have any reason to wish her dead. In fact, all had every reason to want her to continue to live, if only to keep their employment and remain free from possible accusations.

As he crossed the square to his house John found his thoughts instantly drawn away from these puzzles by concern for his daughter Europa and for Peter.

"Mithra," he muttered. Was he getting old to be unable to concentrate on his work, distracted by family matters?

Hypatia answered his knock, tears in her reddened eyes.

"What is it, Hypatia? Peter?"

She wiped her eyes, nodded, and showed him a trembling smile.

"He's cured, Lord Chamberlain! Completely himself again and furious his broken leg won't let him jump out of bed. It's as if one of his angels visited during the night."

Chapter Forty-one

John didn't believe in miracles. How could a smear of lamp oil on a forehead heal? Why would an elderly man who had journeyed to Egypt and obtained a flask of oil be cured while elsewhere in Constantinople other old men, who had never set foot far beyond the city gates, were dying?

He did not believe in omens either. Lightning had struck the column of Arkadios because it towered above anything else in that part of the city. The strike had not presaged the death of Theodora or calamity for the empire.

However, John the Cappadocian did believe in omens. It was said he consulted oracles and sorcerers. Was that why he had arranged to meet with the Lord Chamberlain at the column of Arkadios?

The Forum of Arkadios was comparatively small, populated with ancient statuary, a peculiar gathering of all but forgotten pagan gods and unfamiliar emperors.

John entered the forum warily. There were only a few passersby. The sun was still high enough to press the full weight of its heat down onto the open space.

John was not certain he could trust Anatolius' word that he was not being sent into an ambush, and his lack of trust distressed him.

There was no sign of the Cappadocian.

Had John been tricked?

He walked toward the column. Constructed of dark green serpentine, it rose from a massive base of red granite. A continuous frieze winding around the column depicted the military triumphs of an emperor who, like Justinian, had never ventured onto the battlefield. A sculptor's chisel could make a man a hero as readily as his own sword, and with considerably less risk.

A charred line ran down the side of the column. Where the charring ended, the pavement had cracked and exploded upward. Jagged pieces of masonry lay about, some at the forum's far edge, the result of the lightning strike. Apparently city workers had been too busy with the imperial funeral to begin their cleanup. Those who claimed the top of the column had been sheared off or that Arkadios' image had been reduced to a molten mass had exaggerated.

"Lord Chamberlain."

The voice came to John clearly, yet there was no one nearby.

He looked up and made out a figure standing on the railed platform upon which sat the silver statue of Arkadios.

John went through the door in the base of the column and started up the spiral stairway inside. Shafts of light fell through narrow, scattered openings. The bright, intersecting lances created a confusion of brilliance and shadow on the steep, open stairs. John kept close to the wall, aware of his vulnerability.

No one lay in wait and at the end of his climb he was greeted by the corpulent figure of the Cappadocian. According to rumor, the Cappadocian's oracular advisors had convinced him he would one day wear the robes of Augustus, but this afternoon he wore what might have been the clothing of a beggar, a shapeless brown garment. His broad-featured face was ruddy. He was tonsured, just as described by Pulcheria.

Looking past the Cappadocian John noticed something he had not seen from the ground. The lightning bolt had blasted away half of the platform. A length of railing dangled out into space, resembling the twisted metallic limb of a dead tree. The

Cappadocian stood near the platform's edge, seemingly unconcerned by the steep drop below.

"We won't be overheard here," John observed.

"If Theodora were still alive I would not be so sure of that," the Cappadocian replied.

He might have been tonsured and humbly dressed but John saw the thick, loose lips of a debauchee and the small, glinting eyes of a rodent, a perfect image of the dissolute which monk ascetics inveighed against. Then again, John told himself, that was probably just a result of the man's vile reputation coloring his features.

"You may have more to gain by Theodora's death than anyone in the empire," John said. "Justinian is convinced she was murdered. How long have you been in the city illegally?"

"Not long. Weeks." The Cappadocian surveyed the forum below. "No armed men that I can see. You could have had me arrested, Lord Chamberlain."

"I promised Anatolius I would not."

The Cappadocian's heavy lips curved into an expression between a smile and a sneer. "And you always keep your word, as everyone knows. But naturally I must be suspected of violence against the empress."

"You were not until your presence in Constantinople came to my attention."

"The fact I've been working in the palace kitchens will make me appear even more culpable. There's no reason not to admit what I've been doing. You'd surely find out soon enough. I respect your competence."

"I am surprised no one recognized you."

"No one expects a humble, junior cook to be the monstrous tax collector."

"Where have you been staying?"

"Oh, here and there. I've moved around."

John felt a trickle of sweat snake down his neck. Exposed to the harsh sun, the platform might as well have been on fire. He placed a hand on the remnant of the metal railing. It was hot to the touch and wobbled alarmingly.

"Anatolius believes you decided to return here in the expectation Justinian would soon invite you back anyway, and you wanted to begin regaining properties you had lost."

"That's correct. Your friend is a very capable man. I knew his father well, and so I felt confident I could trust his son. I wished to have some legal matters dealt with before I resumed my duties."

"You expect to resume your duties?"

"Why not? Justinian satisfied the mobs by removing me from the prefecture during the Nika riots, but a year later I was back in charge."

"You've been absent for seven years this time."

"Only because Theodora was involved. Yes, Lord Chamberlain, I had every reason to kill her, and opportunity too, considering how I was employed."

"Why tell me that?"

"Because I didn't kill her. You're a man of principle. When you discover I didn't kill her you will be honest about it. You will do everything in your power to ensure I'm not executed for a crime I didn't commit. If not for your efforts I'd be offered up as a scapegoat. There are plenty of people at court who hate me. I'm counting on you, Lord Chamberlain, to save my life."

"You may be overestimating my influence with the emperor."

"I hope not."

The Cappadocian looked east. From this height Constantinople formed a panoramic complex beyond comprehension. Wherever the gaze fell were colonnaded streets, churches, tenements, squares, monuments, warehouses, mansions. Smoke rose from manufacturies in the Copper Quarter. To the north could be seen the long, narrow bay of the Golden Horn, to the east and south the Sea of Marmara. Above ground cisterns reflected a glare of sunlight. The Aqueduct of Valens cut across the hilly peninsula. At the tip of the city the Great Palace and its gardens could be made out, falling in terraces to the sea shore. Somewhere in the welter John's own home could no doubt be seen if one were to search long enough.

"Magnificent, isn't it?" the Cappadocian said. "Imagine ruling it all."

"Those of us who are not Justinian can only imagine."

"But like his empress, he will not live forever. And who can tell, he may pine away prematurely now his beloved consort is gone. Not that any decent person would wish such a thing, you understand."

John looked away from the scene and back at the Cappadocian, who was smiling to himself. "You can't still harbor ambitions to the throne?"

"Why not?"

"You are one of the most hated men in the empire. The powerful hate the tax collector as much as the poor do."

"And what does it mean that people hate you? It is a sign they envy you, fear you, admire you. Men always hate their betters, but in the end they follow them. I'm no different than you, Lord Chamberlain. I served Justinian. The prefecture was in disarray, ineffective, tied up in tradition. I changed that. I collected taxes that were due, secured the revenues Justinian needed to rebuild this city and recapture Italy. Those who were used to evading their taxes hated me, but who was at fault? Those who flaunted the law or the man who insisted they obey it? Who better served the emperor, the wealthy who balked at paying to restore the empire's glory or the man who forced them to share in the enterprise that benefits us all? They said I was a thief. Naturally. Not to mention a glutton, a pervert, a libertine. Their enemies are always thieves, gluttons, perverts, and libertines."

"Whatever truth there might be in what you say, you would be well advised to return to Egypt before anyone else knows you left. You won't be safe here."

"You are offering to allow me to leave unmolested. Is that what you're saying?"

"I am giving advice."

"We have much in common, Lord Chamberlain. We both know what it is to be hated by Theodora, to be persecuted and plotted against, for no reason beyond her envy, her dread that anyone except her might have Justinian's ear."

John observed the same applied to many people.

"But the two of us, she hated us specially, hated us for years. You know how she had me exiled to Cyzicus and ordained a deacon against my will, how she forced Justinian to confiscate my estates."

"He allowed you to retain enough to live comfortably," John pointed out.

The Cappadocian's dark eyes narrowed and he drew his lips into a tight, plump line, the first signs of anger he had shown. "Live comfortably in the middle of nowhere as a deacon? Even that was not enough for Theodora. When the bishop of Cyzicus was murdered she contrived to have me accused. I was not convicted, because I did not kill the bishop any more than I killed the empress. Yet I was stripped, scourged, and put on board a ship bound for Egypt. In order to survive I had to beg at every port. Think of it. I was reduced to begging."

"Count yourself fortunate. I was once reduced to slavery, although not by Theodora," John replied. "She treated countless people unjustly. I have been thrown into the dungeons. But, like you, I survived. That is all past. Theodora is gone."

John saw the Cappadocian's florid face ran with rivulets of sweat. "You think the past vanishes? Has your long ago encounter with the Persians vanished? Do you think I can forget being thrown into an Egyptian prison? And how, a few years later, she tried to convince two young members of Cyzica's Green faction to testify I had indeed been involved in the bishop's murder? Only one refused even under torture, so she had the hands of both cut off."

John was well aware of the story and did not doubt its veracity. He said nothing.

The Cappadocian ran a hand over his shaved head. The hot sunlight had turned his scalp a fiery scarlet. "You know what is the worst of it, Lord Chamberlain? She used my only child, my innocent young daughter, to lead me into a trap. Think about that. You have a daughter yourself. What if Theodora and Antonina deceived her in order to destroy you?"

He scowled and continued. "Yes, it was Antonina who assisted her. She convinced my daughter Belisarius desired to overthrow Justinian and needed my support. But when I went to the appointed place and spoke to Antonina about the matter, I discovered Narses had been listening with an armed guard. I was seized and sent into exile. Now my poor daughter will carry until the end of her life the burden of what she inadvertently did to her father, simply because she was an unsophisticated young girl."

"Those who hold positions of power can't help but subject their families to the dangers of court intrigue."

"You know that yourself, Lord Chamberlain. I know you suspect me. But when you discover that I am innocent, you will realize we are natural allies, having suffered the same injustices. I remind you that I only know how to cook the sort of nourishment those in holy orders consume. I learned that skill after I entered on my religious career." He smiled and spread his arms, calling attention to his monkish garb. "Antonina, on the other hand, knows how to cook potions and poisons."

"You hid in the kitchens because you could pass for a cook?"

"And also because it is a good place to hear what's going on in the palace. When meals are delivered people are often in the middle of conversations, and servants are regarded as furniture, totally deaf. An hour after the venison in honeyed sauce is placed on the banquet table everyone in the kitchen knows that a certain senator is having an affair with the wife of a prominent official in the prefecture. I had good reason to be in the kitchens, but poisoning Theodora wasn't one of them. Antonina, on the other hand—"

"You aren't the first to point out Antonina dabbles in potions. But then you have as much a grievance against her as you do against Theodora. It would doubtless please you if she were executed or hauled off to the dungeons."

"Certainly. You see, I am frank. Not that Antonina will wield any influence a month from now. How long do you think Belisarius will keep his position without Theodora blocking the ascent of Germanus? A changing of the guard is coming, Lord Chamberlain. I have no grievance against Germanus, nor he against me. The two of us have never opposed one another. In fact, we have much in common."

John directed a thin smile at the fat man. "So you agreed to meet me here to make an offer?"

"No. Not yet. I am merely indicating that I will be willing to make you an offer when I am in a position to do so. But first, you will clear me of wrongdoing, Lord Chamberlain. I have every confidence in you."

Chapter Forty-two

John returned home to find Gaius in possession of both his study and a wine jug. The physician's slurred speech made it plain he had stormed the territory and commandeered the wine some time before and was ready to continue campaigning, given the opportunity.

Already chagrined over the Cappadocian's brazen claim on his services, John was not pleased to find his hospitality had been seized as well.

"What do you think you're doing, Gaius? Did you come here to treat Peter or treat yourself to my wine?"

"John," Gaius said with a hiccup, "I was hoping to find you in residence. Been waiting a while." He laid a finger alongside his red nose and winked. "As you have no doubt deducted. Good at that, John, always have been. But you'll need Mithra's help this time."

"So do you, my friend."

Gaius ignored the remark. He peered around the room as if eavesdroppers were concealed behind its sparse furnishings, "At least I have good news about Peter. He's out of danger. I wish I could say the same thing about myself."

John sat down at his desk and raised interrogative eyebrows at the physician.

Gaius leaned forward and continued in a whisper. "I am not so intoxicated as I appear, John. I can see clearly how Justinian's madness is growing. I hear the head gardener was arrested this morning. A man who has done nothing but served the empire all his life! The talk is he was heard railing about the empress in a fashion he should not have done, but if people will raise their voices in inns, what can they expect? And he knows his plants. Knows which are poisonous, you see?"

"If railing about Theodora were the real reason for his arrest half the city would have been arrested by now. Besides, how could he introduce poison into Theodora's food? He never sets foot in the kitchen."

"Could have had an accomplice," Gaius pointed out.

"And paid him with what to risk his skin? A lifetime of free cabbages, all the roses he likes? However, I can put your mind at rest. I saw him not an hour ago on the palace grounds hoeing the vegetables and looking the same as ever."

Gaius gave a grimace rather than a smile. "Rumor has many heads, cut one off, two grow in its place. You never know when the excubitors will knock at your door, or kick it down, more likely, and you'll be dragged away. It isn't so much death I fear…I've seen enough of death…but the dungeons. As a physician I am too aware of the body's capacity to suffer. I have been summoned to keep alive the poor wretches the torturers weren't yet done with."

He gulped down more wine and burst into tears.

John cast about for a way to divert his friend's attention from the imagined imminence of death. "It's always been that way at the palace. This is nothing new. It doesn't—"

"No, nothing new, nothing new," blubbered Gaius. "How many great men have we seen paraded off to be executed? Senators, generals…"

"Who are you speaking about, Gaius? Exile is much more—"

"Not even religious vestments can save you from the emperor's wrath. Remember the heretic Anthimus? I treated him for an abscess. He was patriarch, then suddenly he was gone. Like magic. Vanished, never to be heard of again."

"None of us are ever entirely safe, Gaius. But consider. How long have you served the emperor? Why would he turn on you now?"

Gaius gave no indication of hearing. "You know Menas replaced Anthimus, so naturally Theodora hated Menas even if she never said so. And with this business of the Three Chapters, Menas had reasons to want Theodora out of the way, before she—"

"You're not making sense," John interrupted.

"You don't think so? I worked at Samsun's Hospice when it was headed by Menas. You don't think they'll be whispering he employed me to do away with Theodora?"

"They?"

"Yes, they. Who is more dangerous at court than they, John? The unidentifiable purveyors of gossip, those who put the wrong words in the wrong ears? They are the scourge of the empire."

John decided his friend was intoxicated beyond reason. He changed the subject. "Tell me about Peter. He is over the worst, you say?"

Gaius wiped his nose with the heel of his hand. "Yes. That is to say barring a relapse. See," he burst into shrill laughter, "I am covering all eventualities. But I think he will mend. Possibly with a more pronounced limp than before, but he'll be able to race up and down stairs again soon enough. He attributes his recovery to holy oil. I suppose it was unbelievable to him my own ministrations might have had some benefit."

"Peter is a Christian," John reminded him.

Gaius snuffled. "If healing were that simple all I'd need to do would be to travel from shrine to shrine collecting souvenirs. Holy water and oil and those blessed coins made from the mud at the bottom of stylites' columns. Just give those to my patients. The Christian ones, at least."

"I am sure Peter appreciates your efforts."

"Perhaps. Well, it might be that the oil had an effect, if he believed it did. What if our thoughts affected our humors?"

John had no opportunity to answer. The conversation was interrupted by rapping at the front door. The sound was not loud, but under the circumstances it might have been a peal of thunder.

"It's them!" Gaius cried, his face, aside from the reddened nose, paler than John had ever seen it.

"I don't think they would bother to knock so politely." John went downstairs, not at all confident it wasn't more trouble for him.

He hoped it would be news from Cornelia, but the heavy door swung open to reveal Joannina, panting and disheveled.

"Lord Chamberlain," she cried, gulping back tears. "Vesta's been taken away! Please help her!"

John drew her in and closed the door.

Gaius had staggered to the top of the stairs. "Don't worry," he called up to the physician. "It's only Joannina."

He lead the sobbing girl into the garden, trying to calm her by assuring her he would do what he could once he knew what her visit was about.

"Vesta, my lady-in-waiting, was just arrested by the excubitors!" Joannina managed to blurt out.

It was fortunate Gaius was safely upstairs, no doubt with his nose buried in a wine cup again, so he did not hear the statement. John encouraged the girl to continue.

"We had been out together looking at jewelry and when we returned, there were excubitors waiting for her. They said incriminating herbs had been found in her room, ingredients for poison."

Though unable to speak, rooms were more forthcoming than many people, John thought. "How did they know they were poisonous rather than cosmetic?"

"I don't know but that's what they said. And they said Vesta had murdered Theodora."

John wondered who had told the excubitors about the herbs.

"Why would Vesta want to murder the empress?" Joannina was saying. "Anastasius and I, our marriage, the empress wished it. Now she's gone and my parents can interfere...it may never happen...my lady-in-waiting was devoted to me, why would she try to thwart it? And now she's in the hands of the imperial torturers and...and...what will happen to her?"

It was a reasonable question, but not one John was prepared to answer, given Joannina was upset enough without knowing any details of what went on in underground cells.

Chapter Forty-three

Justinian was not in the great reception hall or his personal quarters. An assortments of silentiaries, eunuchs, courtiers, and servants sent John here and there and as time passed he couldn't help imagining what horrors the emperor's torturers might already be applying to Joannina's young lady-in-waiting. In his role as Lord Chamberlain, John had been obliged to attend several inquisitions. He had not been able to eat for a long time after any of them.

John finally found the emperor hunched over a table in the imperial library, surrounded by disordered mounds of codexes and scrolls of a religious nature according to the few titles he could make out. Justinian often spent entire nights poring over religious tomes, assisted by theologians in his employ, trying to come to some understanding of the unknowable or, lately, attempting to forge a compromise between beliefs which by their very nature admitted of no compromise. It was a strange occupation for a man who had just sent a girl to be tortured,

Justinian looked up, clearly annoyed. His eyes glittered feverishly. "What is this, Lord Chamberlain? You have broken my chain of thought."

"My apologies, excellency. It is a matter of urgency."

"It usually is an urgent matter, isn't it?" Justinian folded over the corner of the illuminated page of his codex and closed the jeweled cover. "We will dispense with the usual amenities for that reason. Proceed."

"A lady-in-waiting has been arrested after a search of her room led to the discovery of—"

"Yes, yes, I have given orders concerning the girl," Justinian interrupted, fingering his ruby necklace in an absent-minded fashion.

John realized with a shock the emperor was wearing a piece of Theodora's jewelry. A cold chill ran up his spine as if a snake was wriggling up his back. With a silent prayer to Mithra for aid, he said, "I believe this is a grievous error, excellency."

"Do you expect me to countermand my orders?" Justinian asked. "Much blood has been shed on the matter you are investigating. What is a little more if it leads to the truth? You may speak frankly."

"I wish to point out that if the girl dies, we have lost a valuable source of information."

Justinian waved his hand. "Consider this beautiful necklace, Lord Chamberlain. Rubies as red as blood, each connected to its neighbor by a fine golden chain. We might draw a comparison between your investigation and the truth. The golden chain of truth, dotted with regrettably bloody incidents, leading finally to the clasp to be undone, the solving of the mystery." He smiled and fondled the necklace again.

"Still, I am reluctant to shed innocent blood," he went on, a statement of such immense hypocrisy John wondered the emperor did not choke on his words, "and on the other hand we must not lose a possible source of information."

"Indeed, excellency," John agreed.

"Why did they search the room?" Justinian asked.

"I do not know at present," John admitted.

"It is of no importance. What is important, if indeed she poisoned our dear empress, is establishing on whose behalf she was working. The real murderer is whoever hired her, the name of whom my torturers are bound to discover."

"I confess I am worried, excellency. A delicate young girl like that might not survive questioning long enough to reveal her employer. The culprit could well be counting on that."

Justinian acknowledged it was a possibility.

John offered another silent prayer to Mithra and continued his persuasive efforts. "Another difficulty is she could say anything, give any name that occurs, and then I would waste time following a false trail, giving the murderer an opportunity to elude justice."

"Yes, I see your point, Lord Chamberlain," Justinian replied. "We must have a proper inquiry You may rescue her, assuming you arrive in time. I will send for you when I wish to have a full account of what you have learned."

As John bowed himself out of the library, the emperor opened his codex and bent his head over it. He held the sullen red-gemmed necklace flat against his chest, as if again embracing his dead wife.

Chapter Forty-four

John raced down the stone steps leading to the dungeons in a controlled fall and then sprinted along the corridor at their foot. His chest burned with exertion. He had run all the way from the meeting with Justinian.

It was one thing to die in combat but the death meted out in the crude cells he raced past was quite another matter. Though torturers sometimes withheld death, permanent injury was inflicted quickly.

A scream sounded nearby, ascending into throat-aching shrillness and then down into loud sobs mixed with entreaties for mercy.

The air stank of smoke, seared flesh, blood, and less savory odors.

John suppressed a gag.

Turning a corner he saw firelight reflected on wet stones from the open door of the nearest cell.

He hoped the wetness was water.

The scene that met him as he stepped into the cell was much as expected. Vesta lay on the floor weeping raggedly, her clothes torn. A broad-shouldered man bent over her, boot poised to deliver another kick to the girl's side.

"Stop!" John commanded as he crossed the threshold.

The man looked up, his thick lips curling. "Just softening the captive up a little. You can't expect results immediately with some of these women, Lord Chamberlain."

"You haven't begun questioning the girl?"

"No, you're just in time. I've been showing her the hot irons, the knives, and my other pretty toys." The torturer leered in the direction of a brazier and a cluttered table occupying one wall. "So I haven't got around to business. I was waiting for my assistants to arrive so the fun can begin."

Vesta had taken advantage of the conversation to crawl to John and cling to his boots.

"She's not that much of a pretty young thing," the torturer observed, "but men will be men, and I find that afterwards, criminals don't care much any more what they reveal. If you'd care to join—or—uh—watch—"

"Silence! Justinian's orders are she's to be released."

The other looked both surprised and disappointed. "But the irons are just starting to glow! We haven't got started yet!"

"No matter. I am taking charge of her."

The man cursed. "Well, since you are Lord Chamberlain and I am not, I suppose I must agree to it," he sneered. "Perhaps you wouldn't get any pleasure from watching anyhow."

John fixed him with a level stare. He could have the impertinent man subjected to his own toys if he wished it. John said nothing but perhaps the would-be torturer suddenly realized the possibility, because his features turned to stone and he looked away quickly.

John pulled Vesta to her feet and helped her into the corridor.

She was trembling convulsively and clung to him as a child would.

They laboriously climbed the stairs and crossed the palace grounds.

◇◇◇

Hypatia and Joannina greeted them anxiously at John's house.

John let the women take the girl away to an unused bedroom while he got himself a cup of wine. He gulped it down and refilled his cup.

By the time he rejoined the three women, Vesta was wearing one of Hypatia's garments, which fitted the slim young woman almost perfectly.

As she thanked him profusely and incoherently his gaze fell on the purpling finger marks on her arms.

"She's only bruised, master," Hypatia said. "You were in time."

John nodded. He hoped the girl's mental bruises were no deeper than her physical marks. He remembered only too well the feeling of horrific helplessness she had experienced, that he himself had experienced so long ago.

He asked the other two women to leave him alone with Vesta.

When they had he said, "I am sorry to have to ask you questions, Vesta, but the sooner I have answers the better. What are these herbs that were found in your room?"

"I know nothing about them," Vesta's voice quavered. "I am learning how to make salves, perfumes, and cosmetic preparations for my mistress and the ladies of the court. As I told you before, Lady Antonina is instructing me in the work. Please, I'm telling the truth. Don't send me back."

John had an urge to pat the girl's arm comfortingly, but refrained. "I won't," he assured her instead.

He had been informed the herbs were of the sort used in poisons. Was it possible she had been betrayed by someone at court? No one except those on the palace grounds could have had access to her room or even know where it was located.

The simplest explanation was that she was lying.

"You were denounced anonymously, Vesta. I gather the prefect was informed incriminating items could be found in your room. Do you have any idea who might have done that?"

Vesta narrowed her reddened eyes as she pondered the question. "No. No, Lord Chamberlain. Who could hate me so? And why would anyone suspect me?"

"You attended Theodora during her last days," John pointed out.

"Oh, but it was Kuria who was her personal attendant. I was simply helping her. Kuria was with her so much more than I."

"Are you accusing Kuria of poisoning the empress?"

Vesta's eyes widened. "No. But it just occurred to me…"

"What occurred to you?"

"Oh…I…what I said. That Kuria spent more time with her. Please, Lord Chamberlain. Don't question me any further. Who am I? Barely more than a servant. I can't afford to have enemies in high places."

"I don't understand."

The girl seemed to panic. Her eyes widened and she started to leap up but toppled backwards. John caught her before she fell to the floor and eased the unconscious girl onto the bed.

At least she appeared to be unconscious and after her recent experience it would be understandable.

John didn't want to suspect Vesta, but he knew he had no choice.

Chapter Forty-five

Night pressed its dark veil against the windows of John's study.

By this time the house was usually quiet but tonight he could hear footfalls upstairs as Hypatia bustled about caring for Peter.

John had looked in on the servant and listened respectfully to the old man's encomiums to his Christian god and the miracle he had wrought. John could see the attraction of believing the most dire of problems could be solved with a dab of Egyptian lamp oil, that the world was overseen by a loving omnipotent being who was willing to assist His followers if correctly petitioned.

His own god, Mithra, was a general who sent his men into a battle against the the forces of darkness, a battle in which they depended entirely on themselves.

Or so John believed.

He stared at the little girl in the mosaic on his study wall. "Well, Zoe, are you going to help me at least begin to untangle this Gordian knot?"

He swallowed another sip of his bitter wine. "I know your name is not truly Zoe, but you've always answered to it before. At least you don't change. You never grow old. Not like people. Flesh is not glass. Look at Antonina, who is entangled in this whole business. She hides the years cunningly but they are beginning

216 Mary Reed and Eric Mayer

to catch up. Yes, Antonina offers a good starting point. Consider what we have discovered."

He put his wine cup down and began to tick off points on his fingers. "First, Antonina purports to suspect both Germanus and the Cappadocian. Let us bear in mind casting suspicion elsewhere diverts it from yourself."

He got up and paced around the room as he continued. "Very well, then. As far as Antonina is concerned, it would be in her interests for Theodora to remain alive, thereby thwarting Germanus' ambitions for the throne and in the process protecting Belisarius' current role as Justinian's foremost general. Not to mention she hoped to use Theodora to get more supplies and troops from Justinian for Belisarius in Italy. Joannina has the impression that the latter is her mother's main interest at the moment."

Zoe's eyes seemed to twinkle in the trembling lamp light as John looked up at her on his second circle around the room.

"We agree so far, I see. But consider. Antonina is trying to stop the marriage between Joannina and Anastasius, whereas Theodora is adamant that it would take place. Was adamant, I should say. Thus her death means doubt is cast upon the eventuality, which would suit Antonina."

He paused at his desk and took another sip of wine, then resumed his pacing. "However, arguments over a marriage are not a very good reason to risk your life by poisoning an empress. After all, Antonina and Theodora were good friends. Or appeared to be.

"Yet even good friends fall out," he continued, remembering his recent hot words with Anatolius and the surly behavior of Felix. The latter made him think of two other military men: the bitter and intoxicated Artabanes, and Germanus, the rising general.

"Artabanes is frank about his hatred of the empress. Why wouldn't he hate her, forced to live with a wife he does not love and seeing the woman he does love married to another man at Theodora's instigation? And Germanus has every reason to resent

Theodora's efforts in checking his career. Would either of them resort to poison? Neither had direct access to Theodora. Then there's the Cappadocian who worked in the kitchens. The imperial couple's personal cooks have always been held responsible with their lives. Let us suppose Theodora was poisoned with food from the kitchen. Who could have poisoned the meals her cook delivered?"

John shook his head. "Too many guards in the kitchens. Too dangerous. The Cappadocian is too shrewd to take such a risk. Besides, a man used to power would not be likely to perform such a task with his own hands. That trio can be put in the second rank of suspects for now, don't you agree, Zoe?"

The mosaic girl did not disagree.

"Let us examine means and motives next. Was Antonina the culprit? She admits she sent Theodora gifts. Joannina said Antonina had, as in the past, supplied Theodora with potions and cosmetics. She could have sent something poisoned. Equally Gaius could have been responsible by accident by making a mistake in what he prescribed."

He sat down again and thought for a while. "Anyone on the palace grounds could make a potion if they had the knowledge. Anyone could steal the ingredients from the gardens. I could have been responsible, given Hypatia is knowledgeable about herbs."

A thought struck him. Cornelia! She has a hasty temper, and she knew how much Theodora hated him. Surely not. She had left the city shortly after Theodora's death. Where was she? Why hadn't John heard from her?

These thoughts he kept to himself, unwilling to share them even with Zoe.

Obviously he had drunk too much.

He took another large gulp of wine and forced his thoughts away from Cornelia.

"Poison might be introduced by bribing a servant," he continued, aware now of the slight slurring in his words. "So let us consider matters from that angle. Take Vesta. Devoted to her mistress and determined to see her marry that feckless boy

Anastasius. Furthermore, she is being taught to make various preparations by Antonina. Has she learnt to make those that are harmful? She lives on the palace grounds and can easily obtain the necessary ingredients. Then too Theodora's lady-in-waiting Kuria said Vesta always brought a gift of fruit for the empress."

John frowned. "I suppose it would be possible to poison fruit even if Gaius thinks it unlikely, but then Kuria said she and Vesta ate it. She could be lying."

But why would Vesta wish to poison the empress when her mistress' marriage depended on Theodora's continued existence?

"A good question, Zoe," John remarked. "But let us leave it for now and proceed to examine Kuria, also constantly in attendance on Theodora in those final days. Kuria seems unlikely, don't you think? The only protection between her and a life on the streets was retaining her post as a lady-in-waiting to Theodora. And why is Felix behaving in such an odd fashion? What is he hiding? Anatolius has already lied to me. Is there anyone I can trust?"

He laughed softly. "Why, I am even suspecting Cornelia when it is clear Theodora was not murdered in the first place. That is merely Justinian's fancy. Why not suspect everyone of the crime that didn't happen? Is there anyone in the city that didn't want the empress dead? No crime and endless suspects!"

He looked over at Zoe. Her sad expression seemed to say he ought to talk to Felix again. Soon and at length. Even though he is your brother in Mithra and a close friend, he appears to be avoiding you.

"I must speak with Felix," John agreed, draining his wine cup. "It's almost the middle of the night so I should be able to catch him at home. And tomorrow I will question Vesta further. And Kuria too. Vesta said she was with the empress more than anyone. Yes, Kuria might have valuable information. First, though, I will go to see Felix."

◇◇◇

Kuria woke screaming, lying on her back in darkness. She smelled blood and ashes.

Where was she? Was she blind?

The nightmares that had driven her from the refuge of unconsciousness bled into the nightmare that had preceded what she had been certain would be her death.

She gasped at the searing pain as she rolled onto her side. Her body might have been filled with hot coals. It felt as if a spike had been driven into her temple.

Her groping hands stirred ashes. She choked, coughed, spit out a piece of tooth.

Maybe she had died. This was the underworld. Hell. A fitting final destination for a whore.

Why had the beggar insisted on beating her?

She had accommodated enough men she didn't want. That was nothing, really, if only he had not been so brutal. Had not been like a demon.

Well, at least she had stabbed him with her brooch more than once before she passed out. She hoped the pin had hit him in the eye.

Had she? Had he blinded her in return?

She could feel her fine green stola was in shreds and almost ripped off. Oddly, as far as she could tell in her sightless state, her assailant had not taken any of her necklaces, bracelets, or rings.

She rolled onto her stomach with agonizingly slowness, whimpering in pain, hearing the rustle of ash beneath her.

Her bones did not seem broken. She pulled herself around until, suddenly, she was facing a glimmer of light.

She could still see.

She lowered her face and sobbed. "Thank God. Thank God."

Never had she been so devout while at Madam Isis' refuge.

She began to crawl toward the light.

A doorway, she realized, opening into the night. Opening onto the Mese, she remembered.

So she was not blind, not in hell.

"Thank God, thank God," she muttered again.

She crawled straight into the arms of the waiting demon.

Chapter Forty-six

Felix lived close to the Chalke Gate, not far from the main barracks where most of the Great Palace's excubitors and silentiaries were billeted. John was well-known at the house, so though he came calling in the small hours of the night he was immediately admitted.

Felix appeared from the darkness of a hallway, resembling a shade in his rumpled white tunic, running his hands through disordered hair and tugging at his wild beard, as disheveled as if he'd been fighting battles in his sleep.

"Trouble?" he growled.

"That's what I wanted to ask you."

Felix made a grunt of displeasure. "You could have asked me at a civilized hour."

"Except lately you always seem to be hurrying off somewhere," John replied. "And when you aren't rushing away you're hard to find. Your absence from the mithraeum has been noted."

"I've been kept busy. Ever since Theodora's illness worsened Justinian has been nervous. With good reason, if you ask me. When change is in the wind traitors are most likely to take their chance and strike."

The men's voices sounded hollow, lost in the dimly lit marble atrium. Felix did not invite John into a more hospitable part of the house but walked over to the impluvium and sat on the basin's wide rim. The water caught a faint reflection from the single wall torch and cast it up onto the excubitor captain's haggard face. John remained standing.

"I'm sorry, John. I need to be up early tomorrow, and I'm exhausted. I can't spare much time now unless it's urgent."

"You don't consider finding Theodora's murderer urgent?"

"In my opinion Justinian has you chasing a phantom of his own disordered mind."

"And are your excubitors chasing the phantom also?"

"No. We have enough to do without—"

"You haven't been investigating the supposed murder behind my back?"

"No. Why would I?"

"You keep asking the questions I want to ask, Felix."

"What makes you think I've been wasting my time on your investigation?"

"Your excubitors searched the room of Joannina's lady-in-waiting and found supposedly incriminating evidence. I've just rescued the unfortunate child from the hands of the torturers."

"Oh, that. I heard something about it."

John forced himself not to burst out with angry words. He took a step closer to Felix, who showed no inclination to rise or look him in the eye.

"Oh, that, you say. What were your men doing rummaging through her room if you aren't nosing around looking into Theodora's death?"

"A scrap of parchment naming the girl was delivered to the City Prefect, and he notified me as head of the palace guard," Felix replied.

"Is that true?"

"Of course it's true. Why would I lie to you?"

"What exactly did this note say?"

"Exactly? I couldn't tell you, but I gather it was to the effect someone might like to search Vesta's room since they might find something of interest there in connection with Theodora's murder."

"How was this note delivered?"

"By a grubby little street urchin. He handed it over and ran away. As well he might."

"Untraceable then, and surely not written by the boy himself. Do you know any other details?"

"None. Except the note turned out to be accurate."

"You didn't inform me poisonous herbs were found in the room, even though you know I'm responsible for tracking down Theodora's murder."

"I would have as soon as I could, John."

"I'm glad to hear it, my friend. Since you know Justinian has a noose around my neck while I'm engaged on this mad mission of his, I'm grateful you intended to get around to telling me sooner or later, perhaps even before the emperor decided to open the trapdoor under my feet."

John's words were grating, loud. Even as they emerged, he realized they were not the way he would normally have expressed himself, but the tension during the days he had been on this fool's errand was emerging. And then there were worries about Peter's illness and what was happening with Cornelia and Europa.

He would have expected Felix to leap combatively to his feet, but the burly captain continued to sit wearily on the edge of the basin. John wondered if he had been drinking, but his speech gave no sign of it. He, like John, seemed disordered by inner anxiety.

"John, I'm fully aware of your impossible assignment. I fear Justinian may have imposed a lingering death sentence on you."

"Because I will not be able to find someone who doesn't exist? Yet, evidence against Vesta has been found in her room. The emperor seemed ready to believe she was the culprit."

"Why not allow him to continue to think it?"

"You know I couldn't do that, Felix. Let a young girl be tortured, most likely to death?"

"Is her life more valuable than yours?" Felix ran his fingers through his beard, tugged nervously at the neck of his tunic. "You are a man of principle, John. Do you owe your loyalty to a man who has betrayed it?"

"I don't know Justinian means to betray my loyalty. From your behavior I would be more inclined to doubt your loyalty to me."

"You've expressed your own concerns about this impossible investigation," Felix pointed out.

"Perhaps I am being unfair to Justinian. Why would he turn against me?"

Felix continued to stare past John, into the shadows on the far side of the atrium. "Because you're a pagan," he said quietly.

"Because I am a Mithran? Like yourself, like many others at court? You know the emperor winks at pagans and heretics so long as they are useful to him."

"He's had pagans executed." Felix's thick fingers fumbled at the rumpled neck of his tunic, as if he were trying to extricate something tangled in the loose fabric. Perhaps that was what he intended John to think, to make it seem as if the fine gold chain was dislodged accidentally, falling into view against his white garment, and revealing the cross attached to it.

"Is that why you haven't been seen in the mithraeum lately?" John asked.

Felix stuffed the chain back inside his clothing. "It was given to me for a talisman."

"It is the symbol of the Christians' god."

"Yes, and it's a very useful talisman. The world is changing, John. We know demons are everywhere, whether we see them or not."

"You have become a Christian, haven't you?"

Felix shook his head. "No. No. But I've thought about it."

"Because the world is changing? Do you think the gods come and go with the ages like mortals do?"

"It isn't that..."

"You still aspire to a generalship. In today's empire Christians fare better. Is that it? General Belisarius would never have allowed you to get anywhere after that dalliance with Antonina, so—"

"There was no dalliance. She led me on. That was years ago."

"Nevertheless Belisarius hated you, and since you were my friend, Theodora had no use for you either. But now Theodora is gone, she cannot thwart you or Germanus. You think Germanus will supplant Belisarius, and Germanus will be more likely to listen to your entreaties if he thinks you are a Christian. That's it, isn't it?"

"It is a Christian empire, John."

"But as captain of the excubitors you enjoy a higher prestige than most generals."

"You know I have always wanted to command an army on the field of battle."

"Still, at your age…are you certain you do not seek higher honors yet?"

"Now you are speaking like a fool, my friend. Yes, I have been thinking about converting. I have been encouraged to think about it. For now, though, the cross is a good luck charm given to me by a friend."

John suddenly remembered his conversation with Isis who now, just as incongruously as Felix was contemplating, claimed to have converted to Christianity. Could she have given Felix the cross? Or had it been a favorite whore turned penitent turned lady-in-waiting?

"Kuria," John muttered. In the shadowy room he could not make out the reaction, if any, on Felix's lowered face. "Isis thought it was you who kept visiting the girl before she became Theodora's lady-in-waiting. Have you been seeing her again? Isis' girls were required to adopt religious practices when the establishment became a refuge. Theodora wouldn't have taken Kuria into the palace unless the girl at least made a pretense of being devout. Did you get that cross from Kuria?"

"I don't know what you're talking about, John. I'm not privy to all the ins and outs of your investigations. You're thinking out loud."

"You may be right, Felix. But you haven't answered my question. When I first spoke to her, Isis told me you had often sought out Kuria. Then we decided she must have been mistaken, that she must have been thinking of Berta, the girl you visited there long ago. Perhaps Isis was right, after all. Perhaps it had been you seeing Kuria, just as she recalled. And if so, you might have been seeing her while she was a lady-in-waiting, with access to the empress. A young woman who could have poisoned Theodora at your behest."

Felix raised his gaze to meet John's. The dark circles around his eyes were so pronounced they might have been purple bruises. "No, John. I swear it. This cross is from a friend. A woman, yes. You are right there. Someone you don't know. It didn't work out, anyway. Surely you believe me?"

Chapter Forty-seven

John's sleep was brief and troubled. He was repeatedly awakened by confused nightmares that drained away like cloudy wine from a cracked cup before he could recall what they had been about. For all he knew they might contain the solution to Theodora's murder. Most likely they were a meaningless jumble. It was commonly said dreams were messages from the gods. If so, the gods must all be insane.

When it began to get light outside, John was happy to flee his bed, despite feeling more tired than when he lay down. As he went along the hall it came to him that Cornelia had appeared in some of the nightmares.

Surely today she would send word? If not, he would have to... what? If it were not for his investigation he would have ridden immediately to Zeno's estate, but Justinian would not take kindly to his Lord Chamberlain deserting his duties.

"How is Peter?" John asked Hypatia as she served him his usual boiled eggs.

"Almost his old self, master. He's still asleep this morning."

"I told you he was a tough old boot," John said. His nightmares had left a black film over his thoughts, like residue from smoke. Perhaps that explained why he couldn't help thinking how the ill and aged so often rallied a day or so before they died. It was almost as if they knew the end was near and summoned up their final resources to take one last clear look at the world from which they were about to depart.

He chided himself for entertaining such gloomy ideas. Might the thought give rise to the reality? Then he chided himself even more harshly for entertaining a superstition.

John took a bite from a boiled egg. It wasn't cooked enough. He preferred his eggs what most would consider overcooked. Peter knew that. He wondered, had Theodora rallied, given Justinian a glimmer of false hope before the end? There was no knowing, not that it mattered.

Poison, unlike illness, would never grant the dying person one final day to say farewell.

He took a gulp of water to wash down the egg. "Hypatia, you said Vesta picked foxglove leaves and took them to Antonina. Would they have some use other than in making poison? In love potions, for example?"

"Recipes for potions tend to contain a little bit of everything you can imagine," she said, refilling his water cup from an earthenware jug. "I don't know how they work, or whether you they would still be effective if you leave anything out."

"You knew Vesta by sight. Did you ever speak with her?"

"A few times. Once, while I was working in an herb bed, she stopped and asked what could be used as a painkiller for a woman's complaint. Everybody at court asks me questions. I must be interrupted six times a day. I sometimes think I supply more medical advice than Gaius."

John realized he did not know what herbs had been discovered in Vesta's room. He had never taken a great interest in plants. They were stalks with leaves. "There are many herb beds in the palace grounds and all are available to anyone with access to the gardens," he mused.

"Yes, master. Also Gaius has a garden of medicinal plants for his own use but someone could easily steal from it. There are herbs in the garden inside Theodora's quarters too, but you can only get into it from the imperial quarters."

"Is there anything unusual growing there?"

"I don't think so. I wasn't called on to tend it very often."

John hadn't expected Hypatia to know much of use although he had hoped she would.

The last few days had worn him out. He would have been pleased to learn what he needed to know by staying at home.

Unfortunately that was not possible.

Chapter Forty-eight

A s John walked to Joannina's rooms his breakfast sat at the bottom of his stomach like a stone thrown into the Marmara.

The young woman greeted him grimly. "Please try not to upset Vesta further, Lord Chamberlain. She's devastated at being accused of murder."

"Is her room in your quarters?"

"Anastasius' and mine, you mean. No, she lives in the wing with the other ladies-in-waiting. They aren't simply servants. Their accommodations are appropriate to their status." Her bright blue eyes widened in alarm. "Why, if Vesta did live here someone would have had to creep secretly through my rooms to hide those herbs they found in hers. I don't like to think about that."

"Would it have been easier to enter a particular room in the wing the ladies-in-waiting occupy?"

"Relatively. One would still need access to the empress' section of the palace." She paused. "Excubitors would be able to march straight in and place incriminating evidence there."

John asked her why she had suggested such a possibility.

Joannina shook her head and a strand of pale hair fell across her eyes. She brushed it aside. "To find a scapegoat to satisfy the emperor. Then too, it might suit you, Lord Chamberlain, if there was a murderer you could point out."

"If I were responsible for those herbs, Vesta would have been left with the torturers."

"Then perhaps it was someone who wished to distress me. I am fonder of Vesta than I should be."

"I understand that Vesta idolizes you. She considers you and Anastasius the ideal romantic couple."

Joannina's eyes flashed. "Let me assure you she would not commit murder for me. Besides, Theodora's death was the last thing I wanted. The empress championed my marriage to Anastasius. Now my mother will have free rein to put a halt to it. Vesta knows that."

John wondered if Vesta might perhaps fantasize that she might take Joannina's place in the handsome Anastasius' affections if his marriage to Joannina was foiled.

Young people were prone to foolish ideas, John thought, as Joannina led him to the interior garden. It was as if by a certain age people were physically adults but had not managed to free themselves entirely from the phantasmal world of childhood. Outrageous actions might appear perfectly sensible. Then again, it was just as well young people did not yet see reality clearly. If they saw the world as it was they would never dare venture out into it but rather stay in bed with the covers pulled over their heads.

Vesta, looking very much like a child cowering beneath the covers, sat on the bench shaded by the awning beneath which he'd first spoken with her. She had twisted her thin legs around each other and wrapped her arms around herself.

She managed to untangle her limbs, none too gracefully, as John sat down.

"I—I want to thank you, Lord Chamberlain." She gave him a fleeting smile. revealing a chip missing from the corner of one of her prominent front teeth. John did not inquire whether the injury had been deliberately inflicted or occurred by accident during her rough handling. Aside from that, and a few bruises on her face, she looked well enough.

"I don't know anything about the herbs they claim to have found in my room," she told John, in response to his next query. "I don't even know what they were, excellency."

"You sometimes delivered herbs to Antonina. You were not storing any in your room to take to her on your next visit?"

"No, Lord Chamberlain."

"Antonina did not ask you to keep certain herbs in your room?"

Vesta shook her head. Her prominent chin might have been characterized as strong, but at present it was trembling. "No, no, I never saw those herbs, excellency. I was working here all day and when I returned to my room I was arrested. They never even showed me the herbs. I don't believe there were any!"

John did not mention that despite her being released she was still considered the main suspect by the City Prefect.

"Herbs can be found in shops and homes all over the city. A bunch of stalks and leaves is not the same as a bottle of poison," Vesta said. "Do you think they will leave me alone now, Lord Chamberlain? I could hardly sleep last night. I kept expecting footsteps outside my door. It's a terrible feeling to enter your home and find strangers lying in wait for you."

John gazed out into the brilliant sunlight illuminating the garden beyond the soft, light shade beneath the awning. "You told me you visited Antonina with your mistress' knowledge, that Joannina hoped to reconcile with her mother and thought your assisting Antonina might help."

Vesta nodded.

"Did your mistress ever send you with a message for her mother?"

"She did. She asked Lady Antonina to make a healing potion for the empress. Lady Antonina replied that since Theodora was a close friend, she was already doing so. And she was. Theodora was sending me to see Lady Antonina for that very reason, as I must have told you already."

In fact, John recalled her telling him that Theodora had given her notes, that she had not known what they said, or what the packages she had brought back for Theodora contained. Had she been lying to protect herself or simply confused? If Theodora had been trusting enough to take Antonina's potions, Antonina could have easily poisoned her to save Joannina from marriage, if thwarting the marriage was indeed her overriding desire.

"Did you notice if any potions Antonina sent had any effect on Theodora?"

The girl's eyes flashed with anger and for an instant she truly resembled her mistress. "They made her worse, excellency. She would sleep for a short while. When she woke the pain was greater than ever."

"Is that why you pretended to be unsure about whether Antonina had sent potions? Why you told me you didn't know what was in the packages you delivered? Were you afraid the potions had been poisoned? That you had had an unwitting hand in it?"

"No! Not at all! When I said the pain was greater, I meant it seemed greater. The empress expected relief and none came. Nothing she took seemed to give her any real relief. The only thing that helped was when she prayed with the clergyman who visited late in the evenings. She looked more at peace after the visits."

"Who was this clergyman?"

Vesta bit her lip, looked away, then looked back. "Oh please, Lord Chamberlain. I don't think I am allowed to say. I believe the visits were supposed to be secret, and I don't like to tell the secrets of the dead."

"Why do you think they were supposed to be a secret?"

"Because he...the clergyman...wore a baggy robe with a hood pulled forward so you could hardly see his face."

"It wasn't Patriarch Menas?"

"No, from what I could see, his build, his height, I could tell it wasn't the patriarch."

"Did you recognize who it was?"

The girl looked at him pleadingly.

"Vesta, I am certain the empress would approve of you telling me if it helps me find her murderer."

The girl looked worried. "Excellency, it won't help you find her murderer."

John asked her why.

"Because...because...the pope would hardly have murdered Theodora."

John did his best to betray no sign of emotion. He prided himself on being unflappable, but this was a surprise. "Why do you say the visitor was Vigilius if you couldn't see his face?"

Vesta nodded almost imperceptibly. "Once, when the empress was speaking, when I happened to go past the door...I wasn't eavesdropping...she...she said something to him like 'as head of the church' and it shocked me, because I knew it wasn't Menas so who else could she have addressed that way, except for the pope?"

Chapter Forty-nine

"You couldn't seriously suspect me of murdering the empress." Vigilius' prim mouth tightened. John was not certain if the short, white-bearded man was frowning or trying to suppress amusement. "I occupy the throne of Saint Peter. I am God's representative on earth. What did you imagine, that I'd presented Theodora a copy of the scriptures with poisoned pages?"

The two men were walking through the inner courtyard of the Hormisdas Palace, the refuge for Theodora's collection of religious heretics.

When John arrived at the Hormisdas, a scarred flagellant had pointed his bloody lash in the direction of Vigilius' rooms. On his way, John had encountered Vigilius in a corridor.

They went into the courtyard to talk. The air there was slightly less malodorous than that inside the building. The stench created by hundreds of holy men, many intent on humiliating the flesh, in many cases by not washing it, was almost enough to choke John. It reminded him of the smell of a battlefield two days after the fighting ended.

"I do not believe you gave the empress poison," John told Vigilius, not adding that in his experience the rich and powerful did not dirty their own hands.

"As I have explained, I did not visit Theodora. Why would she want to see me? She is responsible for having me detained in the city. She is the one who ordered me to stay in the Hormisdas Palace, this wretched tenement. The empress thought I betrayed her. I had more to fear from Theodora than she had to fear from me."

The Hormisdas Palace had been home to Justinian and Theodora before the former acceded to the throne. Now it was hardly a fit abode for anyone. Over the years Theodora had given sanctuary there to the persecuted of her religious persuasion, monophysites, who would otherwise have been exiled to the far corners of the empire or executed outright, had been granted safety there, bishops and holy beggars alike, clerics who had lived in palatial mansions and zealots who had occupied columns in all weather. The place was filled to bursting and still they came to sanctuary, like cats who knew where to find discarded scraps, thought John, noticing a dark, feline shape slinking through the weeds.

"You have a much better chance of being allowed to return to Rome with Theodora gone," he told Vigilius. "It is a motive, and when I learned you had been a visitor to her sickroom, I could not ignore the information."

"So-called information surely, Lord Chamberlain?"

"It appears Vesta was deceived. Who might the empress request provide spiritual comfort?"

"Menas springs to mind," Vigilius observed.

The courtyard was an overgrown wilderness. Bronze emperors and marble philosophers lay entangled in vines and rank brush, the pedestals upon which they had stood occupied now by ragged stylites whom, John supposed, remained continuously on their low perches just as they had remained for years atop their tall columns. An enormously fat man resembling a huge toad had taken up residence in the dry basin of a crumbling fountain.

"Menas visited her only a few times," John said. "The empress and he reconciled over the years, to an extent, for political purposes. He displaced her hand-picked favorite Anthimus in the patriarch's palace but not in her affections. Although that was years ago."

"Twelve years ago, but the empress never forgets a grudge."

It was true enough, but John said nothing.

Justinian almost never called upon John for advice regarding religious disputes. Perhaps, as more than one person had warned and John had long suspected, the emperor realized that his Lord Chamberlain was a pagan and his views on religion therefore untrustworthy. For his part John was happy to avoid delving into the endless squabbling to which Christians were prone. When he needed to deal with such squabbles as a member of the consistory his approach was to treat them as he would treat any other political disagreement. In the end it was always a question of personalities, power, position, and wealth. That holy men might sincerely be battling to gain theological ground, to enhance the value of their particular beliefs and further their power to impress those beliefs on others, struck John as largely irrelevant.

That was why, when Vigilius began to hold forth on the contentious points of the Three Chapters dispute, John began to excuse himself.

A monstrous ululation interrupted him. It might have been the cry of a holy hermit confronted by the devil himself, but the yowling and hissing that followed identified it as the sound of a furious cat.

There was a scrabbling in the undergrowth and then a small, tan-colored cat burst into view, raced straight over John's boots, and vanished under an ornamental thorn bush. A much larger black feline limped in pursuit.

Vigilius chuckled. "Cyril and Nestorius are at it again. For the most part they are friends. After all, they are both cats. But Nestorius will insist on biting Cyril's injured leg, and finally when Cyril has had all he can endure, well…"

"Strange names for cats," John remarked.

"I'm not sure what wit named them. You will recall the Council of Ephesus supported the teachings of Cyril and anathematized Nestorianism, so since these two are forever fighting in the garden, naturally, we are reminded of—"

"Yes, naturally," John cut in. "I am amazed at the humor of holy men. But I can't detain you any further."

He departed in haste.

It had been a short visit.

Then again how long would one expect it to take to clear a pope of murder?

Chapter Fifty

The stench of the Hormisdas had not faded from John's nostrils before he began to wonder if he had been too hasty in accepting Vigilius' insistence he had not been the hooded man seen by Vesta.

Or had John been too hasty in accepting the accused girl's word she had seen a hooded stranger in the first place?

The odor of the Hormisdas clung to his clothing like smoke. He would have to change.

He usually gave a wide berth to the columns occupied by stylites dotted around the city. When he thought of the religion of the Christians he smelled incense and neglected, unwashed bodies. Mithraism by contrast brought to mind the coppery odor of blood spilled by the sacrificial bull, the smell of raging battle.

He did not understand the attraction of Christianity.

As he neared his house he saw a well-dressed stranger approaching its doorway.

Had a message finally come from Cornelia?

There was no horse to be seen.

The messenger might have stabled his steed.

John picked up his pace, resisting the temptation to break into an undignified run.

The stranger turned at the sound of boots on cobbles and to his disappointment John saw he was clearly not a messenger.

The man's unnaturally thin stooped figure, the soft, unlined face, the gaudy, multi-colored robes, marked him as an imperial eunuch, even before John got close enough to smell the visitor's cloying perfume.

The eunuch addressed him in a tremulous voice. "Please, excellency, you must come with me."

John stopped short of the distasteful creature. The eunuch must have mistaken the Lord Chamberlain's disinclination to come too close for fear because he added, "You were observed speaking with His Holiness and there is information it would be well for you to know. There is no danger. Please accompany me."

"I didn't imagine you posed any danger," John replied curtly. "I will see your master, whoever he might be."

John was not surprised word of his interview with Vigilius had reached other ears before John had arrived home. On the palace grounds everyone could be certain anything they said or did in the open was being observed, not to mention most of the things done and said in supposed secrecy. One could only hope the observer was not the wrong person—or a tool of the wrong person.

The eunuch silently led him back across the square and through the palace complex to the cross-emblazoned doors of the empress' quarters.

John guessed the messenger had come from Joannina.

He was wrong. The scented creature did not take the corridor leading to Joannina's rooms nor did he turn toward Theodora's private chambers, but rather went down a hallway leading deeper into the section of the palace reserved for women. The walls were covered with frescoes depicting luxurious gardens populated with mythical animals.

Eunuchs flitted about the corridors like great, garish birds frightened from their perches. Exotic fragrances saturated the air. Was John being led to the quarters reserved for the ladies-in-waiting? He did not ask, not caring to converse with the eunuch. He would discover their destination soon enough.

When they reached it, set back in a quiet corner down a deserted corridor, a door of heavy carved wood opened into a domed room not much larger than the subterranean mithraeum he frequented. There were marble benches at one end and an altar at the other. Apart from its utilitarian features, the room resembled the interior of the Great Church.

Gilded tesserae glittered on the walls. Silver disks suspended on twisted brass chains sparkled overhead. Columns of green Thessalonian marble, star-speckled porphyry, and silver engraved with shining angels rose around them. A replica of the Great Church's dome surmounted the room. A gold cross shone from the center of the dome and openings around its base admitted the lambency filling the interior. The light, falling in gentle shafts mingling into a golden haze might have been that of the rising sun, but John realized it arose from unseen lamps brightly illuminating a semi-circular, blue painted space surrounding the dome.

A figure rose from a bench. He wore a monk's loose garment, the hood thrown back to reveal ascetic features and sparse white hair. Though he had not seen the man for years, John recognized him at once.

"Patriarch Anthimus." John made a slight bow.

The old man gave a wan smile. "Yes. I know I am supposed to be a pile of bones under the waters of the Marmara, but when I was deposed and replaced with Menas, Theodora, gentle soul that she was, could not bear to see me put to death. She has hidden me here ever since. Justinian has assured me he will continue to abide by her merciful wishes."

The notion that anyone should consider Theodora merciful was as surprising as Anthimus still being among the living, and in the very heart of the Great Palace at that. He was fortunate not to have consigned to the Hormisdas Palace but he probably would not have been safe anywhere else. Given the man's stature, Justinian would have been pressed by political opponents to have him executed.

The former patriarch's presence was another reminder that while the environs of Constantinople were small, they were crowded and concealed many mysteries. It also reminded John that although Theodora was dead, her presence in the city remained very much alive.

"It was you who visited Theodora during her final days, not Vigilius," John stated.

"That is so. Our Lord's faithful followers have lost a great champion but now she is at home with the saints."

"You have spies among the monophysites in the Hormisdas."

"Naturally."

"But why would you wish to clear Vigilius of suspicion? He is opposed to your views. For that matter, Menas might have been suspected next."

"They are both men of God, though they are confused about the actual nature of the one whom they serve. I would not see anyone put to death wrongly. Did not Christ say that as we treat the most lowly of his creatures, so we treat him?"

"You are telling me you live by your beliefs?"

"You sound doubtful, Lord Chamberlain. Well, then, let's say I didn't want you investigating Theodora's secret caller, because it might have led others to me as well. People who, unlike yourself, would not be trustworthy and principled enough to keep my presence secret as Justinian desires." Anthimus smiled broadly, revealing large yellow teeth. "Does that explanation suit you better?"

Chapter Fifty-one

A desultory breeze under a brazen sky summoned hardly enough strength to stir the air, much less countless wisps of straw and drifts of discarded domestic refuse trapped in the corners of colonnades. It was the kind of weather when the brooding sky might soon look down on an outburst of violence.

A good day for a riot, John thought as he crossed the Augustaion on his way to visit Anatolius.

The noise of the busy, overcrowded streets seemed smothered by advancing clouds, pressing down on the city as if determined to extinguish its life. Beggars' beseeching whines sounded muffled, laborers strolled across the square as if they had all the time in the empire to earn a crust, shopkeepers lounged at their doors waiting for customers who were few and far between.

Even those who practiced the legal profession in the law basilica near the Great Church seemed unconcerned that justice was being delayed by their absence from the halls in which it was administered—or at least officially said to be administered. Several men gathered at the foot of the wide steps leading to the basilica's porticoed entrance were engaged in an argument, albeit one conducted at a slower pace than usual.

Anatolius was among the onlookers, but having spotted John left the group and greeted him.

"Anatolius, I expected I'd find you here during the afternoon," John said. "I have a question or two. We should speak where we cannot be overheard."

"The middle of the Augustaion," Anatolius suggested. "No opportunity for eavesdroppers there!"

John retraced his steps until the two reached the spacious square bordered on one side by the bulky, domed mass of the Great Church. A mounted Justinian, gilded bronze, stared down at them from atop his towering column. It reminded John the emperor's eyes were everywhere, but for now he was confident he and Anatolius had not been followed.

They walked toward the center of the square, where they would notice anyone who tried to linger nearby. Gull circled overhead, crying raucously.

"I wanted to talk with you about my conversation with the Cappadocian," John said, "but I had urgent business yesterday."

"It's said you saved the life of Joannina's lady-in-waiting."

"For the time being. Did she tell you herself?"

"Hardly, John. She—"

"I suppose the Cappadocian has already reported our meeting to you?"

"You make it sound as if he works for me. The situation is quite the opposite. He has hired me to represent him. Did he allay your suspicions?"

"What do you think? He admitted hiding in the palace kitchens and everyone knows about the mutual hatred between him and Theodora."

"He had to remain inconspicuous when he returned, given Theodora was still alive at the time, if only barely."

"What do you know about what he's been doing and where he's living since he returned to Constantinople?"

"As I said, he's a client and—"

"I understand that," John said impatiently. "I'm not referring to your legal work for him. I know you want to avoid harming a client. Outside your legal discussions, has he said anything shall we say interesting?"

Anatolius pondered the question. "He has unbent somewhat but not to any great extent. He is a cautious man as well as a vicious one. He did mention his plans are proceeding well, but nothing about what they actually were."

"As you say, a cautious man."

"I've had no indication he's doing anything more than looking into whether he might retain a legal claim on any of the properties that were confiscated from him. A perfectly legitimate pursuit."

"Do you think that's the extent of his plans?"

"I make a point not to think about anything that isn't my business as his lawyer."

"Why is Vesta constantly visiting you, Anatolius? Do you persist in claiming she's there on business as well?"

Anatolius looked confused. "But she is there on business, or so she says." He gazed at the glowering sky. "She's become a trial. She keeps asking for legal advice on the matter of the marriage of her mistress. It strikes me as odd, since usually my clients consult me in person and generally incognito. Many of the matters on which I advise them are delicate in nature so naturally they wish to keep their business confidential. She never asks specific questions. Tell me about this or that, she'll say."

John frowned. "I gather the Cappadocian has called on you more than once. Is it possible Vesta is hoping to meet him at your house?"

Anatolius looked surprised. "I very much doubt it. What possible purpose could there be?"

John admitted he did not know.

"You're working too hard, my friend. Taxing your strength, seeing connections that cannot possible exist. Let's go and have a cup of wine."

John offered only a bleak smile. "Thank you, but no. I would rather you told me where the Cappadocian is staying."

"Ah…yes…I was hoping you wouldn't insist on that."

"I would rather not have to insist, Anatolius, but it is a matter of vital importance that I am able to reach the Cappadocian quickly."

"I see. You're aware that once word gets out that a lawyer has loose lips, his clients desert him?"

"Justinian ordered me to investigate Theodora's death and the emperor's wishes must outweigh your client's welfare. And your welfare too, Anatolius."

"Of course. Understand, I'm giving you the information in strictest confidence. Hopefully my client won't realize where you gained the knowledge. He's been staying with Germanus."

One suspect staying with another. Was John's task becoming simpler or even more complicated? "I doubt he'll be surprised by my sudden arrival," John said. "He must know I'll seek him sooner or later and as long as he's in the city he'll be located eventually."

Anatolius nodded. "He's a shrewd man, the Cappadocian."

"Germanus and the Cappadocian are natural allies. Both had careers blocked by Theodora, now both will return to power." John was thinking out loud. "It's a logical partnership of two men with a mutual interest in seeing Theodora taken to her grave."

Anatolius pointed out it was all speculation.

"I will talk to them both. A fine pair, Anatolius. The rapacious former tax collector and the general who, incidentally, sent one of his bodyguards to warn me of possible fatal consequences if I continued my investigations. Probably he was afraid I would find out he's been hiding the Cappadocian."

He left Anatolius with a curt farewell.

Crossing the wind-blown square he wondered if it had occurred to Anatolius he was now known to have a number of links to persons under investigation, if not actual suspicion?

It must have occurred to him. Admittedly a minority of these persons had more reason to wish Theodora continued to live rather than die.

That was the most puzzling aspect of the whole affair, but setting that aside and placing Anatolius at the center of the web, John could see strands radiating from his friend not only to the Cappadocian, but through him to his host General Germanus, and from Germanus to the once great general Artabanes, now apparently reduced to living in a twilight of intoxication spent mourning the loss of the woman he wanted to marry.

The pattern was complex and confusing, not yet completed. Did Vesta, Anatolius' curiously persistent visitor and Joannina's lady-in-waiting currently being instructed in the secrets of herbal preparations by Antonina, fit into the pattern?

Antonina was a woman whose knowledge surely extended to certain potions that cured their imbibers forever of that most vexatious ailment called living.

Where did she fit?

John hastened toward a confrontation with General Germanus.

Chapter Fifty-two

When the surly underling showed John into a room near the back of Germanus' house, the general and the Cappadocian looked up from a map spread on a table. The long, low table and several chairs were the only furnishings. Surprise was evident on the mens' faces.

"Lord Chamberlain!" Germanus' smile showed too many of his large, square teeth. "An honor indeed. May I inquire what brings you here?"

"My investigation," John replied. "What brings the Cappadocian here?"

"He is my guest," came the reply. "What other reason could there be?"

"Men who are supposed to be in exile are dangerous guests, Germanus. However, I am fortunate in finding you both here. I have questions and I expect answers."

Germanus flushed. "By what right?"

The Cappadocian gave a short bark of laughter. "He doesn't have to give reasons, even if you are Justinian's cousin. After all, a Lord Chamberlain outranks a mere general!"

Germanus suggested the trio go into the garden to avoid being overheard. "A man is not safe from eavesdroppers even in his own home."

John indicated his agreement, although he thought it was a poor general who could not secure his own perimeter. "I have spent much of the last week talking to people who don't want to be overheard," he said, not adding he had just come from the Augustaion where he had spoken to Anatolius, to avoid surreptitious listeners.

"The garden is better than the top of a column, though not by much," the Cappadocian remarked. He lightly patted his tonsured scalp, peeling from exposure to the sun. "We go to great lengths to keep our business private, yet the Lord hears every word we speak, no matter where we are." He gave a wide grin.

John followed the tax collector and powerfully built general into a garden that was almost as stark as the room they had left. Paved with large green marble flagstones, its only decorative features were a statue of Athena leaning on her spear and a fountain to which Germanus led his companions. Long, late afternoon shadows were cast by the western colonnade.

"The splashing helps mask our words," Germanus explained at the lichen-covered lip of the fountain basin.

Was such caution necessary, John wondered? The bulky, unmistakable figure of the Cappadocian in Germanus' house was as damning as any words that might be said. "What is the real reason for your playing host to a man the emperor ordered into exile?" John asked.

"You are thinking of the friendly warning I sent you after we met at the baths," Germanus replied. "You are thinking it was an attempt to persuade you that looking into my affairs was not wise? And that therefore I must be attempting to hide something."

John tensed. He had sensed movement out of the corner of his eye. His gaze swept the surroundings.

There, under the colonnade at the far end of the garden, partly hidden behind a pillar, stood the brawny guard Germanus had sent after him.

"Hiding something or someone." John nodded toward the guard. "The messenger you sent after me is standing over there with his sword drawn."

Germanus slapped his knee in delight. "Do you think I am stupid enough to have you assassinated in my own garden? And there would be no reason anyway. There's an innocent explanation for my extending hospitality to our friend here."

"You've had long enough to think up a convincing story," John said. "Let me hear it."

Germanus looked down into the rippling water in the fountain basin. "Yes. Well, Lord Chamberlain, a wise man plans for all eventualities and that is what we have done. No doubt you recall my friend here was exiled after he was caught at a secret meeting with Antonina, supposedly to hatch a plot against Justinian."

"Everyone recalls that. Belisarius was never involved. It was a trap set by Antonina and Theodora," John replied. "Go on."

"Yes, it was all a deceit cooked up by Antonina to advance Belisarius' interests and thus her own, since she is married to him, although she often forgets that to be the case. And Theodora supported her slanders because she and Antonina were friends and she wanted to get rid of my guest here because…well, who can say? Because she hated him. You can understand that, Lord Chamberlain."

The Cappadocian chuckled. "Do you suppose as a child she was abused by someone named John?"

Germanus did not smile. "I find it hard to imagine that Theodora could ever have been abused. She was always the one doing the abusing. At any rate, after those two harpies entrapped my friend here, he was lucky not to lose his head."

John did not bother to point out that trap or not, the Cappadocian's intentions had been treasonous.

The Cappadocian took up the story. "Now I have returned to the city with my head still attached. I am convinced since Theodora is gone along with her interference, Germanus here will become Justinian's leading general in place of that fool Belisarius. I therefore suggested an alliance for mutual benefit. Germanus and I would work well together, wouldn't you say, Lord Chamberlain? Germanus as conqueror, myself as tax collector helping fund his campaigns. All to the benefit of Justinian.

Everyone is aware of how Belisarius has bungled the Italian campaign, and how the present tax authorities have failed to raise sufficient funding for the effort."

The story was plausible. As Justinian's cousin, Germanus had a greater claim to Justinian's affections than Belisarius, as well as a greater claim to succeed him on the throne. In fact, most expected him to rule after Justinian, although nothing could be made official while Theodora lived. But Germanus must also know the Cappadocian could not be trusted as far as the other end of the garden. So why enlist his aid?

The general was known to take bold moves in warfare. He was not averse to taking risks. Perhaps he did not intend to wait to succeed Justinian.

Germanus and the Cappadocian were beaming at John as if he had just announced they were to be awarded high honors, but their smiles were not completely convincing. Germanus' eyes were narrowed although his back was to the sun, and the Cappadocian's looked as cold as ever.

Before John could respond, he noticed the general's eyes widen as he looked over John's shoulder.

John turned. He half expected to see an armed guard rushing at him, blade drawn.

Instead, he saw Felix, whose expression turned to shock as he spotted John.

"Ah, another old friend joins us," Germanus remarked. "No doubt you are now wondering why the Captain of the Excubitors would visit?"

"I do not think you are turning your house into a barracks for stray excubitors and exiles," John replied, fixing his gaze on Felix.

Felix smiled feebly.

"And you are here because…?" John asked.

"A very good reason, John. There is no doubt Germanus will be given a suitable command now Theodora is out of the way. You see I am blunt," Felix said in a defiant tone. "I am hoping Germanus will give me a command. You know how much I want to return to real fighting, not standing guard to perfumed fops and waiting for Justinian to order the execution of another innocent man."

So Felix had known where the Cappadocian was hiding, John thought. Was that why he seemed to avoid John in recent days, for fear of being questioned about the lack of information following surveillance of Anatolius' house?

"You observe Felix has the soul of a soldier and courage to match," the Cappadocian remarked. "Particularly considering most men his age would prefer to avoid the battlefield."

Felix glared at the Cappadocian. Clearly his allegiance was to Germanus rather than the former tax collector. He turned to John. "Now, my friend, perhaps it is time we discussed what role you shall play in all this."

Chapter Fifty-three

Hypatia spoke frantically almost before the door was fully open. "Lord Chamberlain! Thank the gods you're home! Peter's fallen out of bed!"

She spun around and ran up the stairs, John close behind.

The old servant was crumpled on the floor.

"He cried out," Hypatia explained. "Then I heard a thump."

John knelt down beside the motionless figure. The wrinkled hand he touched felt unnaturally cold. Placing his hand near Peter's face he could feel a wisp of breath.

"At first I thought he was dead," Hypatia continued. "I was trying to get him back into bed when I heard your knock. And yesterday he was doing so well, just like his old self."

Just as John had feared. He had seen too many sick and wounded and elderly revive for a day or two before taking their final departure. "Take hold of his feet, Hypatia. We'll get him back into bed and then I'll go for Gaius."

The limp body, the brown parchment skin, gave an impression of fragility and lightness. In fact, Peter's body was heavy, awkward and uncooperative. They managed to get him settled with difficulty. Hypatia drew the sheet up around him despite the heat in the room.

When she leaned over and pushed strands of hair off his forehead, Peter opened his eyes abruptly. He was staring at the ceiling. "Please, may I speak to the master?" His voice was a dry whisper.

"Of course, Peter," Hypatia told him, stroking his hair.

"Alone. If I might speak to him alone."

Hypatia straightened slowly. "If that's what you want, Peter." There was a catch in her voice.

When she had gone out John said, "I must go for Gaius. We can speak after he gets here."

"No. There's no time, master. Besides, I just saw him. He was going up the heavenly ladder ahead of me. He called back. Beware! I turned and saw a demon reaching for me. It got its claws into my leg. Ah, it burned like fire. I thought my bones would melt. It pulled and then I was on the floor. I had barely climbed a rung, but now that I have set my foot on the ladder I must go back. The angels will pick me up again very soon. I think I have the good deeds for the tolls I must pay. I have tried to live a Christian life."

John pulled the stool to the bedside and sat. Peter was not fully awake, still immersed in his nightmare, he thought. "What is it, Peter?"

"Will you be able to pay the tolls, master? Or will the demons pull you down into the pit?"

"There are no demons here, Peter. You are dreaming."

"Oh no, master. Demons are everywhere. It is when we finally awake that we see them."

"You have been very ill and in pain, Peter. You broke your leg. Gaius has been treating you. These events have become jumbled up into your dream."

Peter slowly turned his head to one side so he was facing John rather than the ceiling. The effort appeared to have been too much for his strength. He closed his eyes and his breath became erratic, a ragged whistling sound.

When John judged he had fallen asleep and started to rise, Peter's eyes opened again.

"Master, I must speak as a servant should never speak to his master, but there is one who is master of both of us and I must..."

"You are a free man, Peter. Speak."

"I fear for your soul. You are a good man. A good Christian but—"

"I am not a Christian, Peter," John said in a quiet voice.

"By your works you are. You live a Christian life. A simple life. You do not crave material things."

"I have estates, Peter. I am a wealthy man. I have little use for wealth, but I have not given it all to the poor."

"I have never seen you pass a beggar without pressing a coin into his hand."

"I worship Mithra, Peter. You know that."

"You call him Mithra. I do not think the Lord cares what name you use for him."

John gave a thin smile. "I fear a clergyman might disagree."

"But why should you care what name you use when you pray, master? Could you not call Mithra Christ? It would not change the way you live your life."

"Peter, you know that is impossible."

"My god has spoken to me, master. Has yours ever spoken to you?"

"A general does not speak to his foot soldiers individually," John replied. "You must sleep, Peter. Gaius will give you something to help you do so."

John began to get up again. This time Peter's hand moved. He managed to draw the Christian sign. "Please wait, master. I will not see you again."

"I do not believe that will be the case," John said, only half-believing it.

"The angels are coming to help me back onto the heavenly ladder. Please, master. I do not want to leave, knowing that your soul is damned to suffer forever. Promise me that you will become a Christian in name as well as by the way you live."

"Peter, I cannot—"

"Emperor Constantine was baptized before he died. It is said that only then was God's true power manifested to him. He threw off the purple and never wore it in his dying days."

"Peter, you must realize I cannot worship your gentle god."

"Ah! They are here!" Peter's gaze fastened on the empty air in the middle of the room. "Only promise me, master, and I will leave the world a happy man."

As John left Peter's room he found Hypatia waiting just outside.

"I'll go for Gaius," he said, and clattered downstairs as she rushed back to the dying man's bedside.

When he reached Gaius' surgery, the door was shut. Gaius did not answer John's knock.

He pushed the door open.

The physician's portly form sprawled untidily against a wall.

Drinking again, John thought. It was not the first time he had seen his friend in such a posture.

The thought had no sooner formed than he realized Gaius was impossibly still. Looking more closely he detected no sign of any of those minute movements of which most are aware without taking particular note.

Gaius' neck felt icy to the touch.

John rolled him over.

The wide open eyes were glazed in death.

Two empty wine jars on the table told part of the story.

He must have been intoxicated to the point of total unreason. Perhaps he had heard a contingent of excubitors coming down the corridor and jumped to the wrong conclusion. If excubitors had truly been coming for him, they would not have left his body lying here.

Whatever the reason, a tiny green glass bottle lying unstoppered in a corner—the bottle Gaius had said contained poison—told the rest of the story.

John had seen death countless times but had never got entirely used to it, especially when it came unexpectedly to a friend.

He went out and found a silentiary, apprised the man of the situation, and ordered him to have another physician sent to tend to Peter. If there was no one readily available on the palace grounds, one could always be found at Samsun's Hospice.

He hoped the new physician would be able to help Peter.

Gaius was beyond help.

On the way home his legs felt as if anchors were attached to them. Slowly crossing the square he saw Hypatia letting a caller into his house.

Had Peter died? Had she called for assistance? From whom?

He realized he was not thinking clearly. He stepped into the atrium to be greeted by an exhausted man in dusty garments. Dirt in the lines of his face and his disordered hair suggested a long ride.

It must be Cornelia's messenger.

"Lord Chamberlain, I've just come from Zeno's estate."

"The child has finally arrived! Is Europa well?"

The messenger gave him a strange look and the breath went out of John's body.

"The mistress' child is late arriving, excellency, and luckily so. I was sent to ask if there has been a mistake of some kind. When will the mistress' mother be arriving?"

Chapter Fifty-four

"I am going to my study. I don't want to be disturbed," John told Hypatia as they stood in the atrium. The messenger had left. He had no information to offer except that Cornelia had never arrived at Zeno's estate.

"Is Gaius on the way, master?"

"Gaius is dead, Hypatia. It appears the fool poisoned himself. I've instructed a silentiary to send another physician for Peter."

He turned and went upstairs to his study, dropped into a chair, and stared blindly at the wall mosaic. He poured a cup of wine, drank it in one gulp, and poured another.

Cornelia should have reached Zeno's estate.

Now he knew why he hadn't heard from her.

No, he corrected himself, he didn't know, because he didn't know why she hadn't reached the estate.

Where was she?

What had happened to her?

His first thought was court intrigue. Had someone abducted her, to protect themselves, to discourage his investigations?

If so, why hadn't he heard from them? Were they waiting to see if John suspected them? If they saw he was ready to level an accusation, then they would offer Cornelia in return for his cooperation.

Germanus had already subtly threatened him. However, the general had not mentioned Cornelia during their conversation about which part John wished to play in the proposed new regime.

Had John's answers been satisfactory?

There was no way around it. John would have to go to Zeno's estate.

But what could he do there? Mostly likely the answer was right here in the palace.

"Lord Chamberlain."

He swiveled around to see Hypatia in the doorway.

"I ordered you not to disturb me, Hypatia," he snapped.

A rail-thin silentiary dressed in a dark green tunic moved past her. John recognized the man as one of Justinian's personal staff.

"It is not the servant who disturbs you, Lord Chamberlain, but the emperor. Justinian demands your presence in the imperial audience chamber." The silentiary sounded regretful, as if apologizing for the curtness of his message, bowed, and departed.

John rubbed his face wearily.

If he took a horse from the imperial stables immediately and rode south, he would be able to beat any pursuers to Zeno's estate. But what assistance would he be to Cornelia if he was eluding arrest? And if he were thrown into the dungeons for disobeying Justinian he'd be of even less use.

He had no choice.

Night was falling as John left the house. Striding across the palace grounds, he felt an ever-lengthening shadow of useless investigation stretching behind him as another fruitless day began to die.

The declining sun gilded the grounds golden-red, added fleeting beauty to palace buildings and flower beds, colored the water in ornamental ponds and fountains, limned the edges of bushes and trees, tinted the high windows of the audience chamber golden, now slowly deepening into orange-red.

Was it significant Justinian had chosen to summon him to the lavishly decorated chamber where emissaries and statesmen were granted brief speech with the emperor, emerging overwhelmed by the sight of beaten gold wall panels interspersed by mosaics depicting the triumphs of Justinian's generals, the sculpted green marble pillars supporting the roof, and Justinian's canopied throne flanked by armed excubitors?

John turned a corner and saw Narses lying in wait, a dwarfish spider dressed in bright blue, waiting by a web represented by the polished oak door of the chamber.

"I see we have both been summoned to the emperor's presence, Lord Chamberlain," Narses observed. "I suspect Justinian is becoming impatient. My advice is to accuse one of Theodora's attendants of murdering her. They all had ready access. Consider. They are open to bribery, being but stupid girls, and not at all important. Easily replaced, and nobody will miss them. More importantly, since I hear your investigation does not go smoothly, it will save your head being parted from your body."

"I will accuse no one without proof," John replied.

"Very well. Adhere to your principles. Bleached bones have no principles. I will be enjoying a fine meal long after you are gone. Shall we go in together or would you care to follow me?"

John shrugged. "If the honor of being first appeals, take it."

Narses smiled. "Together, I think. Silentiary, announce us!"

The two men entered the chamber and began to prostrate themselves as Theodora had always required, but Justinian waved them to desist. He was pacing, red-faced with rage, at the foot of the steps leading up to his throne. John did not think he had ever seen the usually taciturn emperor so visibly angry.

"What have you been doing, Lord Chamberlain?" Justinian shouted. "I ordered you to investigate my wife's death and you have discovered nothing. In the meantime, while you muddle about the city, the identity of the murderer is delivered to me by a mere palace guard."

"Excellency?" John said.

"An hour ago I was handed clear evidence of who was responsible for our dear empress' death. It is my former secretary, Anatolius."

"Surely not the same man known to be a very close friend of the Lord Chamberlain?" Narses put in.

"The same man, as you well know, Narses," Justinian said in a cold voice. "Is this what you have been doing, Lord Chamberlain, trying to hide the guilt of your friend?"

"I cannot believe Anatolius is guilty," John replied. His tone was firmer than his conviction. Given the events of the past few days and Anatolius' devious behavior, could he really be certain?

"Personal beliefs are all very well," Narses pointed out, "but perhaps we should base our opinions on the evidence."

A pleased smile crossed Justinian's face. "Exactly, Narses. The evidence is very strong."

"Allow me to talk to Anatolius, excellency," John said.

"There will be no need for you to interview him," Justinian replied. "Your investigation is ended. He is about to be arrested and will confess to my torturers before he dies. If he refuses to reveal everyone concerned in my wife's death, he will be questioned with increasingly harsh methods until justice is served."

"May we respectfully ask the nature of this evidence?" Narses gave a sly sidelong glance at John.

"It was found in the room formerly allotted to the empress' lady-in-waiting Kuria. It is a copy of a scurrilous poem about my beautiful Theodora, signed by Anatolius and dedicated to his vile mistress. Narses, you told me this disgusting screed has been in circulation for years. It is definitely Anatolius' handwriting. Is Narses' claim true, Lord Chamberlain?"

"It is true that in his youth Anatolius penned some foolish lines. We all do foolish things when we are young," John replied.

Justinian's voice verged on a snarl. "To think his filth has been sniggered over for years while my dear Theodora did so much for so many. Such foul sentiments...I read the entire poem...it revealed his hatred of the empress as surely as if he had announced it at her door. Yes, it is obvious to me his was the hand that was responsible for her poisoning."

"The evidence is most convincing, excellency," Narses agreed.

John had never heard Justinian speak with such anger. It might have been a different man than the outwardly imperturbable emperor with whom he was accustomed to dealing. Was Justinian's uncontrolled fury a measure of his love for Theodora? "What of the lady-in-waiting who possessed the poem?"

"Unfortunately she was dismissed from the palace following her mistress' death. However, she will be quickly found to pay for her part in the monstrous crime."

"She is accused of conspiracy with Anatolius?" John asked.

"Isn't it obvious?" Narses said. "It's plain from her possession of this handwritten poem that she knows Anatolius. Given the man's well-known proclivities, it seems certain they were having an affair. It is obvious he must have given her the poison, knowing she had access to the empress."

Justinian lowered his voice to an icy hiss. "Theodora took that vile creature, a former prostitute, and elevated her to a position of trust as one of her own ladies-in-waiting. And see how she was repaid for her kindness, for her faith in humanity."

"Shall I seek the girl out?"

"Do nothing further in this matter, Lord Chamberlain," Justinian's voice was cold as death. "I set you the task of finding a murderer. Was it so difficult to find that the culprit was Theodora's lady-in-waiting, the one person who saw Theodora most often while she was ill? Leave me, Lord Chamberlain. If I require your services, I will summon you."

Chapter Fifty-five

John was hardly aware of leaving the reception hall. His feet carried him out to the dark palace grounds while his thoughts leapt this way and that.

Dismissed by the emperor, surely he was free to go after Cornelia?

He could gallop off to Zeno's estate.

And yet why should she disappear? The only reason he could think of was because of something transpiring in the city.

Something connected with Theodora's death and John's futile investigations.

Besides which, by the time John reached the estate, Anatolius would have become another victim of Justinian's unfocused rage, as dead as Theodora's cook, the guards outside the room where Theodora had died, her physician Gaius...

Before he realized it John had strode through the Chalke Gate and was on his way to Anatolius' house.

He fixed his mind on his friend's peril. A disinterested magistrate might indeed find Anatolius guilty of arranging Theodora's death. Judging from the poem found in Kuria's room, he had been secretly involved with one of those nearest to the empress, a trusted lady-in-waiting who could have easily administered poison. He had also advised the Cappadocian, who gave every indication of plotting with General Germanus. What reward might a lawyer expect upon Germanus' accession to power, now or later? He might well be appointed Quaestor—the emperor's legal advisor—or be elevated to some other position in the consistory.

Lord Chamberlain, perhaps.

Wasn't this the very sort of connection John had been seeking? A person with much to gain who could reach Theodora through one of those close to her?

Yet facts and logic could not instantly overcome years of close friendship.

Bits of colored glass could be put together one way to form a picture of a demon, whereas in a different combination they might show an angel instead.

Excubitors stood guard at the narrow way leading to Anatolius' house and at its gate. The few passers-by who hurried through the torch-lit darkness took little notice of the situation and in many cases quickened their steps, anxious to leave the area before they became unwillingly involved in the trouble obviously roosting on the house roof.

John was admitted to the courtyard. A group of frightened servants huddled together outside the house. As John arrived, Felix stepped from the doorway. His fierce scowl deepened on seeing John.

With a slight warning nod toward the guards he drew John through the gate out their earshot and growled, "You're too late to warn him, my friend. He's gone."

"Thank Mithra for that! He wasn't at home when you arrived?"

"He was, but unfortunately my men were not exactly discreet as they approached." Felix gave a brief smile. "He must have heard us coming and managed to escape from the back."

It occurred to John that Felix was equally involved with Germanus and the Cappadocian, so he had every reason to allow Anatolius—possibly a co-conspirator—to slip away, quite apart from their friendship.

"No guards were posted at the back of the house?"

"An oversight, I am afraid, Lord Chamberlain," Felix replied with a wink. "We'll find him before too long."

"Do you know where he is?"

"I'll arrange search parties, but first I must question the servants."

"Your procrastination will cause you trouble later on, Felix."

Felix shrugged. "Personally, I don't believe Anatolius has anything to do with your investigation. Any more than I do. In fact, I—"

He bit off his words as a man dressed in clothing announcing his trade to be that of a laborer approached them.

"Yes?" Felix barked at the new arrival.

"I saw a man running away from here, sirs. I work in the Copper Quarter and I was passing behind the back of the house on my way to—"

"Never mind your life story! What about this man you say you saw?" Felix interrupted.

"He was in such hurry I thought perhaps he had been caught thieving. Then I realized he was well-dressed and the well-dressed never run about, do they, sirs? They always have servants to do that for them. Anyhow, it looked so strange I followed him to see where he was going, so I could come back to tell the owner of the house. But seeing the guards I thought it best to report to you first."

"Well?" Felix demanded.

"He ran into the Great Church. Is there a reward for telling you where he is, sirs?"

Chapter Fifty-six

Entering the light-filled building, John stood under a many-pillared gallery and glanced around the huge space under the soaring, many-windowed dome. Light from lamps suspended from the ceiling, set in wall niches, and on tripods, touched the silver seats used by priests and the gold and gem encrusted altar set with richly-decorated sacred vessels. Columns of polished green and white and purple marble pointed colorful fingers to glowing mosaics overhead.

John did not see Anatolius.

Those who sought sanctuary—which surely was Anatolius' intention—often placed themselves beside the baptismal font.

He returned to the narthex and strode quickly along a wide corridor, his boots slapping noisily on the floor's enormous polished marble slabs. At the end of the corridor he passed through the Vestibule of the Warriors, where guards were stationed when the emperor was in attendance inside the church. Felix had positioned a number of his excubitors there to prevent Anatolius from slipping away into the night.

The baptistery sat just beyond the vestibule's exit.

John stepped into the high-domed octagonal room. Lamp-light sparkled on jeweled crosses adorning the outer sides of the font. Waist high and the length of two men, it had been carved from a solid block of marble.

John spotted Anatolius sitting halfway down the steps descending into the basin. He hunkered down at the top of the steps. "Is this what we've come to, Anatolius? A Mithran seeking Christian sanctuary?"

"What could I do, rush to the palace and hide in the mithraeum? I doubt I'll be safe here for long."

"Felix has the church surrounded but he won't drag you out. He takes his orders from Justinian, and the emperor respects the sanctity of churches." He didn't add Felix was even more likely to respect Anatolius' taking refuge at the font, since the excubitor captain might himself be baptized in it before long.

The thought reminded John of Peter's plea that he accept the Christian god. He could not imagine immersing himself in the enormous font, as if he were stepping into a bath at the Zeuxippos. What a pathetic way to acknowledge allegiance to a god.

Fortunately for Anatolius, the font was currently dry.

"I am not sure how long Justinian will recognize my right of asylum," Anatolius said. "The laws specifically bar homicides, adulterers, and ravishers of virgins from enjoying the right, but treason is also a heinous crime."

"Why did you run, Anatolius?"

"I had no choice. When Felix arrived with excubitors I realized he wasn't visiting to arrest my cook, even if he does habitually burn the fish." He forced a bleak smile.

"Flight always gives the appearance of guilt."

"The excubitors were slow in approaching the house and made too much noise. Felix was intentionally warning me, giving me time to get away."

"You don't know why he was ordered to arrest you?"

"What does it matter? If Felix considered it prudent for me to escape, I wasn't going to question his judgment. Every day someone vanishes. If I'd lingered to ask what the charges were I'd be dead by now."

John couldn't argue with that.

Anatolius was leaning back against the font's inner wall. Light hit the top of his head, accentuating his gray hair. The shadows falling across his face deeply sculpted each incipient wrinkle in his tired, sagging features. John suspected he was seeing what Anatolius would look like as an old man.

Provided he reached old age.

John was not certain he could offer any useful counsel. He recounted what Justinian had told him about the poem found in Kuria's room.

Anatolius' grim laugh reverberated in the dry basin. "The follies of our youth come back to haunt us! That cursed poem! Written so long ago and now come to collect payment!"

"It was more than foolish of you to give it to Theodora's lady-in-waiting."

"Kuria wasn't a lady-in-waiting when I first met her, John. Far from it. She was one of Isis' girls. It's touching she kept that little scribble so long."

For a few heartbeats John could say nothing. He remembered what Isis had told him about Kuria's frequent visitor. Had Isis got it wrong? Had it been Anatolius, not Felix, who had sought Kuria out years earlier?

In response to John's query Anatolius hung his head. "Yes, for a time I was obsessed with the girl."

If Anatolius had not been seeing Kuria recently—as Justinian and everyone involved had inferred from her possession of the poem—then he could not have convinced her to poison Theodora to further his ambitions. Ambitions that had also merely been inferred from his involvement with the Cappadocian, and through him, Germanus.

The entire complicated edifice of his friend's guilt collapsed.

"When did you last see Kuria?"

"I don't remember, exactly. It was a long time ago."

"Not within the past few weeks?"

"Not for years. I never had reason to venture into Theodora's part of the palace. I didn't even know Kuria was living there."

"Are you being truthful with me this time?"

"You know I'm always...yes. Yes. This time I am telling you the truth. Ask Kuria."

"I wish I could. She's been banished from the palace. Justinian has ordered her found." John got to his feet. "I'll escort you to him. We'll explain the situation."

"Why would he believe what I say if he's convinced I conspired to murder his wife? I think not, John. I'd rather stay here."

"You'll only be safe here until Justinian loses patience."

"That's probably longer than I would have if I were in his clutches."

"You're probably right. I'll try to find Kuria. Justinian might take her word if he comes to his senses sufficiently to remember how much Theodora trusted the girl."

Chapter Fifty-seven

John was used to being out in the city at night. It held no fears for him. This night felt different. There was a sinister aspect to the shadows. He had the feeling if the sun were to suddenly rise dark forms would be revealed as something other than the familiar buildings and colonnades and monuments he knew during the daytime.

Where in this strange place could Kuria have gone?

When she spoke to John in the palace gardens she was terrified of being thrown out into the streets. Clearly she did not have a plan. If she finally had decided on a destination, who at court would know? What friends would she have had at the palace?

Vesta, John thought. The young women had served Theodora together. Perhaps Kuria had confided in Vesta.

John's house was all but on his way to the womens' quarters. He couldn't pass nearby without checking on Peter, although there was nothing he could do for him, nor, he remembered with a pang, was there anything he could do about finding Cornelia at present.

As he came around the side of the barracks opposite the house he passed a portly, youngish man dressed in the elaborate robes of the clergy.

Why would he be out at this hour unless…

A haggard-looking Hypatia greeted John at the door. "The physician said there was nothing to do but send for a clergyman," she said. Her voice sounded strained but calm. Resigned. Her shoulders were slumped, her normally lively eyes dull.

"Peter is still alive?"

"He woke before the physician got here. It seems it is only a matter of time. He's asleep now. The physician said when he slept again, he would not wake up."

John made no effort to step inside. "I am likely to be away all night, Hypatia. Anatolius is under suspicion. He's taken sanctuary in the Great Church."

"No," Hypatia said "Oh, no." Her words came out in a choked whisper, as if she had found her ability to express grief exhausted.

"You understand, I would stay with Peter but Anatolius needs my help."

"If you want to save Anatolius, why don't you accuse Antonina of the murder? She's an evil woman. How many poisonings has she got away with? Or you could accuse someone else who has escaped justice."

"I could not lie," John said stiffly. "Especially with a person's life at stake."

"But what about Anatolius? Isn't his life at stake?"

Her vehemence surprised John. Did she harbor some affection for Anatolius so long after he had been trying to attract her without apparent success?

"I will see that Anatolius comes to no harm without making a liar of myself, Hypatia."

Her eyes suddenly came alive. "Better that Anatolius die than you should say something that isn't true. For that matter, you would see an old man go to his grave agonizing over your soul—berating himself that he could not save you from the fires of hell—rather than uttering a few comforting words that would make you a liar."

"You were eavesdropping on our conversation!"

"Not intentionally. I simply waited outside Peter's door. I couldn't help hearing what he said. You could have pretended to agree to his final request. After his lifetime of loyalty, what would it have cost you? But, no. You have to adhere to your principles. You always have to be superior, better than other men. And why is that, because you know you aren't really—"

"That's enough! I know you are distraught, Hypatia, but you have forgotten your position. I regret I will not be able to employ you after this outburst."

Hypatia drew herself up and looked John in the face. A smile trembled on her lips. "Would you have me depart immediately then and leave my dying husband unattended?"

"Husband?"

"Yes. The clergyman who visited Peter married us."

Chapter Fifty-eight

A marriage between Hypatia and the gravely ill Peter was absurd. Even if he were not dying, Peter was twice Hypatia's age, but John had no time to dwell on the news.

He brushed by the guards at the entrance to Joannina's quarters. Recognizing the Lord Chamberlain, they stood aside. Anastasius did not.

The tall, skinny young man appeared from an inner chamber, straightening his tunic, black hair rumpled. "What do you think you're doing harassing us in the middle of the night?" he shouted. "We've had enough of this!"

"I am here on the emperor's business."

The young man clenched his fists.

"Anastasius! Stop!" Joannina, emerging from their room, placed a restraining hand on his arm. "What do you want at this hour, Lord Chamberlain?"

"Direct me to Vesta's room. I wish to speak to her."

Before Joannina could answer, her lady-in-waiting emerged groggily from another room

"I heard raised voices," she said. "What…" Seeing John she fell silent.

John noted Vesta wore the same kind of light blue tunica her mistress was wearing. "Why are you here, Vesta? I thought you lived with the other attendants?"

"The excubitors turned her room into a shambles," Joannina said. "Besides, she's too uneasy to stay there, since they've violated the place. I gave her one of our spare rooms."

"Only until we find her a more suitable place," Anastasius said, sounding petulant. "She won't be staying here long."

John wasn't surprised Vesta was upset, considering what she had been through. "Do you have any idea where Kuria might have gone?" he asked her.

"Kuria? She was ordered to leave the palace after—"

"Did she tell you where she intended to stay?"

Vesta shook her head.

"Did she ever speculate about what she might do if she had to leave? Did she mention friends in the city?"

"I...I don't remember, excellency."

"Are you satisfied?" snapped Anastasius. "If so, we'll return to our beds. If you want to pursue this, come back tomorrow."

"Tomorrow will be too late. The emperor seeks to arrest Anatolius. Your lawyer."

Vesta let out a small cry of distress.

"What do mean our lawyer?" barked Anastasius. "Who is this Anatolius?"

Vesta drew her clasped hands up to her face in a gesture of prayer.

John addressed Joannina. "Please take Anastasius back to your room. I must speak to Vesta alone."

Anastasius' took an angry step forward but Joannina's hand tightened on his arm and she gave it a tug. "Come, Anastasius. The Lord Chamberlain is working for Justinian. We don't need to anger the emperor."

Anastasius glared at John long enough to preserve his dignity, then relented and followed Joannina away, grumbling and throwing venomous looks back over his narrow shoulder.

Vesta began to blubber. "Where is Anatolius? What will happen to him? Is he safe?"

"For now. He's taken sanctuary in the Great Church. But I must find Kuria. Justinian believes she poisoned Theodora on Anatolius' orders."

Vesta shook her head wildly. "Oh, no. He would never do that, never! He had nothing to do with Kuria! Not for years and years."

"He was telling me the truth? He hadn't been seeing her recently?"

"No. And I would know. Kuria and I were friends."

John detected coldness in her tone. "You weren't going to Anatolius' house for legal advice on behalf of your mistress, were you, Vesta? You were trying to gain Anatolius' attentions."

She caught her lower lip under her oversize front teeth and nodded morosely.

What he had already guessed had become certain to John when he saw Vesta wore the same sort of blue tunica to bed as Joannina. Vesta had come to the palace from a relatively modest background and being a naive girl, idolized her mistress. She considered the relationship between Joannina and Anastasius the height of romance. She wanted to emulate Joannina in every way, not just in dress. Anatolius had somehow drawn her attention. He was a romantic figure—not the grandson of an empress perhaps, but the son of a senator and a handsome man whose poems still circulated at court. That he was too old for Vesta simply added a spice of impropriety to the sought-after affair, giving it the same illicit savor as her mistress' romance.

"Anatolius did not return your attentions?"

She said nothing, but the tears that welled up in her eyes answered for her.

Chapter Fifty-nine

As John crossed the Augustaion and approached the Great Church he saw light pouring from the baptistery. He pushed through the excubitors in the Warriors' Vestibule, sensing tension among the men. Muttered conversations were too loud, lances and swords were grasped too tightly.

All the lamps in the octagonal chamber where Anatolius had sought refuge were lit. It was as bright as midday. A variety of churchmen had congregated and stood in a double ring around the font.

The diminutive figure of Narses emerged from a knot of excubitors near the doorway and moved in John's direction, a shadowy demon sliding along the floor amidst the coruscating mosaics and glittering jeweled crosses adorning the baptistery. One might have thought such a creature would be banished by the blazing radiance.

"Lord Chamberlain, I am glad to see you. Please advise your friend Felix of the consequences of disobeying a direct order from the emperor."

"Explain yourself, Narses."

The eunuch treasurer simpered up at John. "Justinian has sent me to take over here. I am ordered to seize the murderer." His dark, serpent's eyes glanced over the assembled churchmen. "I don't think they will offer much resistance, do you?"

Felix strode over. "I won't have the blood of any clergy on my hands. My men take orders from me, and I don't intend to relinquish my command."

"Justinian was right to suppose you cannot be trusted," Narses sneered. "In fact, you and that miscreant cowering in here are probably both involved in a plot against him."

Now John understood the reason for the tension he had sensed. The guards by and large were Christian. They would be torn between their loyalty to the empire and their religion and fear of Justinian's wrath. It was ironic their captain Felix, who ordered them to honor their sacred place, was himself a pagan.

Or at least had been hitherto.

"Anatolius is not going anywhere," John told Narses. "So there is no need to be in a hurry. Can you imagine what the reaction will be if you have the priests protecting him slaughtered in the church? Perhaps it is you who has an eye on the throne and might like to see the city set on fire?"

Narses brushed the insinuation aside without raising his reedy voice. "Do you think I am a fool, Lord Chamberlain? I cautioned Justinian a rash act might cause riots. In the end, however, I can only advise and then must carry out his orders. You are Anatolius' friend, which means you are in the best position to prevent bloodshed. Convince him to surrender."

John looked toward the font but could not see Anatolius, hidden behind the massed clergy. Some stared defiantly in their direction, others prayed.

None were armed.

"Why are you hesitating, Lord Chamberlain? Is your allegiance to your murderous friend stronger than your allegiance to the emperor?" Narses said.

"Don't interfere, John," Felix growled. "Anatolius has made his choice. I have made mine."

"And your men?" Narses' asked mildly, "What choice will they make when I directly order them to seize the criminal?"

"I will speak to Anatolius," John said.

Those surrounding the font allowed him to pass. Anatolius was still sprawled uncomfortably on the steps leading down into the dry basin.

"Do you think I should just ask them to bring in the holy water?" Anatolius asked. "They could baptize me and then administer their death rituals. I'd be all set then to fly straight up into that heaven of theirs, where Justinian is sure to send me as soon as I leave here."

It would not be an immediate journey, John thought. Justinian's torturers would ensure it was a seeming eternity before Anatolius was released from his sufferings. "Narses wants you to surrender, to avoid bloodshed."

"Except for my blood being shed. Are you supposed to persuade me to leave sanctuary?"

"Anatolius, swear to me you have not seen Kuria for years, that you are not involved in some plot against the emperor."

"I swear it, John. How many times do I need to tell you? How long have we known each other?"

"A long time, but recently you lied to me."

"We all have duties to honor and—"

"There isn't time to argue. You have no idea where Kuria has gone?"

"No."

"Very well," John said. Then I'll have to find her."

Anatolius let his head drop back against the marble rim of the font, his gaze directed up into the glowing dome filled with stars and angels. "Tell the churchmen to leave, John. There's no reason they should die to protect a pagan like myself."

"They aren't here to protect you, Anatolius. They are protecting their holy space."

Anatolius said nothing and did not move his gaze away from the dome.

When John returned to Narses unaccompanied, the treasurer merely smiled. "You did not convince him, then? I did not expect that you would."

As he spoke there was a commotion and raised voices outside. Narses turned toward the sounds. "Ah, my men have arrived."

Felix cursed.

There was no need to explain. If Narses could not depend on the excubitors there were other forces he could call upon—silentiaries, the scholarae, the City Prefect's urban watch. No matter how defiant Felix might be, it was inconceivable he would order his excubitors to battle other imperial guards.

Unless he were in fact intent on deposing the emperor they all served.

A few of the new arrivals began to filter through the excubitors, moving in Narses' direction. Armed men scowled apprehensively at the weaponless men surrounding the font.

Before Narses had a chance to issue orders, Patriarch Menas entered the chamber. His narrow face, accentuated by the long beard, looked more drawn than ever. He moved as slowly as if his clerical robes were woven of pure gold, rather than decorated with gold thread. He walked past John, Narses, and Felix without a word and interposed himself between the priests and those from the palace.

"I have just spoken with the emperor," he announced. In response to a withering look flung at him by Narses, he added, "You have been overruled, Narses. I order you, in the emperor's name, to refrain from exercising your military skills here for the time being."

"I knew Justinian would never allow his church to be violated," Felix muttered.

Menas looked around and then continued. "The emperor is hoping that the miscreant will recognize his duty toward the Lord and submit himself to justice."

John thought it was unlikely Anatolius would oblige. "What if Anatolius refuses to give himself up?" he asked. "I have reason to believe he is innocent, yet he has already been judged guilty. How long will he survive if he leaves the church?"

"Justinian did not offer me any guarantees on that point," Menas replied. "I intend to pray with this unfortunate man. Perhaps he will recognize his duty."

"And if he continues to claim sanctuary?" Felix interrupted.

The patriarch's face, gaunt as it was, displayed a remarkable lack of emotion under the circumstances. It might have been a saint's face painted on a piece of wood. "The emperor has prayed for guidance. The murderer must surrender himself. That is the Lord's will, and the Lord's will shall be done by sunrise. By whatever means is necessary."

Chapter Sixty

In the middle of the night the Augustaion was a desolate plain receding into darkness beyond the pool of light spilling from the Great Church. The statue of Justinian on his steed, indistinct against a gray sky, hovered on its column like some watchful mythical creature on guard above the roofs and colonnades surrounding the square.

John looked up at the statue as he wondered what to do next. At sunrise Anatolius would be dragged from the church. Whether to the dungeons or to immediate execution, only the omnipresent and omnipotent emperor could say. And Kuria, Theodora's lady-in-waiting, who might be able to convince Justinian of Anatolius' innocence, could be anywhere in the city.

If she was still in the city.

Given enough time he would have questioned people at the palace, sought out ladies-in-waiting other than Vesta who might have known something useful. He would have enlisted the aid of Pulcheria to spread the word among people on the street to watch for the girl. He would have begun to visit likely tenements, seeking her.

But there was no time.

He was crossing the square as he pondered. Where would Kuria have gone? Where could she go? The only life she knew was that of a prostitute and then, very briefly, a penitent at Isis' refuge. Normally John would have expected her to return to the home she had known before Theodora had plucked her from the refuge and transported her to the palace.

But Kuria had slashed a rival, Isis had told him. She would not have such a girl back. So she had said.

Did Kuria believe that?

Would Isis really turn a former employee away?

John's only hope was the answer to both questions was no. It was not a good wager, but it appeared to be the only wager available.

He entered the darkness at the edge of the square, passed through the archway beyond, and set off along the Mese.

Isis greeted him, her face puffy with sleep. She wore a plain linen robe. An enormous silver cross dangled from a necklace and bounced comfortably against her ample bosom.

"I told you I would not take a girl like Kuria back," Isis pointed out after John questioned her.

"I remember what you told me, Isis. Is she here?"

Isis' shriveled rosebud of a mouth quirked into a smile. "Ah, you know me too well, old friend."

"Yes," John agreed, humoring her. "Even as a young woman in Egypt, you always had a heart much too kind for your line of work."

"A kind heart may be lacking in most madams but it never hindered me," Isis replied.

"I guessed Kuria would come here, Isis. She knew you couldn't turn her away."

"Ah, but she didn't seek me out of her own accord. Your informant, Pulcheria, brought her."

John expressed surprise.

"Pulcheria said you had asked her and her friends on the street to keep an eye on a beggar who attacked Hypatia. You suspected he might be more than a beggar. No doubt you will hear from her soon."

"What did she tell you?"

"He's a familiar menace in the area. He camps out near the Hippodrome because he used to be a charioteer, until he fell out of his chariot during a race. He either banged his head on the track or a horse stepped on it. At any rate, it knocked all the sense out of his skull. He's assaulted more than one woman. Always women wearing green, probably because he raced for the Blue faction."

"Why hasn't he been brought in front of a magistrate?"

"He has. Time after time. They all know him from his racing days. He won them a lot of wagers back then, so they always let him off." Isis clucked disapprovingly. "There's nobody less qualified than a magistrate to administer justice. Any bricklayer would be fairer. I'm thankful I don't have to bribe magistrates any longer, now I've changed the nature of my establishment."

Isis paused. "I fear Kuria was hurt, John. Badly beaten. She was lying unconscious all day before word got back to Pulcheria the former charioteer was acting as if he had been up to no good again, that someone had been told by someone else that something or other had been glimpsed by a passer-by. Knowing the rogue's methods, Pulcheria found the girl in a burnt-out shop near his begging spot. Kuria will survive. She's tough. The beggar was reportedly seen bleeding profusely from wounds in his face."

"I'm glad there's someone I can rely on," John said, "even if it is a street woman with a three-legged cat."

"Pulcheria confided to me Kuria was not happy to see her. She kept shrieking that Pulcheria was a demon, no doubt because of her scarred face. Pulcheria told her she wasn't a demon, but her guardian angel. But you said you wanted to see her."

Isis led John through narrow hallways lined with doors to cramped rooms which functioned as simply and well for penitents as they had for her girls when they practiced their former profession.

Kuria lay curled up on a wide shelf that served as a built-in bed on the back wall of her tiny cubicle. The thin mat serving as a mattress must have been a penance for someone used to sleeping on a palace bed. An earthenware plate holding a half-eaten scrap of bread and several olive pits sat on the floor.

The girl whimpered and rolled over, as if the entrance of John and Isis had triggered a nightmare. As her eyes opened she cried out.

"Quiet! You're safe here. Don't you recognize the Lord Chamberlain?" Isis said sternly.

"My apologies for startling you, Kuria," John said. "Isis has told me about what happened. I need some information without delay."

Kuria squirmed into a sitting position. Her triangular little face looked crumpled by fear and confusion. There was a purpling bruise on one temple, scratches down her cheeks, and her lip was split. "What is it you want to know, Lord Chamberlain?"

"Did you entertain Anatolius years ago, while working here?"

"Anatolius?" Isis asked. "I thought it was Felix who favored her? My memory definitely isn't what it used to be."

"Is it true, Kuria? Anatolius says he used to seek you out regularly. He says he gave you a copy of a poem he wrote about Theodora."

Kuria rubbed her eyes. Her wounded mouth quivered as she nodded. "Yes. That's true. About seeing him and the poem. How did you know?"

"The poem was found in your room at the palace," John told her.

"You stupid girl," Isis muttered. "That filthy verse! Didn't I instruct all of you to discard everything of that nature when we changed our direction? You kept it! You had it here in my refuge, before Theodora took you away! And you took it with you, precious to you as it was! If I had known...what was I thinking to take pity on you?"

"Oh, please don't turn me out, madam...I mean...Mother Isis. I...I...couldn't bear to part with that verse. It was written in his own hand."

"You were fond of Anatolius?" John prompted.

"Yes, Lord Chamberlain. I know it was foolish. He's an aristocrat and I was just a, well, even so I was sure he was fond of me. Only it was impossible, the way things were, and I accepted that."

"I doubt it," Isis put in. "Tell the truth, Kuria. Didn't you fancy yourself another Theodora and Anatolius your own Justinian?"

"I know you don't believe me, but the situation was different after I started to work at the palace. I thought Anatolius might see me in a better light. A lady-in-waiting has some dignity. Only…only…" She buried her face in her hands.

"Only what, Kuria?" John asked.

"He was having an affair with Vesta!" She raised her face from her hands and her eyes were full of anger. "The lying bitch was off to his house at all hours, and she pretended to be my friend. It all came out when I showed her the poem he gave me. She was horrified about his gift to me. She blurted out he was hers or words to the effect. Right away she wished she hadn't, but it was too late. I started thinking about her comings and goings. It was clear enough what she was up to."

"When you were attacked, you were on your way to visit Anatolius, to see if you could rekindle the old feelings you imagine he held for you," John suggested.

"Yes. And now I'm in no condition to do so."

John recalled how he had taken her for a helpless, befuddled young girl after their first meeting in the gardens.

He had been badly mistaken.

"Did you tell Vesta about your hopes?"

"Certainly not. I let her think it was over between Anatolius and myself years ago."

Isis snorted with a sound more appropriate to a madam than the head of a refuge. "Girls are all so silly. I'm glad to be out of the business!"

"Kuria," John continued. "Isis told me you attacked a rival not long before you left here, quarreling over a favorite patron. Was it Anatolius?"

Kuria glowered at John but said nothing.

"You placed the herbs in Vesta's room and arranged for the note to be sent to the City Prefect, didn't you, Kuria? Your room must have been near hers, since all the ladies-in-waiting live in the same wing. "

"It served her right, Lord Chamberlain! I almost put it off too long. Right after I got back from the gardens with the herbs I found my door nailed shut. Vesta was naive. After I convinced her I no longer had any interest in Anatolius she started extolling his virtues and confiding how she would soon be together with him. It would be a great romance, just like Joannina and Anastasius."

Kuria's scratched and bruised face twisted into a sneer. "The bitch wanted to be just like her mistress. Like a trained dog, she was. Didn't you notice how she tried to dress like Joannina and wore her hair like her? She wanted her own aristocrat too. Wanted a romance that everyone at court would frown on, just to make it more exciting. She tried to steal my Anatolius from me."

"Ha!" remarked Isis. "You flatter yourself, thinking Anatolius belonged to you!"

"He would have come back to me! He didn't love Vesta. It's easy to feel you're fond of someone in a beautiful room with a soft bed and luxurious furniture, but to feel you love someone on a cold, bare slab like this…" She slapped the utilitarian shelf on which she was seated.

"And you think Vesta a romantic," sniffed Isis.

"As a matter of fact," John said, "Anatolius and Vesta were not having an affair. He was at his wit's end trying to avoid the girl. He's old enough to be her father, or yours for that matter, Kuria."

Kuria's looked at John hopefully. "Are you sure they—"

"It doesn't appear to concern you that your jealousy placed Vesta in danger," John said in a cold voice, "but doesn't it bother you that you've put Anatolius in danger?"

Kuria's face clouded. "But why?"

"Have you forgotten what that poem says about Theodora? The emperor is convinced Anatolius plotted to kill Theodora with your assistance."

Isis chuckled grimly. "If everyone who pointed out Theodora was a slut was plotting against her…" She broke off abruptly and stared at John. "That means the emperor will have his men looking for Kuria."

Chapter Sixty-one

There was as yet no sign of dawn when John emerged from Isis' refuge and set out at a trot for the palace. The black shapes of ox-drawn carts making night deliveries materialized from the darkness and creaked past. A dog barked frantically as he went by its resting place, a niche sheltering a statue of a once illustrious general.

John had lost all sense of time. He was afraid to look at the sky for fear he would see it brightening.

But even as he raced to save Anatolius, his thoughts kept turning toward Cornelia.

What had happened to her?

Where was she?

He imagined her imprisoned somewhere, having been abducted. Terrified, perhaps injured.

He recalled his own abduction, lying in the dark in the carriage, not knowing its destination, expecting only that the trip would end in his death.

What might Cornelia be feeling right now. Or worse yet…

No, he forced his thoughts away from the idea. And yet he had seen so much violent death he could entirely prevent unbearable images from forming in his mind.

But what would be gained by harming Cornelia? If someone wanted to use her to protect themselves against John's investigation why had he heard nothing?

He realized he could not afford to let his mind wander away from the most pressing problem—the imminent danger to Anatolius.

Cornelia might be in just as much danger.

The hours were flying by.

He tried to convince himself Cornelia's disappearance must be connected to his investigation, that continuing his pursuit of Theodora's murderer, clearing Anatolius of wrongdoing would in the end serve Cornelia.

He must go directly to Justinian. The emperor must be made to believe Kuria's explanation for the incriminating herbs she had left in Vesta's room. Vesta, whose frequent visits linked her to Anatolius, who was linked to his client the Cappadocian and the Cappadocian's ally, Germanus. The men arguably had reason to want Theodora dead, but neither had access to the empress. Remove Vesta and the whole imagined plot fell apart. And besides, Vesta wanted Theodora to live, so that her mistress Joannina could marry Anastasius.

It was obvious.

Provided one believed Kuria.

Provided the emperor would pay attention to her. John pictured the pathetic girl on her hard bed in the refuge's narrow cell, her meager half-finished meal on the earthenware plate. Why would the emperor pay attention to her?

Because she had been a protegée of Theodora. A favorite. Surely he would pay attention, or at least delay any action against Anatolius until he heard the girl's story. He would feel he owed as much to his late wife.

Isis was right now helping her get clean and chastely outfitted, readying the wretched girl for the imperial audience John hoped to arrange.

But if Justinian believed Kuria and allowed Anatolius to go free, where would the emperor turn his ire next?

Many in the city held a grudge against Theodora. More than half the court might imagine advancement for themselves in her absence. Everyone John spoke with pointed him toward one of their enemies, as if their word would be sufficient to dispose of them.

Kuria had been more cunning than the aristocrats, for only she had supported her self-serving accusation through physical evidence: herbs which could not lie about their purpose.

Objects were more trustworthy than people. They did not seek to mislead, but neither did they readily offer up what they knew.

If dawn was breaking it was still concealed beyond the black bulk of the palace as John arrived back. The reception hall where he had met Justinian was vacant except for smoky phantoms created by smoldering lamps.

"He did not ask for guards to be summoned to accompany him yet he's walking on the grounds, Lord Chamberlain," said the silentiary on duty. "It makes it very difficult to ensure his protection."

Yes, John thought, it would also be difficult not to be able to sleep at your post for fear the emperor might suddenly appear and catch you at it.

Where would Justinian be?

There was nowhere in the palace the emperor's nocturnal journeys did not take him. On the night John had gone to the mithraeum he had encountered Justinian in the kitchens. Surely, however, one place he would never miss visiting was the room where Theodora had died.

The room was empty.

John stepped inside. So deep was it in the interior of the palace, Justinian had not bothered to keep a guard on the door. Compared to the riches all around there was hardly anything of value here. The dismantled bed sat in the corner, as he had last seen it, beside the marble-topped table and wooden chest. The only light was from a wall lamp several paces down the corridor.

He turned slowly to survey the room.

With a start he noticed two men staring at him with shining eyes.

No, it was only the icon depicting the healing saints.

The air smelled sweet, as if someone had been burning incense.

He completed his survey. As before, the room did not lie to him, but neither did it tell him anything.

Theodora had not left its confines for weeks. She could only have been killed by one who had entered here, as John had, but unlike this night, the room had been closely guarded and few had gained admittance.

John had hoped to explain to Justinian that Vesta, who had served Theodora, had not, as the emperor had apparently convinced himself, murdered her at the behest of Anatolius, on behalf of Germanus and the Cappadocian. And, John reminded himself, Felix, for hadn't he been visiting Germanus too? Nor had the murderer been the lady-in-waiting Kuria, whose word— if Justinian accepted it—would exonerate Vesta and Anatolius.

Very well. Who had entry to this small room? The two ladies-in-waiting had spent a great deal of time with Theodora. Gaius visited often, but now he was dead he could not satisfy Justinian's wrath even if John were inclined to blacken his friend's memory.

He looked at the grim-faced holy men depicted in the gilded icon. They had seen the murderer.

Christians believed that saints interceded in earthly affairs, and that their power was more concentrated in the vicinity of holy icons, relics, and the like.

But Cosmas and Damian did seem inclined to aid a Mithran Lord Chamberlain.

John turned his gaze elsewhere.

Spartan as the room was compared to most of the palace, it was luxurious compared to the cell in which he had interviewed Kuria. Theodora's deathbed had been soft.

There came to John's mind an image of the plate in Kuria's cell. The half-eaten bread, the olive pits.

He opened the inlaid wooden chest, crouched down, and pushed aside bottles and pots until he came to the carefully wrapped bundle he sought. Cushioned inside the fabric was the lidded ceramic jar from the imperial kitchens he had seen when he first examined the contents of the chest at the beginning of his investigations. An image of an olive tree was embossed in the clay.

There was a footstep behind him.

"Have you stooped to robbing the dead, Lord Chamberlain?"

John turned.

In the half light, the emperor's scarlet boots looked the color of blood.

Chapter Sixty-two

"You may stand, Lord Chamberlain," said the emperor. "We are all equal in the presence of death."

John got to his feet.

Justinian gave a sardonic smile. His gaze fell to the jar in John's hands. "You would make a poor thief. The shelves of the kitchens are lined with such jars. Once their contents are gone, they are worthless clay. Like our own flesh."

Though the words were spoken lightly, John detected a tightening around the emperor's eyes.

"Excellency, I wish to speak about Anatolius."

Justinian gave no indication he had heard. He looked around the room. "The plasterers will arrive soon," he said quietly. "This is the last opportunity I or anyone else will have to see this accursed place before it is sealed off forever. The dust of years will fall silently where my dear wife suffered and died, covering everything with a soft mantle of memory. A strange thing to contemplate, is it not?"

A strange time to engage in poetical ruminations was John's opinion. "I must respectfully request Narses be instructed to allow Anatolius to leave the Great Church in safety. I have evidence Anatolius was not involved in the empress' death."

Justinian leveled an expressionless gaze on John. "Proceed."

John recounted Kuria's confession.

Justinian paced as he listened. Then he closed his eyes briefly. "Kuria. Yes. My dear Theodora's favorite lady-in-waiting, one she trusted. She raised her up from a terrible life."

"The empress could not have misjudged the girl's character," John suggested.

The emperor patted the frame of the bed. "I agree. But who then? Who was the culprit?" He paused. "That murderous drunkard Gaius. Of course! He killed himself, a sure admission of guilt. Perhaps he realized your long friendship would not protect him?"

"It is my belief his death was a mistake while he was intoxicated," John replied.

"It was made plain to Gaius that retaining his head depended upon his remaining in a fit state to treat my wife." Justinian glanced in the direction of the icon of the healing saints. "When he was elsewhere it was doubtless a different matter. On reflection, it seems obvious he made the last batch of Theodora's painkilling medicine far too strong, fatally strong. Therefore I have decided her death was due to an overdose, brought about by the physician's carelessness. Unfortunately the culprit is beyond justice."

John shifted the jar he held from one hand to another. "Her death was then an accident, not murder?"

Justinian sighed and nodded. "It seems so, Lord Chamberlain."

"Excellency," said John, praying to Mithra his tongue would not tangle the words he had to say. "If I may give my opinion, I believe it was not an accidental overdose. Nor was it murder by an enemy's hand."

Justinian's gaze had moved back to the icon. "Her agony was unimaginable, Lord Chamberlain. I saw it all, shared it all. I never left her side. I fed her personally as long as she could take nourishment, helped her drink her medicine. Toward the end she took nothing but painkilling potions. By then they had lost their effect. It was torture, Lord Chamberlain."

"It is true, excellency, you attended the empress constantly. Of all those I have spoken to in the course of my investigations, no one spent as much time with her as you."

The expression Justinian turned on John was so utterly devoid of emotion as to appear, under the circumstances, totally inhuman. "Explain yourself, Lord Chamberlain."

John raised the jar slightly. "Olives. This jar contained olives. Who would eat olives in the presence of the empress, who could not even eat the fruit she was sent? Surely you would never have done so."

"One of the attendants," Justinian replied.

"They would not bring a jar of olives into the sickroom. This jar is from the kitchens. I know you are familiar with the kitchens. I saw you there one night not long ago."

Justinian said nothing.

"Do you require me to be more specific?" John asked, asking Mithra to protect him.

Justinian's face remained a rigid mask. "I have asked too much of you, Lord Chamberlain. I will summon you later when you are less tired. You may go."

John remained where he was. He needed to finish this, now. He could not wait any longer to find Cornelia, no matter how much he might anger the emperor.

And he was about to anger him.

"Excellency, you had the most and the easiest access to the empress," he said. "You also had the strongest motive for hastening her death. The motive of mercy. You just pointed out she was being tortured. As I said, her death was neither an accidental overdose nor murder by the hand of an enemy."

There came to him an image of the wall painting at Antonia's house, the copy of the Ravenna mosaic, the empress holding the chalice.

"A cup of sorrow for one may be a cup of blessing for another," he added.

Justinian's eyes blazed as if they opened onto the pits of hell. "I should have your throat cut and your body entombed in this room. Explain yourself before I order it."

"Gaius kept increasing the amount of the empress' painkilling medicine," John replied. "Toward the end it ceased to help.

There was no escape from her torture. The more painkiller the empress was given the more her pain increased. How could that be? Because after it became apparent it was not possible to relieve her agony, you were no longer giving her the proper amount."

Justinian remained silent.

"Instead you were pouring part of it into this jar, one you'd taken from the kitchens. Gaius had been exceedingly careful not to bring a fatal dose into the room. Nobody could possibly know that you were saving the painkiller. You wanted to make certain you accumulated enough to relieve the empress of her suffering."

The emperor stared at him, his face unreadable as a blank sheet of parchment. Though the room was hot, John felt enveloped with cold. He shuddered.

Mithra, I am about to be condemned to death. Guard my family, he prayed.

The emperor's voice issued in a faint draught from all but motionless lips. "A pretty explanation indeed, Lord Chamberlain. Now explain why I would order you to find a murderer if the murderer were myself?"

Why? To hide his actions? Had he wanted John to present him with a scapegoat? Or because he had been deranged and had not, until now or some time after the act, admitted to himself he had taken his wife's life? Had he wanted John to convince him that someone else had murdered Theodora?

"I did not say you were a murderer, excellency."

"Then…?" Justinian pressed.

"I believe you did not want to see the empress' torture prolonged," John said, wishing Theodora had shown such mercy herself to those she had sent to the underground dungeons."It was an act of mercy."

Justinian forced his lips into a mockery of a smile. "You have been a valuable servant to me, Lord Chamberlain, but tonight you have brought an end to your time here."

Chapter Sixty-three

Hypatia sat with Peter—her husband Peter—all night. She had pulled a stool to the side of the bed and taken one of his still hands in her own. The physician told her Peter would not wake again when he went back to sleep, and Peter had fallen into a deep slumber before the clergyman who married them left.

Peter had mumbled the appropriate words. Had he truly known what was happening? At the same time he was taking his vows he seemed to think he was climbing the ladder to heaven.

He was half-sitting, propped up on the pillow. His hand was cool. She could hear him breathing faintly, with an occasional long pause between breaths. Hypatia waited every time, holding her own breath, until his breathing resumed.

She kept brushing his wispy hair back into place. His forehead felt as cool as his hand. In the soft glow from the sleeping city outside the open window he might have been any age.

What a strange marriage, ending before it began. Like a baby who died at birth, whose life consisted of a single cry and an inscription on a tombstone.

She had always felt a bond with Peter, as if they were family, without realizing it.

Was it foolish for her to marry an old man? She ran a finger over the back of his hand, feeling the fragile bones through the parchment skin. It was better they had married. The Lord

Chamberlain should have married Cornelia long since. Did he suppose there would always be time?

The night passed. Outside the window dawn replaced the soft night glow of the city. Hypatia was gradually aware she could again discern Peter's bedside table, the amulet she had given him, the lucky coin from Derbe, the pilgrim flak with the oil she had thought miraculous for a brief while. The cross on the wall came into sharper relief.

Her eyes burned and for an instant, as sunlight began to filter into the room, she was sure the increasing light formed a cross over the sleeping Peter. She blinked and it was gone.

No doubt it had been a transitory effect of sunlight and her own exhaustion.

Then the hand she held spasmed.

Suddenly it was clenched tightly around her hand, squeezing painfully.

Then the pressure released.

Peter opened his eyes and looked at her.

"Hypatia. I have just had the strangest dream." His voice was strong. His eyes were clear.

How long Hypatia might have remained speechless she would not know because almost simultaneously with Peter's awakening there came a pounding at the door. Up on the third floor the noise was barely discernible but it startled Hypatia like a thunderclap.

She rushed downstairs. She could hardly see for the tears of joy blinding her.

What wonderful news she would have for the Lord Chamberlain when she let him in. She had forgotten their argument.

Blinking back tears, stifling sobs, she fumbled with the bolt and finally threw the door open.

The caller was not the Lord Chamberlain.

◇◇◇

It was later that morning before Hypatia learned what had happened to John.

He gave her a hurried summary of his meeting with Justinian as they stood in the atrium.

His first question upon entering the house had been about Peter.

"He's sitting up and having something to eat, master. Complaining I undercooked the eggs."

John had braced himself for bad news. "He sounds like his old self," was all he could think to say.

"He's entirely himself. He really has recovered. It's a miracle. Isn't it wonderful?" Hypatia smiled. "His god has decided to grant us some time together, or so Peter says. And how can I not believe him?"

For Peter's sake John accepted Hypatia's tearful apologies for her outburst and reinstated her in the household. Hypatia worshiped the gods of Egypt as John knew. He wondered if Peter would seek to convert her to his own religious views. "I am happy for both of you, Hypatia."

He and Hypatia had exchanged their news in a rush. There was no time to waste. No time for John to visit Peter.

He put his hand on the door and looked around the atrium, wondering if he would see it again, half expecting it to dissolve like a dream. He was enveloped by a sense of unreality. If he were to reach out his hand it might pass through the scene as it would pass through the reflections in the water in his impluvium, or perhaps come up against a hard, cold, mosaic.

He had experienced this sensation after his mutilation by the Persians. Surely, he had thought, it must be a nightmare. The world could not have changed so much, so abruptly and inexorably. But he had never awakened, and gradually he had stopped waiting.

"I'm leaving immediately for Zeno's estate to find out what has become of Cornelia," John told Hypatia.

"That won't be necessary," said a familiar voice.

He turned, startled. Cornelia came down the stairs. Her clothing was mud-spattered.

"I arrived back not long ago," she said. "All that rain delayed us right from the start of the trip. The roads were flooded. We got stuck in mud, then a bridge had been washed out. It was my fault, ordering the driver to try a side road. We ended up in a ditch with a broken axle and had to stay at an inn waiting for the carriage to be fixed. By the time we got to Zeno's estate a messenger had already been sent asking when I would arrive. I turned right around and came back immediately."

She put her arms around John.

"I may as well not bothered to go," she said. "I was no help at all. Our grandson was being born as I arrived. He is named John."

"You really should have stayed," John said, holding her tightly.

"Europa and Thomas and John are doing well. I knew you would worry and I didn't want you to be distracted from your investigation, and given I could get here as quickly as another messenger, well…" She kissed his cheek.

Over Cornelia's shoulder, John saw Hypatia looking uncertain if she was free to go, trying to remain unobtrusive.

Cornelia put her head on John's shoulder. "Why does it all need to be so complicated?"

John gave a thin smile and put his arm around her shoulders. "It doesn't have to be, not any more. We have always talked about living in Greece. You can start to pack, Cornelia. I am free to leave the city at last. The emperor has relieved me of my position."

Epilogue

Early morning sunlight poured into John's study, warming him as he stood looking out the window, waiting for Cornelia to finish packing.

Today they were leaving for Greece, to be followed in due course by Thomas, Europa, and the infant John.

Turning, John smiled at the mosaic girl Zoe.

"Yes, Zoe, Peter and Hypatia will be with us too. They at least are constants in a time of great change," he informed her.

He resumed pacing back and forth across the empty room, as he had been doing off and on since Cornelia had banished him while she was making the final preparations for departure.

"It will go faster if you aren't looking over my shoulder," she'd told him.

The house was even more bare than it had been. So John had gone to his study, where there was no longer a chair, and looked out the window and paced and talked to Zoe.

"A time of great change," he repeated. "Not just Theodora's death, though Mithra knows how that will affect the empire. Felix is still talking of converting to Christianity. And Anatolius is convinced he was saved from death because he took sanctuary in the Great Church and says he is thinking along the same lines."

He gazed at the mosaic girl with whom he had spoken so often. "Gaius is gone and Isis is running a refuge. The world is certainly changing, Zoe."

He resumed pacing.

"And speaking of Gaius, it's strange Peter would believe he saw him climbing the heavenly ladder before anyone knew he was dead. Then there's Peter's holy oil. Did it really heal him as he believes? Gaius once claimed fate was just another competitor of his. I should have liked to have heard Gaius' thoughts when he learned Alba, who swore by white food, choked to death on the black olives Gaius presented him."

He took another turn around the sunlit room and continued. "I was not paying as close attention as I should have to what I heard during my investigation, Zoe. I overlooked more than one nudge in the right direction. Pulcheria pointing out the same jar can contain wine or poison, for example, and Gaius mentioning the same plants can be used for good or ill, to kill or cure. Then there was Antonina's servant, who believed the goblet Theodora held in her mistress' wall painting foretold the blessing of the ending of her agony."

He paced back to the window and looked out across the palace grounds. Seagulls wheeled and squawked over treetops and the familiar tramp of military boots announced the departure of a company of excubitors.

"I shall miss you, Zoe. We have shared many confidences over the years."

"And now it's time to say goodbye, John," Cornelia said from the doorway. "Everything is packed and loaded." She came to him and put her arms around him. "It will be a new life and a better one, John. You no longer serve Justinian. You are free."

They left the study. The thud of the house door closing quivered upstairs through the hot air. Cloud shadows briefly dimmed the sunlight pouring across the mosaic girl's face, seeming to animate her features and creating a brief, sad smile on her glass lips.

Afterword

Nine For A Devil was—as they love to say in book blurbs—torn straight from the screaming headlines of the summer of 548, or would have been if anyone in Constantinople had invented newspapers. Empress Theodora in fact died around the end of June from a disease which, to judge by the sparse description left to us, was most likely cancer. What the historians all failed to note —— even the sixth century writer Procopius who never met a scandalous rumor he didn't like—is that there were a lot of real historical figures who had possible motives for killing the empress.

Theodora's death allowed General Belisarius and his wife Antonina to prevent the marriage Theodora had arranged between their daughter Joannina and Theodora's grandson or, according to some sources, nephew, Anastasius. Although Theodora's meddling might sound farfetched, Procopius, as translated by Richard Atwater, avers that:

"She [Theodora] made the boy and girl live together without any ceremony. And they say she forced the girl against her will to submit to his clandestine embrace, so that, being thus deflowered, the girl would agree to the marriage, and the Emperor could not forbid the event. However, after the first ravishing, Anastasius and the girl fell warmly in love with each other, and for not less than eight months continued their unmarital relations."

Antonina arrived in Constantinople, seeking military aid for Belisarius, around the time Theodora died. Some sources say she arrived after the empress' death, but we side with those who say simply that she arrived too late.

Perhaps it would have been better for Belisarius, if not for Antonina, to have allowed Joannina's marriage to take place. The historian Philip Stanhope says that whether Joannina eventually married someone else or whether Belisarius' line even continued is unrecorded.

Another general, Justinian's cousin Germanus, had indeed long seen his career impeded by Theodora, who all her life maintained an enmity to Justinian's side of the family. In 550, with Theodora gone, Justinian was finally allowed to favor the man whom many expected to succeed him on the throne. He appointed Germanus to head the ongoing invasion of Italy. Unfortunately, Germanus fell ill and died on the way, giving Theodora a posthumous victory in the family feud.

The situation of the general Artabanes, prevented by Theodora from repudiating his Armenian wife to marry the patrician he had rescued from rebels in Libya, is as described, melodramatic as it may seem. We cannot confirm with absolute certainty that Artabanes had a borderline drawn down the middle of a house he shared with his estranged wife, but we are sure Procopius would have been happy to tell the story if he had thought of it.

Artabanes may well have been disgruntled enough to be suspected of the empress' murder. Later in 548 or early 549 he actually became embroiled in an attempt to depose Justinian. The scheme was easily foiled and Justinian, acting inexplicably as he often did, granted clemency to the conspirators. Artabanes resumed his military career. He was sent to Italy, no doubt pleased to get away from his wife.

During 548, and for years before and afterwards, the empire was agitated by the religious controversy known as The Three Chapters. We refrained from any attempt to detail either the theological or political subtleties of the matter. In our defense we cite Edward Gibbon who, in *The Fall of Roman Empire,* referred to "The famous dispute of the Three Chapters, which has filled more volumes than it deserves lines…" Suffice it to say that Justinian hoped to broker an agreement between the various religious factions but ultimately failed, leading in time to the schism which still exists between the eastern and western churches.

As part of Justinian's effort to unite the church, Pope Vigilius was invited to Constantinople for a full and frank discussion, or kidnapped, depending on which historian's interpretation you prefer.

Emperors knew how to negotiate in those days. Vigilius was detained for eight years. He was finally allowed to leave the city in 555 but died before reaching Rome.

As for the monophysite Patriarch Anthimus, after he was deposed for his heretical views, the empress kept him safely hidden in her part of the palace where his presence was not discovered for twelve years, until Theodora's death, if you believe John of Ephesus.

John the Cappadocian, the much maligned tax collector, was hounded by Theodora for years, even after she managed to have him removed from power and exiled. The tale of woe he relates to John is entirely factual. In a sense, the Cappadocian was a real life counterpart to our Lord Chamberlain, a powerful man, close to the emperor and trusted by him, whom Theodora hated and relentlessly sought to destroy.

While Procopius states that John the Cappadocian "… remained in prison till her [Theodora's] death, after which he was allowed by the Emperor to return to Constantinople, a free man…" we calculated that a cunning fellow like the Cappadocian—knowing Justinian would allow him to return anyway—would surely have come back early. It isn't surprising that Procopius failed to notice the Cappadocian lurking for a few days in the imperial kitchens. He failed to notice the former patriarch Anthimus hiding in the palace for twelve years.

Unfortunately, we must believe Procopius when he tells us that the Cappadocian had to be content with remaining a priest, despite his continuing ambitions. We can't help but wonder if the formerly powerful official visited Theodora's sarcophagus in the mausoleum next to the Church of the Holy Apostles. And if so, who did he count as the victor in their struggle?

From the foregoing it might be concluded that it is not so difficult making fiction out of history since so much of history is fiction to begin with.

However, having said all that we have, we can hardly shy away from two final items. We have to admit that from 541 to 552 the captain of the excubitors, the imperial guard, was a man name Marcellus, rather than a bushy bearded German called Felix who has held that position for many years in our books. All we can do is wave our poetic license, properly and impressively done up with various official seals! A detective needs a friend in law enforcement. We needed the excubitor captain to be friends with John and, frankly, Marcellus wouldn't give the Lord Chamberlain the time of day.

Which brings us to the matter of "Lord Chamberlain," a loose translation of the name of a high palace office, praepositus sacri cubiculi (head of the imperial bedchamber). At one time or another, the famous eunuch Narses probably held this office, amongst others such as treasurer. However, official titles multiplied endlessly and the duties attached were often nebulous. Narses, for example, was eventually sent like Belisarius, Germanus, and many others before him, to lead the armies in Italy, perhaps on the theory that if all else fails, try an eighty year old eunuch. Given all this, we decided it did not fly in the face of history to claim that Justinian had a close advisor with the title Lord Chamberlain of whom no record remains. John, like his authors, was a private person who preferred to live out of the public eye, and being a shrewd man, he succeeded.

Glossary

Dates are AD unless otherwise stated.

BLUES
See FACTION.

CARROT
Orange carrots did not appear until well after the Roman era. Roman carrots were white or purple.

CICERO (Marcus Tullius Cicero) (106—43 BC)
Prominent Roman orator, politician, lawyer, and philosopher.

CITY PREFECT
High-ranking urban official who governed Constantinople and nearby areas.

COUNCIL OF CHALCEDON
451 church council, its determination that Christ has two natures, fully human and fully divine, in one person, was rejected by many eastern churches, resulting in a schism which has lasted until the present day.

COUNCIL OF EPHESUS
Refers to three church councils, the second of which, held in 449, was repudiated by the COUNCIL OF CHALCEDON.

COUNT OF THE CONSISTORY
Member of an imperial advisory council made up of high state officials.

CHRISTODORUS (fl. 6th century)
Egyptian-born epic poet also noted for his epigrams.

DALMATIC
Loose overgarment.

EXCUBITORS
Imperial bodyguard.

FACTION
Supporters of the BLUE or GREEN chariot teams, taking their names from the racing colors of the team they favored. Great rivalry existed between them, and brawls between the factions were not uncommon, occasionally escalating into city-wide riots.

GALEN (c. 130 - c. 201)
Celebrated Greek physician whose writings on medical topics greatly influenced the profession for centuries.

GREAT CHURCH
Colloquial name for the Hagia Sophia (Church of the Holy Wisdom). The first Great Church was dedicated in 360 and burnt down during civil unrest in 404. The rebuilt church was destroyed during the Nika Riots of 532 and replaced by the existing Hagia Sophia, constructed by order of Justinian.

GREENS
See FACTION

HIPPOCRATES (c. 460 BC - c. 377 BC)
Known today as the Father of Medicine, Greek physician Hippocrates was considered by his contemporaries to be one of the foremost practitioners of his profession.

HIPPODROME
U-shaped race track. It featured tiered seating accommodating up to a hundred thousand spectators. It was also used for public celebrations and other civic events.

NONNUS (fl. 5th century)
Greek poet. His epic Dionysiaca (Dionysius) is comprised of over forty books detailing the history of the god.

NUMMUS
Smallest copper coin in the early Byzantine period.

MITHRA

Sun god said to have been born in a cave or from a rock. Mithra is usually shown in the act of slaying the Great (or Cosmic) Bull, from which all animal and vegetable life sprang. A depiction of this scene was in every mithraeum. Mithra was also known as Mithras.

MITHRIDATUM

Legendary antidote against poisons, said to have been invented by Mithridates VI (d. 63 BC), ruler of Pontus on the southern coast of the Black Sea.

NIKA RIOTS

Much of Constantinople was burnt down in 532 during the riots. They took their their name from the rioters' cry of Nika! (Victory!) and almost led to Justinian's downfall.

PLINY THE ELDER (Gaius Plinius Secundus) (c. 23-79)

Roman naturalist and author. He died during an eruption of Vesuvius, having traveled to the area to observe the event.

PRAETORIAN PREFECT

Civil official responsible for a Praetorian Prefecture. There were two prefectures in Justinian's time, the Prefecture of Illyricum and the Prefecture of the East, the latter of which John the Cappadocian headed. The prefect's duties included collection of taxes, construction of public works, the public post, and the provisioning of the army.

SAMSUN'S HOSPICE

Founded by St. Samsun (d. 530), a physician and priest. Also known as Sampson or Samson the Hospitable, he is often referred to as the Father of the Poor because of his work among the destitute.

SEE THEODORA AT DAWN

According to the Secret History by Procopius (490? - c. 560) glimpsing Theodora was considered an ill omen, particularly if it happened at dawn.

SCHOLARAE

Imperial guard that by the time of Justinian had become largely ceremonial

SILENTARIES

Court officials whose duties were similar to those of an usher, and included guarding the room in which an imperial audience or meeting was being held.

STOLA
Ankle-length garment worn by women.

TESSERAE
Small cubes, usually of stone or glass, utilized in the creation of mosaics.

THREE CHAPTERS
Writings by three fifth century theologians concerning the nature of Christ. Justinian condemned the writings in an attempt to find common ground between religious factions. His efforts proved futile, however, resulting in a drawn out controversy and the eastern and western churches subsequently drifted apart.

TUNICA
Undergarment.

To receive a free catalog of Poisoned Pen Press titles, please contact us in one of the following ways:

Phone: 1-800-421-3976
Facsimile: 1-480-949-1707
Email: info@poisonedpenpress.com
Website: www.poisonedpenpress.com

Poisoned Pen Press
6962 E. First Ave. Ste 103
Scottsdale, AZ 85251